BARLOCH

To Feed The Fire

Diarmid MacArthur

A Barloch investigation

Copyright

S

SPARSILE
BOOKS

To Joan and my girls, with love.

Prologue

They deserved it—they all deserved it!

He clutched the box of matches tightly, excited yet half afraid. But they deserved it. No one got to treat him like that. All he had asked for was a job, a chance...but that bitch had put paid to his chance.

He took a match from the box, his hands shaking as he held it against the rough side. It would only take a stroke...he knew the drill; he had already had a trial run.

He felt a feeling of power, like a beacon in an otherwise powerless existence. He grinned in the darkness; they deserved it—he'd show them!

He pulled the match towards him, watching it ignite, aware of the sharp, sulphurous tang over the smell of the paraffin. He dropped it, watching, waiting!

The crackle of burning wood, the spiral of thick smoke billowing in the clear night air. A shout from nearby, a door opened.

He lifted the half-full can and threw it into the heart of the rapidly spreading flames.

Running now, time to go, time to leave the remaining paraffin to feed the fire.

Chapter 1

It was unseasonably warm for mid-April; Constable Alan McInnes lay on the narrow, rather uncomfortable bed, his hands clasped behind his head as he stared up at the cracked, stained ceiling. Although it made sense to occasionally sleep in the little police house that he was in the process of renovating, he missed his home comforts. Most of all, he missed his mother's cooking.

He had shed his pyjama top and, as the bed had no covers, he lay on the recently-purchased ex-army blankets, clad only in his baggy, striped pyjama bottoms. Although the young man was exhausted, sleep eluded him, his mind troubled. He should have been happy but happiness, like sleep, seemed an elusive commodity.

It had been several months since he had finally proposed to Nancy Wright, the local schoolteacher who was, undoubtedly, the love of his life. To his joy, and to his great relief, she had accepted and a subsequent chat with her father to ask his permission for her hand had elicited the same response. Needless to say, his mother Isa was delighted and even his taciturn father had grudgingly offered his congratulations.

Following the rather harrowing events in the normally peaceful little West Renfrewshire village of Barloch, the end of 1959 had seen Alan undergo a particularly gruelling interview with the area chief superintendent at Paisley's police headquarters. He had passed his sergeant's exams earlier in the year and, despite the tempting offer from Inspector McGinn of Paisley's

CID, he had decided to remain as a uniformed officer at Bar-loch. Sergeant Tait, his superior, had indicated that he planned to retire this year and Alan hoped to be promoted and take over the running of the local office.

Donald Tait lived in a semi-detached house next door to the police station, half of which had lain empty for some considerable time. A rather cold winter had caused a pipe to burst and, although it had been mended, there seemed to be little spare funds to carry out any renovation of the property. Tait had suggested that, as and when Alan gained his promotion, the house should probably be his for the taking and available to move into once he and Nancy got married. Despite his previous misgivings, it had seemed an ideal opportunity.

Alan ran his hands through his short, dark hair; he had been spending a great deal of his spare time in trying to make the rather decrepit police house habitable, sometimes, as tonight, sleeping in the only furnished bedroom. Despite all his hard work, Nancy still hadn't shown a great deal of enthusiasm. A new estate of attractive, modern houses was currently being constructed on the edge of the village, just across from the school where Nancy taught, and she had obviously set her heart on a brand-new property rather than the damp and draughty one next door to her husband-to-be's superior officer!

Donny Tait: Alan let out a long, despairing sigh. Despite the sergeant's previously indicated intention to retire, so far he had shown little or no further inclination to do so. In fact, he seemed to have gained a new lease of life! Between Alan and his mother, Isa, as well as fellow-constable Kerr Brodie, they had finally persuaded Tait to attend an optician in Paisley, where he had been prescribed a pair of bifocal spectacles. The grin on the older man's face when he turned up for duty in a pair of gold, police-issue glasses had been a sight to behold, but it had obviously caused the sergeant to re-think his plans and the issue of retiral hadn't been discussed since much earlier in the year.

Then, to add to his troubles, there was the re-kindled and burgeoning friendship between his mother and Sergeant Tait... Alan turned on to his side, facing the drab, green wall. He wouldn't—he daren't—think about that.

He was physically tired too; there had been a recent spate of arson attacks in the village and although these hadn't been particularly serious, they had caused considerable damage, not to mention local alarm. Ten days previously, a decrepit allotment shed had fallen victim, rapidly followed by a paint store at the site where the new houses were being erected. The latest, at the start of the week, had seen the school janitor's shed fall victim, its recently creosoted timbers igniting and causing an alarming conflagration. Fortunately the school was spared, the shed being located at the rear of the playground, but the community was shocked at the thought of their beloved, Victorian-era building almost falling victim to fire-raisers. Investigations were ongoing but Alan suspected it was little more than a bout of juvenile delinquency that was at the root of the problem and, if truth be told, he had made little progress in catching the culprits. The fires had all taken place late at night and, in deference to Sergeant Tait's age, plus the fact that Kerr Brodie, the other Barloch constable, was on holiday, Alan had been on call on all three occasions, resulting in three long, sleepless nights. He gave a grim smile in the near-darkness of the room; he liked his sleep and the ungodly hours of CID work were, most definitely, not for him.

~~~

Alan was finally in a deep slumber and, although his dreams were jumbled, it seemed that, somewhere, someone was banging. He heard his name being called and he opened his eyes, instantly alert.

'Mr McInnes—Mr McInnes—quick, there's a fire!'

Swearing under his breath, he fumbled for his pyjama jacket, and rushed, barefoot, down the un-carpeted wooden stairs, almost slipping on several occasions. The banging started again.

'Aye, I'm comin'—no need to batter down the door!'

He opened the front door to find Angus Wilson, proprietor of the local baker's shop, standing on the doorstep, clad in white jacket, trousers and hat.

'Mr Wilson—what's the matter—a fire, you said?'

'Aye, Ah was on ma way to get the ovens lit when Ah seen it—doon at the goods yard, so it is.'

Alan's heart skipped a beat—his father was the night watch-man at the local railway yard.

'The goods yard?' he repeated. Wilson nodded his confir-mation.

'Aye.'

'Have you called the fire brigade?'

'Aye, Ah went back hame and got the wife up, she's awa' tae the phone box doon the road, so she is.'

Before Alan could respond, a sleep-laden voice called out.

'Here, whit's a' the commotion?'

Sergeant Tait was standing at the doorway adjacent to Alan's, a disreputable dressing gown wrapped around his sturdy frame.

'Mr Wilson says there's a fire down at the goods yard.'

Tait paused before replying, realising, like his constable, the implications.

'Well, ye'd better get yersel' awa' doon, then. Ah'll get on some claes then get the motorbike oot. Ah'll see ye doon there.'

Tait stepped back inside and banged the door shut as Alan turned back to the baker.

'Right, thanks, Mr Wilson. I'll get dressed and get down the road.'

'Aye, richt ye are...'

Wilson paused, then gave Alan a sympathetic look.

'Yer faither's on watch the nicht, is he no'?'

Alan nodded.

'Ach, Ah'm sure he'll be fine—as likely as no' he's knocked the brazier over an' the hut's caught alicht. Dinna you worry'.

But, as Angus Wilson turned away and Alan closed the door before running back up the stairs, he was trying in vain to calm a rising sense of alarm. Given the current warm spell, it was quite possible that Gilbert McInnes hadn't bothered lighting the watchman's brazier.

~~~

As Alan pounded down School Street and across Barloch's Main Street, he could smell the acrid smoke of the fire. A few minutes later, he heard the distant jangle of an approaching fire appliance, giving him a modicum of relief. Passing under the three railway bridges that spanned Kirk Street, he turned left and jogged up the ramp leading to the goods yard. He could hear the crackle of the flames now, their orange glow reflecting on the dilapidated buildings. He reached the yard to find a handful of people standing well back from the raging fire but, even at a distance, he could feel the intense heat. Two wooden goods wagons were well alight and the flames were beginning to lick around the brake van that sat between them and the rudimentary buffer-stop. One of the onlookers turned at Alan's approach.

'Alan—thank God ye're here, son, it's lookin' pretty damned serious! Ah'm fair worried it spreads tae oor buildings.'

Alec McGeoch, the local coal merchant, had premises about

11

twenty yards from the fire and Alan could see the look of concern on his face, as the adjacent garage contained his two coal lorries.

'Could you not move the lorries out, Mr McGeoch?'

The coal merchant shook his head.

'Left the bloody keys at hame—Ah'm feart tae leave an' go back for them, jist in case!'

The lights were on in the little coal-office and he suspected that Mrs McGeoch was inside, probably preparing to remove anything of importance. Despite McGeoch's words, Alan felt helpless—there was really little that he could do at this stage.

'The Brigade's on its way, Mr McGeoch, they'll soon have it under control.'

'Ah bloody hope so— like Ah said, Ah'm worried it spreads...'

He stopped mid-sentence.

'Here, is yer faither no' supposed tae be on duty the nicht?'

'Yes...yes he is. Erm, have you seen him?'

McGeoch's expression of concern deepened.

'Naw, son, Ah havenae...look, here's the fire engine comin' the noo.'

Alan followed McGeoch's gaze to see a red Dennis fire-tender grinding its way slowly up the incline, closely followed by Sergeant Tait astride the police Velocette motorcycle. Tait, wearing his hastily donned uniform, dismounted and came to stand by Alan's side as the firemen alighted and began their preparations. After laying down the long canvas hoses, one of their number ran back down the slope to where the nearest hydrant was situated. Within minutes, the hoses snaked into life and strong jets of water were soon playing over the burning wagons, raising a cloud of dirty steam into the night sky. Alan turned, noticing that a few curious locals were now making their way up the approach ramp and, thankful for the diversion, he shepherded them away from the scene.

Leaving the seemingly enthralled onlookers with strict instructions not to come any closer, Alan walked back to join Tait and McGeoch; Mrs McGeoch, who was now standing beside her husband, was clutching a sheaf of paperwork. She managed a grim smile at his approach, but remained silent. She, too, knew that Alan's father remained unaccounted for.

Within a short time, the firemen had succeeded in taming the flames and the smell of wet, charred wood was strong in everyone's nostrils, clinging to their clothes and hair. One of their number was using his axe to cut away the still-smouldering wood of the furthest wagon when he stopped and called the senior officer over. After a brief confabulation, the officer approached Alan and Sergeant Tait, drawing them aside. He lowered his voice, wary of the curious onlookers.

'Listen, lads, Ah'm afraid it's worse than we thought...'

Tait gripped Alan's arm as the fire officer continued

'...we've found a body in one o' the wagons.'

~~~

Alan was sitting in McGeoch's coal office as if in a daze; Mrs McGeoch had made him a cup of strong, sweet tea and now stood behind him, her hand on his shoulder, as he stared unseeingly at the wall.

'C'mon son, dinna' dwell on it, it micht no be...'

Alan looked up at her, his eyes glistening.

'Who else would it be, Mrs McGeoch? There's no sign o' him anywhere.'

He choked back tears; despite their differences throughout the years, Gilbert McInnes had been a good father to him. However, it was the thought of telling Isa, his mother, which was troubling him most. As if reading his thoughts, Sergeant

Tait spoke, his own voice choked with emotion.

'Ah'll go up an' speak tae yer mother, son. Leave a' that tae me...'

He paused for a moment.

'...an' Ah think Ah'll need tae call in the CID. Ah cannae handle this by masel'—Ah've had enough bodies in the village tae last me a lifetime!'

He fumbled in his tunic pocket for his notebook, then turned the pages, frowning at his writing before handing the book to Mrs McGeoch.

'Here, Ellen, could ye dial this number for me please—Ah've left ma spectacles up the road.'

Chapter 2

Detective Inspector Gordon McGinn, of Paisley CID, was not best pleased at being awakened in the middle of the night; nor was his wife, who, half asleep, was grumbling rather incoherently about 'wakin' up the wee man.' However, Sergeant Tait's terse narrative had the effect of a cold shower, galvanizing him into action. With a weary sigh, he pulled the covers back, shoved his feet into his comfortable, worn slippers and, as quietly as he could manage, headed downstairs and into the kitchenette, where he lit the gas ring then used the same match to light a Capstan full strength cigarette. He wasn't heading anywhere until fortified by tea and nicotine.

Half an hour later, unshaven, bleary-eyed and filled with concern, he set off in the police Wolseley, heading for the village of Barloch. He liked Alan McInnes and had hoped that he might have joined his as a detective, but the young constable's recent engagement had set him along a more traditional route. McGinn gave a grim smile; a newlywed couple could well do without this sort of nonsense! The smile vanished as he recalled the reason for his nocturnal journey.

The road to Barloch was a route that the inspector knew only too well, having spent over a week there the previous year investigating the murder of a father and his stepdaughter. Stopping at a deserted road-junction, he lit another cigarette; at least that crabbit bugger, Nisbet, wasn't there to complain about his nicotine habit! As quickly as the thought arose, however, it was followed by a pang of guilt; had it not been for the inspector's tragic demise, McGinn would, most likely, have remained in the position of sergeant for the foreseeable future.

He made a right turn off the main Largs road and eased over the little humpbacked bridge that led along the side of the Bar loch and into the village. Little wisps of mist appeared and vanished, like the witches and ghouls of Tam o' Shanter's famous tale and, as the headlights illuminated their ethereal shapes, he imagined that Barloch probably possessed a few more ghosts after last year's macabre events. Moments later he turned into Kirk Street then right onto the slope leading up to the goods yard. He could see the fire engine still in attendance, although the flames seemed to have been quelled, as well as the ubiquitous crowd of thrill-seekers that always appeared when there was a fire. Such was human nature, he mused. He stopped the car and, as he exited, the familiar bulk of Sergeant Tait approached, his hand outstretched, his voice sombre.

'McGinn—oh, sorry, Inspector, Ah forgot—good tae see you again, though Ah wish it wisnae under these circumstances.'

'Aye, indeed; and McGinn's fine, Tait, let's not get too bothered over protocol.'

The customary Masonic handshake having been exchanged, Tait gave the inspector a fuller account of the evening's events, the detective nodding as the story unfolded.

'I see; and are we sure it's Gilbert McInnes that's in the wagon?'

'Weel, Ah cannae say for certain, but he should have been on duty an' there's nae sign o' the man anywhere.'

'Hm, it certainly doesn't look good. I'll need to have a word with the fire officer in charge.'

'Aye—that's him ower there.'

McGinn crossed the yard to where the chief officer was supervising the coiling of the hoses. Tait watched as they exchanged a few words, then the inspector crossed towards the coal office. Tait followed, the two men pausing outside the door.

'Right, he can't really shed much light on it, he says that the body is lyin' face down at the end o' the far away van. Identification might be difficult at this stage so it's probably best that we wait until the police doctor arrives. How's McInnes bearin' up, d'you think?'

Tait shook his head sadly.

'He's taken it richt hard, McGinn. Ah've said Ah'll speak tae Isa, but Ah'll leave it the noo, let the poor woman get her sleep. She'll have a difficult few days ahead o' her.'

'Aye, she will. Look, I'll away in an' speak to the lad, you wait out here and keep an eye on the onlookers. I've got the nasty feelin' that we're lookin' at a crime scene.'

~~~

McGinn entered the small office, where Mrs McGeoch was still standing with her hand on Alan's shoulder, speaking softly to him. Alan looked up and made to stand, but McGinn pushed him gently back down.

'McInnes, I'm very sorry—Sergeant Tait's filled me in.'

Alan merely nodded.

'Dr Miller's on his way. We can wait until he arrives then...'

He stopped; then what? Alan would have to make a positive identification and, judging by his apparent mental state at present, that might be the final straw. The young constable didn't deserve this.

'...well, let's just wait and see, eh?'

Mrs McGeoch favoured McGinn with a weak smile.

'Cup of tea, Sergeant?'

'Aye, that'd be grand, Mrs McGeoch, thanks.'

He certainly wasn't going to correct her about his rank at this point in time.

~~~

They were sitting in a sombre silence, the small room filled with a haze of blue smoke from Mrs McGeoch's and McGinn's cigarettes. Alan was staring at the desk, clutching an un-drunk cup of tea in his hand. Suddenly, the door burst open and a large man with a bushy beard stormed in. McGinn recognised him as Bert Oliphant, the stationmaster, and the man appeared highly agitated.

'Good God Almighty, whit a bloody to-do! Twa bloody wagons gone—an' a brake van half burnt oot as weel! Ah tak' it there wis naebody hurt?'

The ominous silence, as well as the expression on the other occupants' faces, told Oliphant that his assumption was most certainly not the case. He gave McGinn a questioning look.

'Whit—whit's happened; for God's sake, tell me!'

McGinn put his cup on the table and beckoned Oliphant outside, closing the office door behind him.

'Whit the hell's happened?' repeated the stationmaster.

'I'm afraid the firemen have found a body in one o' the vans. We haven't made a positive identification as yet, but as McInnes's father should have been on duty and as he appears to be missin', we're workin' on the basis that it's him.'

Oliphant gave McGinn a strange look and shook his head.

'But it canna' be him—Gilbert phoned in sick this afternoon! The thing is, Ah knew there wis twa goods vans comin' the day, an' that they had stuff for the pubs an' for the shops—spirits an' cigarettes an' the like. So, ye see, when Gilbert cried aff, Ah wis concerned aboot leavin' the vans unattended overnicht so Ah asked Alex Combe, the porter, tae cover the shift...'

He broke off, his eyes widening.

18

'Oh, dear God—if it's no' Gilbert, then it must be Combe!'

'You're absolutely certain about this?' asked McGinn.

'Aye, Ah spoke tae Gilbert masel'. Said his leg wis playin' up—ye ken he lost a leg a while back, a shuntin' accident?'

McGinn nodded.

'Weel, he said it had kept him aff his sleep the nicht before an' that he wisnae up tae daein' his shift. Combe's aye lookin' for some extra money so Ah asked him tae fill in.'

The man looked stricken.

'Then it's a' ma fault— it wis me that sent him doon here...'

'Now, Mr Oliphant, you can't blame yourself, you were only doin' your job to keep the goods safe. Look, if you're absolutely certain, we need to get back in and put poor McInnes out of his misery.'

~~~

Having broken the news to Alan, who was immediately favoured with a maternal hug from Mrs McGeoch, Inspector McGinn was outside having a smoke, allowing the occupants time to come to terms with their sense of relief—and, of course, their dismay at Alex Combe's probable demise. He stood in the yard, surveying the aftermath of the fire, wondering where he would make a start; after all, this would be the first investigation into a suspicious death that he had led since his promotion. Although his initial gut feeling told him that he was dealing with a murder, he gave a wry smile; Nisbet would have reprimanded him for this assumption at such an early stage. Somehow, though, he felt sure that his instincts would prove to be correct. He dropped his cigarette, grinding it out with the toe of his shoe—despite the hour there was work to be done.

~~~

Aware of a lightening of the sky, McGinn looked at his watch—it was nearly five a.m. He had taken statements from the fire officers and had allowed them to get on their way. Dr Miller was currently attending the corpse, Bert Oliphant having been called upon to make an initial identification, and the ambulance men were in attendance, awaiting the doctor's permission to remove the charred remains. Having done all that he reasonably could until daylight, the inspector intended to return home for a few hours of sleep before proceeding with his investigations. However, he needed someone to remain and ensure that the crime scene, if such it was, remained untouched. He wondered if Alan McInnes was up to the job.

When he re-entered the office, the constable had certainly regained his colour and was now standing, in conversation with Mrs McGeoch. Oliphant had been allowed home, McGinn having told him that he would take his statement in the morning. Although the stationmaster was clearly distressed, he had undertaken to perform the unpleasant task of advising Mrs Combe that her husband had died, a task that McGinn himself detested. He nodded at Alan, who gave him a wan smile in return.

'Feelin' better, McInnes? '

'Aye, sir, I am.'

'Is Sergeant Tait away home?'

'Aye, he felt there wasn't much he could do at this stage.'

McGinn was slightly put out—the sergeant should really have sought his permission before leaving the scene. He shrugged; it probably wasn't worth making a fuss over.

'Anyway, must've been a hell of a shock for you, mind. Still, just shows the pitfalls of jumping to conclusions, eh? Inspector Nisbet used to say never to assume anythin' and he was pretty much correct—no, don't worry, we all do it, me as much as anyone. Look, I need someone to keep watch tonight, just until I return later on. Are you up to it?'

Alan nodded.

'Aye, sir, I'll be fine now. Erm, what about the—'

'Don't worry, the ambulance is there now, once Dr Miller's finished and the photographer's done his job, they'll remove the remains—'

He was interrupted by a knock at the door. Dr Miller entered, his jacket and trousers smeared with soot.

'Well, I have to say it's not a pretty picture, but I can tell you one thing.'

As Mrs McGeoch handed the doctor a cup of tea, McGinn asked, 'What's that, Doctor?'

'I'll know more once I have the poor chap on the slab, of course, but I'm pretty certain that we're looking at a case of murder, although the final determination will be yours, naturally. Despite the damage inflicted by the fire, the man has a large impact wound on the rear of his head, consistent with a blow from a wooden club or perhaps a leaded cosh. At the very least he was unconscious when he was placed in the wagon. I'll be able to tell when I examine the lungs, see if there's been any indication of smoke inhalation...oh, I beg your pardon, madam, I'm very sorry. I didn't mean to upset you.'

It was Ellen McGeoch's turn to lose her colour; she sat down heavily.

'Och, dinna' mind me, Doctor, Ah'm just no' used tae such talk.'

'And neither you should be—again, I apologise Anyway, Inspector, that's me done, I've instructed the ambulance boys to take him to the mortuary. I'll do my work, clean him up a bit and we can get a formal identification, although the station-master had a look and, as you know, confirmed that it was indeed Alex Combe. He says that the usual watchman has a prosthetic lower leg and our corpse was fully limbed... oh, I'm sorry again, madam. Anyway, I'll be in touch once I've carried out the postmortem. Good night—well, good morning now, I suppose. Might be lucky to catch a few hours' sleep.'

McGinn broke the ensuing silence.

'Right, I'll be away as well. I'll need to speak to you tomorrow, Mrs McGeoch, just to see if you noticed anything prior to tonight. You sure you're okay, McInnes?'

'Aye, sir, I'll be fine.'

'Ah'll make you up a flask and a wee chocolate biscuit tae see you through' said Mrs McGeoch, rising once again to the task of providing food and drink. 'Ye'll be in the wee watch-hut?'

Alan nodded, once again offering a silent prayer of thanks for the sparing of his father.

Chapter 3

Connie Lumsdale opened her baby-blue eyes, lay for a moment and then, with a feline purring sound, stretched the limbs of her lithe young body. Unaccustomed to the luxury of a comfortable double bed, she was determined to make the most of it, although, as with most such luxuries, there was a price to be paid. She turned her head to the left and, realising that the bed beside her was empty, she rolled onto her right side, stretched across to the bedside cabinet and lifted the attractive box labelled Sobranie Cocktail Cigarettes. Selecting one with pale blue paper, she lifted her matches, lit the cigarette and inhaled deeply the exotic, Turkish tobacco smoke. She rolled on to her back once more, watching the blue wisps curling towards the ceiling and wondering vaguely where Jock Wallace, her lover for the night, had got to. It seemed to her that it was too early to be rising, then she giggled; no doubt the man was answering a call of nature—after all, he was old enough to be her father! But, as she took another deep draw on the cigarette, she became aware of Wallace's raised voice, laden with expletives, in the adjoining room. A few moments later, she heard the crash of the telephone receiver being slammed down; hastily she stubbed out the cigarette and pulled herself up in the bed, running her fingers quickly through her peroxide curls before arranging the covers neatly around her lower body. However, as Jock Wallace barged in to the room, clad in a grubby vest and trousers supported by bright red braces, one look at his face told Connie that their liaison was at an end.

He glared at the pretty young woman, as if unable to recall why she was there.

'Richt, hen, get her claes on, party's over.'

She smiled sweetly up at him.

'Are you sure, baby? There's plenty of time for—'

'Ah said, get yer stuff an' beat it.'

Connie knew when to quit. She dressed hurriedly, slipped on her high heels and lifted her bag, stuffing the box of cigarettes into it—she was certainly not leaving those behind. As she headed for the door, Wallace lifted his wallet and pulled out a sheaf of one-pound notes, peeling a number off and handing them to the girl without a word. She smiled sweetly at him—he was certainly a generous client, one that she hoped to meet in the future.

'Will I see ye again, Jock?'

The big man shrugged disinterestedly.

'Who knows?'

As far as Wallace was concerned, Connie Lumsdale was history, at least for the moment. As far as Connie was concerned, it had been a rather lucrative night's work.

As soon as the door had closed, Wallace sat down at the dining table, uncorked a bottle of Red Hackle whisky and poured himself a generous glass. He needed to think and whisky always helped, even at this ungodly hour. The news that the caller had brought had not only infuriated the big man, it had also worried him.

He returned to the untidy bedroom and recovered his wallet, vaguely aware that it seemed to contain less money than he remembered—had that little tart pinched some? His lips twitched in a vague smile, admiring her cheek, but his mind soon returned to the considerably more serious matter in hand. He sat down, refilling his glass before lifting the telephone receiver; there was a very difficult call to be made and, as he took out the now rather dog-eared business card that he had been given nearly six months ago, he paused for a moment, recalling the events that had set him upon this new path.

~~~

Completely out of the blue, he had received a phone call from a Londoner giving his name as Dicky Brand. This brash Cockney had asked if Wallace would be interested in meeting him and his associates for dinner to discuss some 'mutually beneficial business'. Wallace was immediately on his guard; a parochial being, he had never ventured much further afield than Rothesay and he also had a strong mistrust of anyone with an accent originating anywhere further south than Ayr. However, once Brand explained that the meeting would take place in Glasgow and that it would be very much to the big man's advantage, Wallace's curiosity was aroused and he had finally agreed.

Although he was not a particularly intelligent individual, he had sufficient brain power, as well as considerable and notorious physical presence, to oversee a large, thriving criminal empire in Glasgow and its environs. He had always lived by his wits and his fists but recently he had harboured a sneaking suspicion that things were changing. The River Clyde's dockyards were quieter than they had once been, offering less opportunity for pilfering. The police had become more efficient, making life considerably more difficult for those, such as himself, engaged in nefarious activities; and there was a new breed of criminal on the streets, young, smart, dressed in flashy suits and keen to make a reputation for themselves—at any cost! But Jock Wallace knew no other life and he wasn't going to give in that easily.

As he slugged down some more whisky, he cast his mind back to that meeting.

Brand had suggested that they dine at Glasgow's exclusive Malmaison restaurant, situated on Hope Street beneath Glasgow Central Station. Wallace, and his wardrobe, were unaccustomed to such grandiose surroundings, but a visit to Slaven's, Glasgow's well-known tailor, had ensured that he was suitably, if slightly uncomfortably, attired. Taking a tram from his South Side flat, he had arrived, finding himself staring nervously up at the glass canopy emblazoned with 'Malmaison'. This was unfamiliar territory to the big man.

As he approached the door, a thin man with slicked black hair, a pencil moustache and clad in a smart tails-suit, opened it with a flourish, speaking in a somewhat exaggerated French accent.

'Bonswarr, Monsewer. Je swee Marcel, ze maitre d'. Do you' av a reservacion?'

'Eh, Ah'm...I'm here tae...to meet friends.'

'Ah, I see, an' zeyr name, seel voo plet?'

'Erm, it's a Mister Brand.'

The waiter beamed.

'Ah, mer-see, monsewer, right zis way.'

As Marcel beckoned him inside, Wallace felt like a fish out of water. The palatial surroundings, the distant, accomplished tinkling of a grand piano, the smell of French haute-cuisine... however, he straightened his broad shoulders, adopting his customary swagger and air of confidence; no Londoner would get the better of Jock Wallace!

The maitre d' led him through the busy restaurant until they approached a pristine, white-clothed table, adorned with silver and crystal; a highly-polished candelabra containing five candles sat as a centrepiece. As Marcel pulled out his chair the three people already there rose to greet him, one of them extending his hand.

'You gotta be Jock—a pleasure, sir! Dicky Brand, at your service. 'Ere, let me make the introductions.'

Dicky Brand was a suave Cockney in his mid-forties, clad in an expensive, if flashy, pin-striped suit. His thick brown hair was beginning to grey at the temples, giving him a somewhat distinguished air, and he fitted easily into the ambience of the exclusive restaurant. Accompanying him was his sister, Elsie, a few years younger and somewhat less suave. Attractive but with a harder edge, her manner was guarded while her brother's verged on being garrulous. The third member of the party was introduced simply as 'Jan', a tall, thin and cadaverous individual who hailed, apparently, from Rotterdam. Throughout the evening, he barely spoke a word but his eyes roamed restlessly, as if looking for any hint of trouble. Despite his own undoubted physical presence, Jock Wallace still felt decidedly out of his depth.

Marcel returned and handed them their menus but, to Wallace's horror, he found that all the dishes were named in French. Sensing his discomfiture, Dicky Brand winked across at him.

'You leave this to me, Jocky-boy. I'll order for all of us—that okay, sis?'

'Yeah, that's fine, Dicky, y'know what I like,' agreed Elsie, with a smile that failed to reach her cold, grey eyes; the enigmatic Jan merely nodded. It wasn't long before a large plate of oysters arrived, resting on a bed of ice and garnished with capers and lemon.

'I do love a nice oyster.' Dicky squeezed lemon juice on to one before tipping it into his mouth. Wallace followed his lead, almost gagging as the raw, gelatinous shellfish slithered down his throat; he preferred his fish cooked and in batter. A glass of chilled white wine sat next to him and he washed the offending mollusc down with a copious swallow, trying not to grimace at the acidity.

Once the oysters had been consumed, the plate was removed, Wallace having struggled his way through three of the shellfish. As they awaited their Chateaubriand, Dicky leaned across in a conspiratorial manner; Jan's eyes continued to scan the room as he toyed menacingly with his steak knife.

'Right, Jocky, me old son, on t'business...'

Rather theatrically, he glanced right and left, as if ensuring that they wouldn't be overheard.

'So, I'm lookin' for an associate up 'ere, norf o' the border so to speak, an' they tell me that you're the very man...'

~~~

The evening had progressed, the wine had flowed, a rich Chateau Neuf-du-Pape being served with the succulent, rare steak. That had been followed with what Wallace took to be a chocolate pudding although, like the rest of the meal, it came with an unpronounceable French name and was too rich by far for his tastes. Brandy, coffee and cigars concluded their repast, following which Dicky picked up the not-insubstantial bill and they rose to leave.

'Right, me old son, we're puttin' up in this 'ere hotel, headin' back to the smoke tomorrow. Listen, Jocky, it's been a pleasure t'make yer acquaintance. Think it over and gimme me a bell.'

As they parted, Dicky handed Wallace his business card and the big man placed it in his wallet. As he exited the restaurant, Marcel gave him an ingratiating smile and somehow Wallace felt obliged to pass the man a couple of pound notes, receiving an insincere 'ah, mer-see monsewer' for his trouble. Glad to be finally out of the restaurant, Wallace strode down the steps muttering vague insults about 'the bloody French'.

Once outside in the cold, smog-filled October air, he walked down Hope Street before crossing the road to where a dark lane ran along one side of the Alhambra Theatre. A few paces in, he leaned his arm on the wall and vomited violently, ridding his stomach of the rich food to which it was unaccustomed. A passing couple gave him a disgusted look, but he ignored them, his mind focused entirely on the evening's discussion. He was well aware that, if he decided to accept Brand's offer, he would be moving in much bigger circles...and with much bigger fish!

~~~

Wallace emptied the glass of whisky in a single swallow, turning Brand's card over in his beefy fingers for a few moments. In the intervening months, his conversations with his new associate had been minimal, the Londoner suggesting that the less they spoke, the better. Any communications were brief and contained the bare details of what Brand termed 'a shipment of goods'. The system had worked very well and Wallace was starting to see a good return on his investment.

Until now.

~~~

The big man hung up the phone, wiping sweat from his brow. Wallace's news had caused Brand's normally oily tones to take on a harsh edge, giving rise to comments such as 'not liking mistakes' and 'compensation'. He had felt his hackles rise but had managed to control his temper. On top of this fairly catastrophic loss, there had already been a few issues with the distribution of supplies and Wallace had gone to great lengths to assure the Londoner that alternative plans were in place: unfortunately this wasn't true. Admittedly, some weeks back, one of the big man's associates had made what seemed to Wallace to be a rather ridiculous suggestion and he had dismissed it out of hand. Now, as he refilled his glass and crossed to the couch, dropping himself heavily into it, his brow furrowed. Maybe it wasn't such a stupid idea after all. After a few minutes of thought, he fell asleep, the glass dropping onto the couch and spilling its contents.

~~~

He awoke with a start; a sound was jangling somewhere, intruding in his dreams and grating on his nerves. He crossed to the window and looked outside; in the street below, a group of laughing children, enjoying their Easter break from the tedium of school, were crowded around a pale-blue van, some of them clutching ice-cream cones, others with bags of sweets. A few teenagers were there too, trying unsuccessfully to look nonchalant as they bit messily into their slightly more sophisticated wafers and single nougats. As the van moved off, the name emblazoned on the rear of the van struck a chord somewhere in his mind. The chimes sounded once more, a discordant rendition of a tune that seemed vaguely familiar to him, beckoning customers from near and far. Suddenly, his dour countenance was lightened by a smile as he recalled happier childhood memories, of hot summer days at resorts such as Dunoon, Rothesay and Saltcoats. As a young boy, he could never understand why the ice-cream didn't go right down inside the crisp brown cone and he recalled breaking the tip off and making a miniature version of the treat. He shuddered, recalling his present predicament; he had no time for such foolish memories and he was about to turn away when a thought occurred to him: what could be more innocent than an ice-cream van? After all, their customers clearly didn't just consist of kids; teenagers and the occasional adult were to be seen queueing for a frozen treat.

He sat on the couch once more, his mind racing. He wasn't normally given to intuitive thinking and he was self-aware enough to realise that his imagination was somewhat limited; but this? In the absence of any reasonable alternative, it seemed that the idea mooted by his associate might just be the answer to his immediate problems.

He sat for a while, cogitating, calculating and smiling as his scheme took form until, finally, he stood up, crossed to the sideboard and removed one of the drawers. Attached to the rear was a small and battered address book, a book that the police would have been delighted to lay their hands on. Wallace was astute enough to have garnered the details of most of Glasgow's—and its environs'—criminal fraternity; he flicked through the pages until he found the entry he was seeking—the name that he ice-cream van bore. He returned to the telephone, lifted the receiver and dialled the number. After four rings, a heavily-accented voice responded.

"Ello, Carleveri's."

Wallace cleared his throat.

'Aye, hullo. Could I speak to Mr Bruno Carleveri please?'

There was a pause.

'Who will I say is calling?'

'Jock Wallace.

'Uno momento, I will see if 'e is available.'

Wallace tapped his fingers impatiently on the desk; finally, a gruff, even more accented voice spoke.

"Ello, Bruno Carlaveri speaking.'

'Mr Carlaveri, it's Jock Wallace here.'

There was a silence, as if the Italian was considering whether to proceed with the call. Finally, he responded.

'Si, Mr Wallace, what-a can I do for you?'

'Mr Carlaveri, Ah have a business proposition that you might be interested in.'

'Really? An' what-a make you think that, Mr Wallace?'

Wallace immediately wondered if he had made a mistake. He had only met Carlaveri once, at the funeral of a fellow criminal, the attendance at which was expected rather than requested. He knew that the Italian ran a powerful business empire including the manufacture and supply of ice-cream. Carlaveri's attendance at the funeral had suggested that other, less honest, dealings also took place.

'Ah'll cut tae the chase, Mr Carlaveri. Ye see, Ah—'

Carlaveri interrupted..

'Mio amico, if you have a proposition for me, then I suggest that-a we meet, si? I do not-a like discussing such matters on the telephone.'

~~~

Alan was desperately trying to keep awake as he sat in the narrow and uncomfortable watchman's hut, well aware that, although normally occupied by his father, that night it had provided the last modicum of sanctuary for Alex Combe. The arrival of the first train for Glasgow had provided some relief, the ageing steam locomotive giving its sharp whistle before chuffing slowly along the track, its soot-stained carriages click-clacking dutifully behind. Soon afterwards, he had heard the early bus for Paisley grinding its way along Main Street; but he could resist sleep no longer. His eyes had just begun to close when he heard the crunch of footstep and, jerking himself upright, he looked round the edge of the hut to see Sergeant Tait approaching.

'Sergeant—didn't expect to see you this early!'

'Ach, Ah couldnae get back tae sleep an' I reckoned you could dae wi' a break. Away you up the road an' tell yer mother an' father what happened afore they hear it from someone else.'

'Are you sure? I can stay on a bit longer.'

'Na, you try an' get some sleep afore McGinn gets ye roped intae more foot-sloggin'. Ah'll tell him you'll be down a wee bit later.'

Gratefully, Alan stood up and stretched, his limbs stiff from sitting on the hard wooden bench.

'Okay, Sergeant, I'll head up the road an' I'll see you in a wee while. What time is it anyway? I rushed out and forgot to put on my watch.'

Tait consulted his own watch.

'It's just after seven—if ye're lucky, ye'll get yer head doon for a couple o' hours.'

~~~

Alan made his way wearily up the hill that led to his family home. He opened the door as quietly as he could but, unsurprisingly, Isa McInnes was already up and about. He entered the kitchen, where she was busy at the stove, and she jumped at the sound of his footsteps. She looked over her shoulder as she turned the sausages that were sizzling in the pan, their aroma filling the small kitchen and causing Alan's mouth to water..

'Oh, Alan, you gave me a right start! Here, aren't you meant to be on duty soon? What brings you up here at this time of day?'

The smell of her cooking should have been sufficient answer but instead he asked, 'Erm, is Father up yet?'

She gave him a questioning look.

'He's just having a shave, he'll be down in a minute or two.'

'I heard he called in sick yesterday.'

Isa turned away from the stove to face her son, placing her

33

hands on her hips.

'Aye, he did—how did you hear that?'

'I was talking to Mr Oliphant, he told me.'

Alan could see the glint of suspicion in his mother's eyes.

'And when were you talking to Mr Oliphant—surely he'd have been off duty?'

'Erm, look, Mother, let's wait until Father gets here.'

With a grunt of dissatisfaction, she turned back to the stove. A few minutes later, Gilbert McInnes entered.

'Aye aye, an' to whit dae we owe the pleasure this mornin'—or are ye just lookin' fur a feed?'

'Mother, can you turn off the gas a minute, I need to talk to you both.'

After a moment's hesitation, Isa complied, taking a seat beside her husband at the small kitchen table. Alan cleared his throat nervously then began, lapsing into a more formal 'on-duty' style of speech.

'Right, I'm very sorry to have to tell you but, last night, an accident occurred...'

~~~

Once Alan had finished, there was a stunned silence. Gilbert stared at the tabletop, wringing his hands together, while Isa dabbed at her eyes with the corner of her floral apron. Finally, she spoke, her voice quavering.

'I'll go down and sit with Mrs Combe for a wee while this afternoon. I'll bake her some scones.'

She stood up quickly and opened the larder cupboard; as always, when tragedy struck, Isa's thoughts turned to providing for the victims—it also gave her something to keep her mind occupied. Finally, his father mumbled what Alan took to be his commiserations, then got up and made his way back upstairs.

'Mother, are you all right?'

Isa didn't turn round.

'Yes, yes, son, I'm fine, just keeping myself busy, I just can't help thinking that it could so easily have been...'

She burst into a flood of tears and Alan pulled her slight frame into his arms.

'Aye, I know, Mother, please, don't dwell on it. Providence works in strange ways—you always told me that.'

She nodded, her head buried in her son's broad chest.

'Yes, I did, didn't I.'

She pulled away, dabbing her eyes once more.

'Och, this'll never do, I need to get on with thon baking.'

~~~

In the end, Alan managed just over an hour's sleep, leaving him feeling worse than he had before he went home. He had a quick shave before wolfing down a couple of Isa's freshly baked scones, washed down with a mug of scalding tea. He stood up, pulling on his uniform jacket; without thinking, Isa reached up and, with maternal affection, straightened his tie. As she did so, she couldn't help but notice the dark circles beneath his eyes.

'Och, son, could you not have got a wee bit more sleep? I'm sure they wouldn't have minded.'

'I'll be fine, Mother; anyway, it's the Easter weekend, I'll be off so I'll get a long lie on Saturday. I'll see you tonight.'

He gave his mother a quick peck on the cheek, then he was gone. Isa sat down with a sigh; she knew fine well that, if that man McGinn had anything to do with it, her son's long lie would be but a figment of his imagination.

Chapter 4

Thursday started out as another bright sunny day, no doubt much to the delight of the parents and children enjoying the Easter holiday. Detective Inspector McGinn, however, was feeling not the least uplifted by the unseasonal hot spell; he had hoped to take a few days off to spend with his wife and young son, but the previous evening's events had put paid to that. Having parked the police Wolseley on Kirk Street, in case its wheels disturbed any possible evidence, he was standing at the top of the ramp leading to the Barloch railway yard. He lit his customary Capstan and, inhaling deeply, surveyed the sorry scene. Across the yard, Sergeant Tait was in conversation with the stationmaster, Bert Oliphant, as they regarded the burnt-out remains of the goods wagons; even from a distance, he could determine their sombre mood, their shoulders slumped as, no doubt, they discussed the tragedy. McGinn exhaled smoke then sniffed; the tang of charred wood lay heavily in the bright morning air and he tried to dispel from his mind the suggestion that there may be an underlying, more unpleasant smell of burning lurking. He dropped the cigarette, grinding it out with his toe then, as an afterthought, he bent down and picked up the butt, not wanting to contaminate the crime scene. He crossed the yard, the other two men turning towards him.

'Mornin' Tait—Mr Oliphant. Everythin' okay here—well, you know what I mean? An' where's McInnes?'

Tait nodded dourly.

'Aye, weel, if ye can ca' it okay; Ah sent McInnes hame aboot seven—Ah couldnae sleep masel so Ah came doon an' told him tae gang up the road an' get some shut-eye; the poor laddie's worn oot. Anyways, Ah wis jist sayin' tae Bert here that he mustnae go blamin' himsel' for whit's happened.'

'Aye, that's easy enough for you tae say, Donny,' replied Oliphant, 'but—'

McGinn interrupted; while sympathetic, there was no time for wallowing in self-recrimination. He suppressed a smile, however; the relationship between Sergeant Tait and Constable McInnes was interesting, to say the least.

'Tait's right, Mr Oliphant, you were only doin' your job an' we all know the implications if it had been Gilbert McInnes that had been on duty. Best thing is to keep busy—now, can you get me an inventory of what was in the wagons? It would help to know exactly what was in them—if this was a robbery that went wrong, then we need to know what the thief might have been after.'

Oliphant began to speak but the arrival of a car drew their attention and McGinn turned. A careworn blue Standard Eight drew in beside McGeoch's coal office and its occupant stepped out, walking over to meet them; a sallow-complexioned young man whose most noticeable features were his crew-cut bright red hair and his freckles.

Inspector McGinn still had to make his mind up about Detective Sergeant Niven Fairbrother. The younger man was certainly enthusiastic, having transferred from Glasgow in January of that year following his promotion. He seemed to be a reasonably competent policeman and detective, yet McGinn had misgivings that he couldn't quite put his finger on. Was it the modern-cut, rather flashy suits that Fairbrother sported? Was it his slightly supercilious air—he had, apparently, attended a rather 'good' school and he had a habit of using words the meaning of which

McGinn wasn't entirely sure. Or was it, perhaps, the fact that the man wasn't a member of The Craft, McGinn's handshake having been consistently unreturned? Fairbrother approached, a suitably grim expression on his face.

'Morning, sir—bit of a catastrophe here last night, I understand. You should have called me, I'd have been happy to attend.'

The younger man's enthusiasm grated somehow on McGinn's fragile temperament.

'Aye, well, not much we could do last night, Fairbrother. Oh, this is Sergeant Tait, of the Barloch office, and Mr Oliphant, the stationmaster.'

Sergeant Fairbrother duly shook hands with Tait and Oliphant, both men giving McGinn a surreptitious and knowing look at the lack of Masonic engagement. He turned back to his superior.

'So, what's the state of play, sir? Where'll we make a start?'

'Well, Fairbrother, at the moment I'm workin' on the basis that this was a robbery that went wrong, resultin' in an assault an' a death. I've asked Mr Oliphant to provide details of the inventory and I'm waitin' for a couple of forensic lads to arrive—although I doubt there's much left to examine, given the extent of the blaze.'

'And what about the victim?'

Sergeant Tait raised an eyebrow—Fairbrother's tone almost made it seem as if it was McGinn who was the junior of the two men. However, the inspector wasn't one to be bested.

'That's all in hand, Fairbrother. Dr Miller should be carryin' out a postmortem this mornin'; we're fairly certain that it was the night watchman, Alex Combe.'

Oliphant winced slightly at the mention of the deceased's name as McGinn continued.

'The doctor's initial findin' is that Combe received a blow to the head before he was placed in the wagon, which was subsequently set alight. I'm just about to have a look at the wreckage, although I don't want to disturb anythin' before the forensic boys get here. '

The sound of footsteps crunching across the yard caused them to turn once more; Alec and Ellen McGeoch were approaching. Despite the tragedy, the business of supplying coal to the residents of Barloch would, no doubt, continue as usual. Alec McGeoch was glowering at the car parked outside his office, clearly wondering to whom it belonged.

'That's a job for you, Fairbrother; you can take a statement from the McGeochs and their coalmen, see if anyone noticed anythin' suspicious over the last few days.'

'Like what, sir?'

McGinn snapped back at the young man.

'Use your damned imagination—strangers in the vicinity, anythin' unusual or out of place. You shouldn't have to ask!'

As Fairbrother turned away, Tait gave McGinn an odd look and the latter experienced a twinge of remorse; he was tired and, if truth be told, very slightly worried at the responsibility of the investigation, but what concerned him more was the fact that he had sounded for all the world like his predecessor, the late Inspector Nisbet.

~~~

McGinn consulted his watch; it was just past ten-thirty. The forensic examiners, two serious and earnest young men, had been and gone, having given the wreckage of the vans what McGinn considered to be a cursory examination. They declared that, due to the ferocity of the conflagration and the resulting destruction, the likelihood of finding fingerprints, or any other useful evidence, was pretty much zero. They had taken a few samples from various parts of the debris, for what purpose McGinn was unsure. The only useful piece of information that they had imparted was that the door and padlock of the nearest van, although badly charred, remained intact, indicating that the second van had been the target. He remained unimpressed; as far as he was concerned, these modern forensic methods were a poor substitute for good, old-fashioned police work.

Aware of another figure approaching, he looked towards the entrance ramp, where Alan McInnes was striding towards him. McInnes gave a smile of greeting but, before he could stop himself, McGinn snapped.

'Nice of you to make an appearance, McInnes.'

The young constable looked crestfallen as he mumbled that Sergeant Tait had said to get a few hours' sleep before coming back on duty. Again, McGinn regretted his harsh words; his own tiredness was making him irritable but that shouldn't be an excuse. After all, he had been the one that had asked the young constable to stay on duty in the yard.

'Aye, fair enough, you're here now. Right, let's get a look at those wagons, see if we can find anythin' the forensic lads missed.'

Alan hesitated as McGinn turned.

'Erm, Inspector.'

'Aye, McInnes?'

Alan handed McGinn a brown paper bag.

'My mother sent these down—she thought you might be needin' something to eat.'

McGinn looked in the bag—there were two rolls filled with cooked bacon; although almost cold, the smell caused his mouth to water. A slow smile spread over his face.

'Aye, we can always count on your mother to feed the troops! Thanks—an' be sure to pass my thanks to Mrs McInnes.'

'I will, Inspector.' Alan replied, looking slightly more cheerful.

'How did they take the news?' the inspector asked, masticating a mouthful of bacon roll.

'Well, my mother was pretty upset, understandably—she says she'll go and visit Mrs Combe this afternoon. My father...'

He shrugged and McGinn nodded.

'Aye, a man o' few words, as I recall. Still, he'll feel it sore, McInnes. Just because he doesn't say much, it'll have come as a hell of a shock to him. After all, there but for the grace of God...'

The expression on Alan's face halted him mid-sentence.

'Aye, erm, sorry—right, let's get over an' have a wee look.'

McGinn popped the last of the bacon roll in his mouth as they headed over to the burnt-out goods vans; the bag containing the second roll was stowed safely in his jacket pocket. The van furthest away, the one in which Combe's body had been found, had been reduced almost to the chassis, the fire had burned so fiercely. The floor was piled with ash and a tangle of unrecognisable debris.

'Right, McInnes, those forensic lads haven't been able to tell us a great deal so far. They reckon there'll be no prints, the doors have all burned away so we have no idea whether the door was jimmied or if the lock was picked. What they did say is that they think that some form of fuel was used and they've found a badly burned can—paraffin, they suspect...'

Alan made to interrupt, causing McGinn to frown.

'Aye—what is it?'

'Well, sir, it's probably just coincidence but there's been some cases of arson in the village over the last few weeks. We've found empty paraffin cans at the scenes and we think that's what had been used to start those fires.'

'What was set alight?'

'The last was the school janitor's shed, on Monday there—he'd

41

just newly creosoted it and it went up like a torch. Before that, a storage shed at the new housing estate and an old shed up at the allotments. '

'Hm. You're probably right about it bein' a coincidence—I wouldn't necessarily say that they were connected to this, sounds more like kids havin' what they think is fun. I'd say it's pretty certain that we're investigatin' a theft and a murder here, goin' by what the doctor said. D'you have any leads for these incidents?'

'None, sir, and I tend to agree; there's one or two bad families around here, unfortunately, an' the kids tend to run wild at times.'

They stood for a moment surveying the remains of the two vans and the grey, reeking piles of ash and mangled pieces of metal scattered across the sodden, scorched wooden floors. They approached the van where Combe's body had been found and McGinn poked at the debris with his toe.

'Right, let's see...God, it's a mess. Forensics were right enough, I doubt we'll get bugger all evidence here.'

A shout caught their attention and they looked up to see Bert Oliphant approaching, making his way across the railway tracks and clutching a sheaf of papers; he was slightly out of breath when he reached them.

'Inspector, Ah've brought ye the manifest fur the vans.'

'Ah, good stuff, Mr Oliphant.'

McGinn stepped back on to the adjacent stone-built goods platform and took the sheets from the stationmaster.

'I was wonderin', Mr Oliphant, why isn't there a goods shed here? Usually these yards have a small facility at least.'

Oliphant hesitated for a moment, casting a concerned glance in Alan's direction.

'Aye, weel, ye see, there was an accident a guid few years back, a bit o' a misunderstandin' between the shunter an' the engine driver. The vans got pushed through the back wall an' the roof came doon. The shunter—weel, erm—'

'It's all right, Mr Oliphant,' interrupted Alan, turning to Mc-Ginn. 'You see, that was when my father got injured. He managed to jump clear but he tripped and his leg got run over by the wagon, it was too badly injured to save so they had to amputate it.'

'Christ, son, that must have been terrible for you all, I'm sorry. '

'Och, it's all right now, sir, but it was pretty bad at the time. The railway tried to say it was his own fault but the union got a lawyer on to the case and he got compensation, it's all water under the bridge now. But, as Mr Oliphant says, that's what happened to the shed and they never bothered replacing it.'

Oliphant shook his head sadly.

'Aye, seems tae me they're runnin' things doon a' the time, no' replacin' things, no' investin' in anythin'. Ah mean, take the rollin' stock—'

McGinn interrupted; he didn't have time to listen to the trials and tribulations of railway officials.

'I understand, thanks Mr Oliphant. Right, McInnes, let's see if there's anythin' worth seein'.'

As Oliphant made his way back across the tracks towards the station, they clambered once again up on to the wagon, McGinn consulting the manifest.

'Right, seems this one contained boxes of cans an' dried food-stuffs, a couple o' sacks o' potatoes, boxes o' cigarettes, three cases o' whisky an'...'

He looked up at Alan.

'...two dozen bottles o' turpentine for a local decorating firm, plus a dozen cans o' paraffin for the Co-operative.'

'So it would have gone up like a torch.'

'Aye, it would, McInnes, just like the janitor's shed.'

'Do the forensic lot think the paraffin used was one of the cans in the wagon, or was it brought?'

'Good point, McInnes; let's have a shufti and see what we can find, eh?'

Alan began poking his foot about the floor, acutely aware of the slightly less charred area where Combe's body had lain. He crouched down and scraped away at the ash, pulling out melted pieces of glass and laying them on the floor, working away for a few minutes.

'Inspector?'

'Aye, McInnes?'

'Take a look—here.'

McGinn crouched down beside the constable.

'What've you got?'

'Well, the manifest said there were three dozen bottles of whisky—I reckon this is them; although most of them are broken and melted I've dug out all I can find—they're still pretty much in the one place.'

'And?'

'I'm pretty sure there's a couple missing.'

The two officers spent a few more minutes sifting through the ash but found nothing of any further significance, the fire having destroyed pretty much everything inside the van. McGinn dusted his hands and stood up.

'Aye, I think you're right enough, McInnes. From what I can make out it seems like there are a couple o' bottles missin', although I don't know if that'll be of much help.'

Alan scoured the debris for a few more moments then got to his feet.

'But why would the thief just take a few bottles if they came to steal the lot?'

McGinn gave him a long look.

'How would you feel if you'd just killed a man and were about to set his body alight?'

~~~

McGinn and Alan continued their search, discovering the melted remnants of twelve cans of paraffin, still where they had been stacked.

'Looks like the fire might have been premeditated then. If the villain knew there was paraffin an' turpentine aboard, would he have bothered bringin' his own?' asked McGinn. He stepped off the remains of the van, wiping his hands once more on his already ash and soot begrimed trousers. As Alan followed, he noticed an unfamiliar, smartly-dressed figure approaching; McGinn made his way towards the stranger but, as Alan made to follow, something on the railway tracks below the van caught his eye. He clambered down and, scraping aside some of the charred detritus with his foot, he bent down and picked up a broken glass bottle that had been partly concealed. The label was still attached and he looked at it for a moment, his brows furrowed in thought.

'Inspector!'

McGinn turned to face him.

'What is it, McInnes?'

'I think you should have a look at this.'

McGinn gave a grunt of exasperation and turned back towards the van, where Alan showed him the piece of glass he had lifted.

'What d'you make of it, sir?'

McGinn took the broken glass and looked at the label.

'Vat69, eh? Well, this might account for at least one of the missin' bottles.'

'Look at the label—it's upside down.'

'Aye, which means it was intended for a pub, McInnes—the bottles sit upside down in the gantry.'

'Yes, they do. D'you want to keep this, Inspector?'

McGinn took the remains of the bottle.

'Aye, maybe best, just in case. So much for the forensic boys, eh!'

The stranger was now standing beside the ruinous van and McGinn jumped down beside him.

'Fairbrother—this is Constable McInnes, Barloch office. McInnes, this is detective sergeant Fairbrother, my new assistant.'

Alan felt an unreasonable pang of jealousy, but nodded dutifully.

'Sir.'

Fairbrother extended his hand and Alan gave the customary handshake which, to his surprise, wasn't returned.

'Good to make your acquaintance, McInnes. Right, sir, I've spoken to the McGeochs and their coalmen. No-one appears to have noticed anything out of the ordinary recently. I've taken all the statements, got them all signed. What would you like me to do now?'

McGinn rubbed his chin. He realised he hadn't shaved that morning.

'I suggest we instigate a door-to-door in Kirk Street, round about the entrance to the yard at any rate. See if anyone noticed a stranger hanging about over the last few days, it's a pretty close-knit wee community, everyone knows everyone else. If you don't have any luck, we'll probably need more officers if we're goin' to extend it. McInnes, is that other constable of yours on duty today?'

'Kerr Brodie? No, sir, he's on leave, won't be back until next Monday. It's just Sergeant Tait an' myself.'

McGinn swore under his breath.

'Then I suggest you go with Sergeant Fairbrother and ask about. As I said, keep it to the houses at this end of the street. I'll go an' take Bert Oliphant's statement then we'll meet back at the office and see what's what—hopefully cadge a cup of tea off Sergeant Tait! I'm parched with all that damned ash.'

Chapter 5

Constable McInnes and DS Fairbrother crossed Barloch's Main Street, walking in a rather disheartened silence. Having elicited no useful information from the occupants of the terraces and tenements in lower Kirk Street, they were now en route to the local police station. Admittedly, many of the residents were at their place of work but the few souls that they had spoken to—housewives, young mothers, the retired—had neither seen nor heard anything untoward that seemed relevant to the investigation. Alan, however, hadn't been sure exactly what they should be looking out for and he had voiced his concern to the CID man. Fairbrother had favoured him with a rather supercilious smile.

'Oh, come on, McInnes, think about it—first of all, there are hardly any motor vehicles in the village, so if someone had driven up to have a look at their intended target, they should have stood out like a sore thumb. But, as far as I can see, the locals mostly appear to be half-inbred at the very least—there's a decided village 'look', if you ask me!'

Alan could feel his hackles rise; he certainly wasn't warming to this rather smarmy detective sergeant, especially with the knowledge that the position could, quite probably, have been his for the taking. With some considerable difficulty, he tried to make his reply sound respectful.

'That's a bit unfair, sir. I mean, I do know that, in the past, a lot of these parochial villages and communities tended to marry cousins, but it doesn't mean that—'

Fairbrother cut him off.

'Anyway, that aside, everyone appears to know everyone else—they certainly all seem to know you, McInnes! Surely any stranger skulking about, casing the joint as they say in the movies, would have stood out a mile. No, it's been a waste of time, I'm afraid. Either they're too stupid to notice or they don't give a damn.'

Alan clenched his fists as they turned on to the path leading to the office. Angrily, he pushed the door open and stepped inside, ignoring the look that Fairbrother gave him as the constable barged in front of him.

'Ah, just in time,' said McGinn. 'Sergeant Tait's just bringin' out the tea. Any luck?'

McInnes shook his head, a sullen expression on his face as Fairbrother answered.

'None at all, sir, the residents appear to be pretty damned unobservant, in my opinion; and if they have noticed anything, they're too ignorant to take any notice—'

'Here, we'll have nane o' that' interjected Tait, as he arrived with a pot of tea and four cups. 'These are decent, honest, hard-workin' people doon here, there's no need tae go castigatin' them in that manner.'

'Tait's quite correct, Fairbrother' agreed McGinn. 'Just because they're not necessarily up to your high standard of education doesn't make them dishonest—or ignorant, for that matter...'

He broke off suddenly, leaving a rather awkward silence hanging in the small, smoke-filled office. Alan noticed Fairbrother's face turning scarlet, whether with anger or embarrassment, he wasn't sure. After a few moments, McGinn spoke again, the somewhat bitter tone of voice having left him.

'Anyway, it's been a hell o' a long night an' we're all tired—at least some of us are—let's have a cup o' tea. Cures all ills, so they say!'

Tait poured the brew, a dark expression on his craggy features; Fairbrother, however, appeared not to notice. McGinn took a sip from the steaming mug.

'Right, let's assess the situation so far.'

~~~

As far as Alan could determine, the situation wasn't particularly encouraging; all they knew for certain was the name of the victim, Alex Combe. No fingerprints had been detected, there had been no witnesses to the crime. No-one had seen anything suspicious in the days leading up to the fire; and, apart from a single bottle of whisky, it seemed that nothing had actually been stolen. McGinn swore softly.

'This is shapin' up to be a bugger o' a case. I'll speak to the Super, see if we can get a few more uniformed officers down, but I don't know what, exactly, we're goin' to be lookin' for.'

'Has this happened before?' asked Fairbrother. 'I mean, have there been previous thefts from the goods yard?'

Tait, unable to conceal his hostility, glared at the young detective, then turned to Alan.

'There wis a theft near the end o' last year, wasn't there, McInnes? Same thing, a goods van was broken into.'

'Aye, that's right, Sergeant, I think they got away with some electrical goods for the Co-operative, if I remember correctly.'

'And you never got anyone?' asked McGinn.

Alan shook his head.

'No, sir, same as this time, no-one saw or heard anythin'. It was carried out at night, just like this one, there were no leads an' the case just went silent—we suspected that the thief wasn't a local.'

McGinn frowned.

'Was there no watchman on duty on that occasion?'

'Ach, it's the usual story, Inspector,' replied Tait. 'When auld Tam Dawson retired, they didnae replace him. It's just Gilbert noo, Alan's faither, an' he cannae cover a' the shifts—if they need someone then Bert Oliphant just asked wee Alex...'

His voice tailed off as his thoughts turned to the deceased.

'My father says that a lot of the deliveries are coming by road nowadays,' Alan continued. 'British Railways seem to be running the goods yard down—you can see that for yourself. He reckons it's only a matter of time before they close it altogether. '

They drank their tea in silence for a few moments, then McGinn spoke.

'So, how would the thief have known what was in the vans? I mean, if it had been the first van, it was just a load o' mixed goods an' the like, nothin' of any particular value. How would he know that the second van contained the booze an' tobacco?'

Tait thought for a moment.

'Weel, ye'd need tae ask Bert, but someone could maybe have had a look at the inventory, that would have told them whit was comin' doon in that day's train. Could have been someone up in the Glasgow goods office too, Ah suppose.'

'Is it not more likely to have been this man Oliphant?' asked Fairbrother. 'After all, he would have had access to the inventory, someone could easily have slipped him a back-hander for that information.'

He turned to McGinn before Tait or Alan could object.

'Might be worth having a chat with him, Inspector, lean on him a bit, see if he maybe took a bribe...'

Tait immediately jumped to Oliphant's defence.

'Here, Fairbrother, ye cannae just come doon here an 'start acccusin' all an' sundry o' bein' on the graft! Ah've known Bert Oliphant for many a year, the man's as honest as the day is long. Ah can vouch for him—he's had mair than enough upset over a' this, dinnae you be causin' him any more grief wi' yer unfounded accusations!'

'Right, just calm down, lads' interjected McGinn, as Alan gaped at his sergeant's outburst; it seemed that Tait, too, was no fan of Niven Fairbrother. 'Look, Fairbrother's got a fair point—and I'm not accusin' Oliphant of anythin', Tait, but we have to investigate all possibilities here. The thief must have known that the van was worth robbin', after all. We'll have a chat with Oliphant, see if anyone other than him had access to the inventory. If not, we can start lookin' at the Glasgow goods office—or wherever the van came from. I dare say Oliphant can provide all that information. Don't forget, we're all on the same team here, we all want to catch the person that carried out the attempted robbery and was responsible for Combe's murder.'

He moved towards the door.

'Fairbrother, I want a word wi' you—outside.'

~~~

Despite the forced silence between them, neither Alan nor Sergeant Tait could hear any of the discussion that ensued, apart from McGinn's raised voice on several occasions. After a few minutes, the two CID men returned, a chastened expression on Fairbrother's sallow features. He cleared his throat.

'Erm, Sergeant Tait, I apologise for jumping to conclusions regarding Mr Oliphant. I just wanted to ensure that every avenue of suspicion was investigated; I didn't intend to accuse him of anything.'

Tait nodded, puffing on his pipe.

'Aye, weel, apology accepted, Fairbrother, an' we'll say nae mair aboot it.'

McGinn breathed a silent sigh of relief before he spoke.

'Right, now the question is, what next? We've got damn all to go on at the moment, other than we know the deceased to be Alex Combe. No-one at the coal yard saw anythin' suspicious an' the door-to-door hasn't provided any information.'

He paused to light a Capstan, the blue smoke he exhaled adding to the fug in the office.

'McInnes, I want you to head down to the station an' see if Oliphant can provide us with any clues as to who else may have had access to the inventory. Once we know where the stuff was sent from we can question the yard staff an' see if anyone's lookin' a bit guilty.'

He took a deep draw on the cigarette.

'An' I wonder if Oliphant can tell us who the goods were for? Could even have been someone on the staff of one o' the pubs; if they knew there was spirits or tobacco comin' they might have tipped someone local off.'

He looked at Tait.

'D'you know the landlords hereabouts, Tait?'

'Aye, Ah do; they're a' local folk an' it's likely that they were a' waitin' for a delivery, what wi' the Easter weekend comin'. Ye see, a lot o' the locals will be aff this weekend an' spendin' a bit more time in the pubs.'

McGinn rubbed the stubble on his chin.

'Hmm; unfortunately, that also means it might have been more common knowledge than usual; doesn't take much reckonin' to figure out that the pubs will be stockin' up for the weekend. Look, are there any locals who might be capable of carryin' out this crime? And I don't just mean the theft—is there anyone you can think of who might be capable of commitin' murder to cover their tracks?'

Both McGinn and Alan shook their heads, the latter answering McGinn's query.

'No, I don't think so, sir. The only one would have been the man Campbell and he's no longer with us, as you know. Anyone else around here—well, there's just a bit of petty thieving now and then. I don't think there's anyone that'd be capable of killing someone...'

His voice tailed off and Tait took up the narrative.

'McInnes is correct—remember, we're jist a wee village an' it's highly unlikely that anyone could hae been capable o' killin' poor Alex Combe—after a', most folk aroon' here wid ken him pretty well, he's lived here a' his life. Naw, Ah dinna think this wis the work o' someone local.'

'Fair enough,' replied McGinn. 'I just wanted to make sure. Right, McInnes, get off and question Oliphant and mind what I want you to find out. Tait, if you can give me a list of the publicans—and anyone else who might have been waiting for cigarettes or booze— then you, Fairbrother, can go round and question them, see if there's anyone they might have a suspicion about. The sooner we get a bloody lead, the better, before it all goes cold.'

~~~

Jock Wallace was seated in one of his favourite haunts, Aldo's Fish Restaurant in Glasgow's Paisley Road West. The restaurant attracted a variety of patrons; young mothers who fed the delicious golden chips, cooked in beef dripping, to their grateful offspring; commercial travellers drinking tea and smoking endless cigarettes as they complained of diminishing orders; the occasional pensioner, there as much for the company as for the food. As far as Wallace was concerned, it offered a safe and anonymous rendezvous for his clandestine business dealings; it also happened to be owned by his potential new business associate, Bruno Carlaveri.

He pushed the remains of his fish and chips across the table, lit a cigarette and consulted his watch; ten minutes until the man he was meeting was due to arrive. His feelings were mixed. For many years, Wallace had been all but autonomous in the running of his Glasgow-based criminal empire and he was reluctant to relinquish that power. However, circumstances had changed and, following recent events, this seemed as good an opportunity to recoup his losses and expand his interests as any. Rather nervously, he puffed away at the cigarette, aware of the door to the restaurant opening. Looking up at the large mirror that hung on the rear wall, the image of his visitor appeared between the gold-painted words 'Aldo's Finest Fish'. He stubbed out his cigarette and stood up.

With a mane of greying hair, slicked back in a rather dated Brylcreem'd quiff, a bushy moustache, and dressed in a light grey suit that looked as if it might have been fashioned from silk, Bruno Carlaveri looked every inch the powerful businessman that he undoubtedly was. Wallace knew that the Italian owned a considerable number of chip shops and cafes across Glasgow, as well as a large ice-cream factory. Although these were all legitimate businesses, Wallace suspected that many were used as a cover for dishonest activities, such as prostitution and the reset of stolen goods. As the Italian approached the table, the big man shook Carlaveri's proffered hand.

'Mr Carlaveri.'

The visitor replied in a strong Italian accent.

'Mr Wallace. How are you?'

'Aye, dae'in' fine, thanks. Yersel'?'

'Si, bene—very good, mio amico.'

They sat down, Carlaveri hitching up his smartly-pressed trousers and making Wallace feel ever so slightly scruffy, despite having donned the suit he had purchased for his visit to the Malmaison. Carlaveri looked across towards the serving counter, snapped his fingers and called out.

'Due espresso.'

A young man with a thin face and olive skin replied.

'Si signore, subito.'

Carlaveri reached into his jacket pocket and removed a pack of cigars, offering one to Wallace. The two men lit up in silence as the coffee arrived. Carlaveri nodded at the waiter.

'Grazie, Luigi.'

'Prego, signore.'

The Italian took a sip of the coffee, regarding Wallace above the rim of the little espresso cup.

'So, what is it that you think I can do for you?'

Wallace leaned across the table, lowering his voice.

'Ah understand that you have a fleet o' ice-cream vans.'

Carlaveri chuckled amiably.

'Si, that is-a correct. Surely you are not wanting to go into the ice-a cream business, Mr Wallace.'

Wallace smiled back.

'No, somethin' a hell o' a lot more lucrative, Mr Carlaveri. A hell o' a lot more!'

~~~

At first Bruno Carleveri had laughed at Wallace's suggestion but, after some consideration—and some very persuasive talk from the big man— he had agreed about the pure simplicity of it all.

'Mr Wallace—may I call you Jock?—you might just 'ave struck on an excellent idea. In time, I might 'ave thought of it myself, then again I might not, who knows? But I think that, with a bit of organisation, it-a could work. Now, you say that you 'ave a delivery arriving tomorrow, si? And that you need to distribute this delivery quickly?'

'Aye, that's right. My friends doon south have a man comin' up on the train.'

'Hm, I see. And you 'ave someone to collect this delivery? Someone that you can-a trust?'

Wallace paused before answering.

'Erm, Ah'll be daen' it masel'.'

Carlaveri drew his dark eyebrows together in a frown and shook his head.

'That is not wise, my friend. What if someone is watching? How will you know that this—this courier, we will call him— is-a what he seems? He may be an undercover policeman; you do not know.'

This hadn't occurred to Wallace; he shrugged, trying to make light of the suggestion.

'Aye, weel, Ah get yer point, but Ah'll just have tae take ma chances tomorrow, Ah suppose—the arrangements have already been made. Ah'll maybe get one o' my boys tae pick it up in the future.'

He leaned across the table and lowered his voice.

'Ah'm sure ye understand, Mr Carlaveri, it's gettin' harder tae find folk ye can trust these days, all the young yins, they're a' wantin' tae branch oot on their own.'

The Italian nodded.

'Si, my friend, I understand, but let me give you some advice. You just have to make sure that they are fully aware of the consequences if-a they do try to double-cross you. You have to assert your authority, show them who is really the boss.'

Carlaveri ran his fingers across his throat, giving Wallace an evil grin as he did so.

'Capiche?'

Wallace sat back and nodded; Carlaveri clearly wasn't averse to using extreme violence when required.

'Aye, Ah get yer drift.'

'Bene. So, I take it you are not-a just handed these goods—surely that is too obvious?'

'Naw, Ah've tae wait by the old shell in Glasgow Central station, the man comes tae meet me, we shake hands an' he passes me a left-luggage ticket, it's aw' quick an' easy, Ah wait a bit then Ah go an' pick it up.'

'I see. So, what-a have you been doing to collect these goods up until now?'

Wallace had been hoping that Carlaveri wouldn't ask this question.

'Erm, weel, the parcel gets sent up on the train, just as ordinary goods. It goes tae a wee local depot an' Ah pick it up, like. All under an assumed name, it's usually pretty safe. Naebody asks any awkward questions or nothin'.'

Carlaveri nodded sagely.

'Hm, I understand; so what-a makes you want to change this arrangement, Jock, if it has worked so well?'

Wallace wondered if the Italian had heard something; he could feel beads of sweat breaking out on his forehead.

'Erm, weel, there wis a wee incident...'

'Ah, an incident...'

Wallace explained as briefly as he could manage, not wishing to reveal the extent of his failure. Carlaveri nodded sympathetically.

'That is-a most unfortunate, Jock, most unfortunate indeed. Like I said, you need to ensure that everyone knows who is boss, si? And it sounds to me as if your-a method of distribution is not very reliable either.'

'Aye, weel, Ah've come tae that conclusion masel', Bruno. See, there's been one or two wee problems here an' there an' it takes a while tae get the goods oot tae the customers. Ah'm thinkin' that ma idea wid make distribution a lot easier an' quicker.'

The truth was that Wallace needed to recoup his losses very quickly indeed; Dicky Brand had made that abundantly clear. Carlaveri puffed on his cigar for a few moments.

'So, let us assume that I agree to your idea. You said that you 'ave more goods arriving tomorrow?'

'Aye, like Ah said, Ah had a wee talk wi' ma man in London just this mornin'. He has a fresh shipment for me, it's comin' up on the train tomorrow afternoon.'

Carlaveri blew a large smoke ring towards the ceiling.

'I see, I see. But this is-a still a big step for me, Jock, and a big risk. We will need to discuss the financial...'

He spread his hands and shrugged.

'...well, you understand, mio amoco?'

Wallace understood only too well and he responded with a rather feeble grin. Carlaveri's earlier comments regarding his method of collection already had him worried and now they were moving on to the nitty-gritty of the financial split.

'Aye, weel, Ah wis thinkin'—'

'Fifty-fifty.'

'Eh? Ah wis thinkin' more along the lines o'..'

Carlaveri's features hardened as he leaned across the table.

'Fifty-fifty, take it or leave it, amico mio.'

Wallace had little choice; Carlaveri had the upper hand and he knew it.

'Aye, weel, if that's your terms, Bruno, then Ah don't seem tae have much choice.'

Carlaveri grinned.

'You are a wise man, Jock Wallace, you know a good thing when you see it.'

Wallace tried to hide his anger; he had hoped for better terms but he wasn't really in a position to negotiate, especially with

Dicky Brand breathing down his neck. The Italian seemed to sense his disgruntlement and gave an oily smile.

'I am sorry if you are disappointed, Jock, but this is-a just business. Anyway, I am sure that, if we work together, the rewards will be plentiful—for both of us! Do not worry, amico mio, everything will be fine! Maybe I am-a just being over-cautious regarding your arrangements, but we both 'ave a lot riding on this, do we not?'

'Aye, we do, Ah suppose. Look, Ah take it you'll be able tae have everythin' ready at your end if Ah get the goods tomorrow?'

Carlaveri nodded.

'Of course, leave it with me, Jock, I will organise it immediately, rest assured. Yes, I think that this is a very good idea of yours! He lifted the cup of espresso and raised it towards Wallace.

'Salute, amico mio, here's to a long and prosperous association.'

Wallace did likewise, trying not to grimace at the taste of the strong, bitter brew.

~~~

Once Wallace had left the restaurant, Carlaveri sat for a few moments, finishing his cigar. Finally, grinding it out in the battered metal ashtray, he stood up and made his way to the door, giving the manager a peremptory nod. Bruno Carlaveri had unlimited credit in his culinary empire!

Once outside, he looked right and left, making sure that Wallace was not in sight. He knew that the red-faced, sweating man in his ill-fitting suit was little more than a thug, a dinosaur whose world was diminishing. Carlaveri possessed considerably more knowledge than Wallace realised; he also strongly suspected that Wallace's slightly bizarre, if clever, idea was probably not

60

his own, although it might just prove to be a stroke of genius. Anyway, he would run with it for a while and, once his network was in place, he would get in touch with Wallace's suppliers in London and bypass the big man altogether. After all, he did not see the need to share his profits with the likes of Jock Wallace. Carlaveri smiled and walked towards the shiny black Rover 90 parked at the kerb; perhaps if this business deal went well, he could afford an upgrade.

Chapter 6

The inevitable cigarette clamped between his lips, Inspector McGinn perused the neatly-handwritten list of people who may have had access to the manifest for the two goods vans. He squinted through the haze of blue smoke.

'Right, at least we've somethin' to be goin' on with here, although it seems a pretty meagre inventory to commit murder for. There's also precious few at this end that had access to the inventory. Combe, of course, Oliphant...'

He looked up at Alan.

'...an' then' you'll have realised that there's your father an' all, McInnes. He might no' have had access to the manifest but, as watchman, he would have had an idea as to what the vans contained. '

Alan nodded

'Aye, I'd already realised that, sir. D'you want to come up the road an' have a word with him now?'

'Aye, might as well.'

He was interrupted by the door opening; Fairbrother entered, sweating profusely and with a look of near-despair on his sallow features.

'Well?' asked McGinn, rather abruptly, Alan thought.

The sergeant shrugged.

'Not a great deal to report, I'm afraid, sir. As with the local residents we spoke to, they were all a bit cagey, don't seem to like strangers in their midst, it seems. However, I have managed to get a list of names—most of the public-house staff, it seems, would have known that a delivery was due. I suppose we could interview them.'

'Aye, I suppose we could but it'll take ages. I've spoken to the Super and he's goin' to let us have a few uniformed officers tomorrow. Once they arrive, we can speak to the staff at the pubs, but we'll also need to get on to College Goods depot up in Glasgow, that's where the delivery originated. We'll likely need the Super to clear it with the City o' Glasgow lot first, though, they might not be too happy with us turnin' up on their doorstep, askin' questions.'

He turned towards Tait, who was puffing ruminatively on his pipe.

'Is there someone that can keep an eye on things down the road—not that there's a hell o' a lot to keep an eye on, mind.'

Tait nodded sagely.

'Aye, a couple o' McGeoch's boys said they'll stay the nicht, just in case. Ah think McGeoch's mair worried aboot his ain place, although it's no' likely that anythin' further'll happen.'

'I doubt it, right enough, but I'd just be happier if an eye was kept; after all, it is a murder scene.'

He frowned, rubbing the dark stubble on his chin.

'Right, we may as well call it a day at that—McInnes, I'll come up the road with you now and we can have a wee chat with your father. Erm, will you mother be home?'

Alan smiled to himself as he replied in the affirmative; he had the sneaking suspicion that Inspector McGinn was ever so slightly afraid of Isa McInnes!

~~~

Alan opened the door to his house and, as he followed McGinn into the hallway, a delicious smell of cooking assailed their nostrils. Alan's stomach rumbled and he realised that he was starving. His mother called from the kitchen.

'Is that you, Alan? You're home early; come away ben the kitchen, dinner won't be too long...oh, Sergeant, I didn't realise that you were here too.'

Her tone had turned slightly frosty; Alan glanced at his superior, quickly realising that the man had no intention of correcting his mother regarding his rank.

'It's Inspector McGinn now, Mother!'

'Oh, I'm sorry, Inspector. Congratulations, I'm sure.'

'Thanks, Mrs McInnes' said McGinn. 'My, that smells delicious—what's on the menu tonight?'

Although McGinn clearly had a lot of making up to accomplish, a compliment aimed at Isa's cooking was a good start. She managed a slight smile.

'Och, it's just stovies—they're Alan's favourite. Erm, you'll have had a long day— would you like some?'

There was a short pause before McGinn replied, half-heartedly shaking his head.

'That's kind, Mrs McInnes, but my wife'll have something ready when I get up the road.'

Isa cast a sidelong glance at the inspector; the disappointed expression on his face brought out her best maternal instincts.

'Yes, I'm quite sure she will, but I do need someone to have a wee taste to make sure I've added enough salt.'

'Oh, well, in that case...'

A few minutes later, McGinn was seated at the kitchen table, tucking in to a bowl of that simplest of Scottish meals, potatoes, onions and sausage fried in beef dripping. Isa looked on, her hands on her hips, a smile hovering on her lips. Between mouthfuls, McGinn looked up and grinned.

'Honestly, these are the best stovies I've had, Mrs McInnes. Absolutely delicious.'

He took another mouthful, chewed, then continued, poking his fork at the dish as if to make his point.

'Y'know, there's those that can make proper stovies an' there's those that...'

Isa shooshed him.

'Och, away with you, it's just a knack that a mother has, making the best of what they've got to feed their family. A wee drop more?'

As Alan watched Isa spooning another helping into McGinn's bowl, he felt a lump rise in his throat. He knew fine well that Isa would have made just enough for the three of them and that Inspector McGinn was happily—and innocently— devouring his mother's dinner.

~~~

They were waiting in the living room as they heard Gilbert McInnes clumping his way down the stairs. The door opened and he nodded at his son; even since that morning he appeared to have aged, no doubt as a result of realising just how easily it could have been him lying in the burnt-out guards van.

'Good afternoon, Mr McInnes,' said the inspector, his tone friendly.

'Aye, guid afternoon tae yersel.'

Gilbert dropped wearily in to his easy chair, the two officers sitting down opposite the older man.

'How are you feeling, Mr McInnes—I believe you were unwell yesterday?'

Gilbert glowered down at the prosthetic leg that was just visible below the hem of his trousers.

'Bloody leg wis playin' up—think there's an infection in the damned stump.'

'You'll really need to see the doctor; you don't want it to get any worse, Father. '

Almost imperceptibly, Gilbert McInnes's face twitched at the use of the word, although McGinn noticed it. As usual, the reply was in the form of a complaint.

'Ach, bloody quacks, whit'll they dae—jist put me on some stupid pills.'

McGinn interrupted.

'Your son's correct, Mr McInnes, you really don't want it to get any worse. Look, if you don't mind, I want to ask you a few questions about the tragic incident this morning.'

A suspicious look crept over the older man's face.

'Oh aye—whit kind o' questions?'

'Just what we've been asking everyone else, Mr McInnes. Did you see anyone suspicious hanging about the goods yard in the days, or weeks, leading up to the crime?'

Gilbert shook his head.

'Ah'm only there fur the nicht shift an', even at that, there's bugger aw shifts these days. Onywey. Ah never saw anythin'oot the ordinary.'

Alan cringed at his father's abrupt manner but McGinn seemed unperturbed.

'Fair enough. Now, as you will know, the second van contained an amount of alcohol and tobacco; we are working on the basis that the thief was intent on stealing this and was likely disturbed by the unfortunate Mr Combe.'

This time, McInnes senior visibly cringed at the mention of the deceased's name but McGinn continued, his voice taking on a harder edge.

'Now, I am aware that you would, at least, have had an idea about the inventory, or manifest, for the goods vans, Mr McInnes; might you have mentioned it to anyone, in the pub, or elsewhere? Even just the fact that you were on watch duties would indicate that there was somethin' worth stealin' in the vans, would it not? Did you mention your shift to anyone?'

Gilbert McInnes glared at the inspector.

'Here, whit the hell are ye implyin'? Are ye tryin' tae say that Ah tipped someone aff?'

'I'm not implying anything, Mr McInnes, but you must remember that we are dealin' with a murder enquiry and I need as much information as I can gather to allow our enquiries to progress and hopefully apprehend the murderer. So, I'll ask you again, would you have mentioned any of this to anyone— anyone at all?'

Gilbert shook his head.

'Naw, Ah never; anyway, wha wid Ah have mentioned it tae? Ah hardly go oot these days, Ah mostly jist bide at hame.'

'What about your wife, Mr McInnes—did you maybe mention anythin' about it to her?'

Alan clenched his fists in anger—surely his mother should be beyond reproach? Before he could interject, Gilbert burst out.

'Don't be a bloody fool, man, Isa's got naethin' tae dae wi' anythin', an' Ah never said a word tae her.'

McGinn gave McInnes senior a scrutinising look then stood up.

'Okay, Mr McInnes, thanks for your time. If you do happen to think of anything you can add to our enquiries, you can let me—or your son—know.'

~~~

Alan was still bristling as he showed the CID man to the door but McGinn gave him a friendly pat on the shoulder.

'Don't take it too hard, McInnes, you know that I've got to be fair an' treat everyone the same way. It doesn't mean I suspect your father—or your mother, for that matter—of anything.'

Alan forced a smile.

'I understand that, sir, it was just when...'

'Aye, when I said about your mother—an' I'm sorry, maybe that was a bit below the belt, but it's what I'd have asked any other witness so, once again, I have to be seen to be fair. Anyway, you away and get your dinner then get a decent sleep; those stovies were delicious! I'll see you in the mornin'— let's hope Friday brings somethin' fresh to the case, eh?'

~~~

Alan closed the door and joined his mother and father in the kitchen. As he sat down, he realised that there were three generous helpings of stovies sitting on the oilcoth-covered table and he looked at his mother.

'Here, mother, I thought you'd given the inspector your share!'

She fussed with her knife, wiping it on her apron as she replied

'Och, I'd made a wee bit extra for Donny Tait, I was going to take it down to him after dinner. I really don't think he's feeding himself properly.'

Gilbert McInnes grunted his disapproval and clattered his cutlery noisily against the bowl—the customary response when Tait's name was mentioned in the McInnes household.

~~~

Inspector McGinn drove the police Wolseley through the suburbs of Johnstone, puffing on his Capstan as he mulled over the case. Fairbrother sat silently beside him, his window wound down half-way to relieve the fug that had built up inside the vehicle. Remembering the late Inspector Nisbet's intolerance to his smoking, McGinn hadn't commented; anyway, he was too wrapped up in his own thoughts. He knew that the

Superintendent would be looking for a swift result—after all, the public detested a murder, especially that of a seemingly blameless victim such as Alex Combe. He was also only too well aware that, as a newly-promoted Detective Inspector, he would be under close scrutiny by his superiors, his performance being carefully weighed and measured. Finally, he glanced across at his colleague.

'So what d'you make o' it all so far, Fairbrother?'

The sergeant appeared surprised at being asked his opinion. 'Me, sir?'

'Aye, well there's only the two of us, isn't there?'

Yet again, he could have bitten his tongue; why had he taken such an irrational dislike to this young man? Was it his education, his slightly aloof demeanour, his rather proper manner of speech which made McGinn feel ever so slightly inferior? Or was it because he had hoped that McInnes would have joined the CID? The young constable had shown considerable insight in their last case, even if he had failed to follow correct procedure. McGinn had harboured great hopes for McInnes but it seemed that the young man preferred the quieter office of a rural constabulary. Given recent events in the normally tranquil parish of Barloch, however, he might now be regretting it! Fairbrother replied.

'I don't really know what to make of it yet, sir. I'm going to stay on at headquarters and write a preliminary report, then look it over, see if anything becomes more apparent. If that's all right?'

'Aye, of course, that's fine. Y'know, it just seems madness to commit a murder, all for the sake of a few cases of whisky an' some fags. I mean, even if the thief had been caught, he'd have got away with maybe a year or so. Now, if he's charged with murder then he could still be facin' the rope. Doesn't make any sense.'

'I suppose not, sir, but that's the criminal classes for you. I very much doubt if they stop to think of the juxtaposition between their actions and the rewards.'

McGinn felt his hackles rise once more at Fairbrother's slightly pompous statement; despite that, however, he tended to agree.

Chapter 7

Alan awoke to find his mother shaking him gently by the shoulder. He prised his sleep-sticky eyes open as she spoke.

'C'mon, son, you've slept through your alarm—you don't want to be late!'

He sat upright, instantly awake. He had gone to bed at nine o'clock the previous evening and had slept for ten hours without stirring

'God, what's the time, mother?'

'Och, don't worry, it's only just gone seven, you'll be fine. I'll leave you to get washed, your breakfast's cooking, don't be too long!'

As he carried out his ablutions, Alan thoughts turned to the case so far. Like Inspector McGinn, he found it peculiar that a thief would risk so much for such a small reward. Even with his limited experience of such crimes, it didn't seem to make much sense. As he made his way downstairs, a vague thought came into his mind and, as he ate his breakfast, his idea developed. Fortunately, Isa McInnes respected her son's silence during his morning repast and, by the time he pulled on his police overcoat, he had resolved to put his thoughts to Inspector Nisbet. Suddenly, he stopped himself—it was, of course, Inspector McGinn. He'd best not make that mistake!

~~~

Fully refreshed and adequately nourished, Alan made his way down School Street and reached the Barloch police office at eight-thirty to find the police Wolseley already sitting outside the door. A police van was parked in front of it, with three uniformed officers leaning against it, chatting and smoking. Alan greeted them as he passed.

He walked up the path and opened the door; McGinn was deep in conversation with Sergeant Tait, obviously planning the day's actions; Fairbrother nodded and made his way outside, presumably to give instructions to the uniformed constables. McGinn and Tait looked up at him through the tobacco-laden atmosphere, Tait removing his pipe from his mouth.

'Mornin', McInnes—have ye caught up on yer sleep?'

'Aye, I have, Sergeant. Erm, Inspector, could I have a word?'

McGinn looked vaguely irritated at the interruption.

'Aye, what is it, McInnes?'

The young constable swallowed hard, remembering several previous instances where he had overstepped the mark. He chose his words carefully.

'Well, I was thinking, sir, you know that you'd said it seemed strange to commit murder just to cover the theft o' tobacco and alcohol?'

McGinn gave him a shrewd look.

'Aye, what of it?'

'Well, you see, it crossed my mind that, maybe, it wasn't the tobacco and alcohol the thief was after.'

Tait interjected.

'But there wisnae anythin' else on the manifest worth stealin', McInnes. Paraffin, turps, a pram, some ironmongery goods, a few cases o' provisions—whit else wid the thief be lookin' for?'

'That's the thing, Sergeant, I wondered if, maybe, he'd already found and taken what he was after, then set the van alight to cover his tracks.'

A short silence ensued; McGinn, his brows furrowed in

thought, lit a fresh Capstan from the stub of his dog-end. The door banged open, heralding Fairbrother's return.

'Right, I've instructed the uniformed officers, they're going to carry out a more thorough door-to-door and see if anyone noticed anything, either the other night or over the last few weeks...erm, have I missed something?'

McGinn continued to frown..

'Aye, just maybe. Let me get this straight, McInnes—you're suggestin' that the thief had already stolen what he came for, got disturbed by the unfortunate Mr Combe, carried out the murder then set the van alight?'

'What, in heaven's name, made you come up with that suggestion, McInnes?' asked Fairbrother, in his customary condescending manner.

'I don't really know, sir, it was, well, like I said, when the inspector had suggested that it wasn't worth killing someone for some fags and booze—it made me start thinking...'

McGinn cut Alan off; although his tone was harsh, there was a twinkle in his eye as he spoke.

'Aye, well, it wouldn't be the first time you've done a bit o' thinkin', McInnes, and it got you in some bother last time, if I recall. However, it also led us to an arrest.'

Alan looked rather sheepish at the slightly back-handed compliment; McGinn drew thoughtfully on his cigarette for a few moments more then continued.

'Right, I think McInnes may have a reasonable point, although what the thief was after remains to be seen. Again, if he was prepared to commit murder for it, the goods must have had some considerable value. Listen, Tait, I need some local knowledge here—I want you to go back through the manifest with a fine-tooth comb and look at each of the addressees. Tie them up to the orders, see if there's anythin' that doesn't look right.

Everyone should know what they were due to have delivered but if we find somethin' on the manifest that doesn't correspond to an addressee, or somethin' that's obviously missin' from the wreckage, then we could be on to somethin'. McInnes, you help him, you know the locals as well as the sergeant. Fairbrother, you come with me, we'll go an' have a word with the station-master and see if he can shed any light on this.'

Fairbrother looked slightly put out as they left the office; no doubt his feelings would have been exacerbated had he seen the surreptitious wink that McGinn gave to Alan as he passed.

~~~

Alan and Sergeant Tait spent an hour or so going over the manifest, tying up the goods that had been in the vans with the names that they knew. Barloch was a small village, both officers had lived there for most, if not all, of their lives and, between them, they could identify every name and address. Everything appeared to be in order; everything except one entry. Tait lit his pipe and puffed thoughtfully.

'That's odd, McInnes. A' the entries tie up—we ken each an' every one, all except this wan name.'

He pointed the stem of his pipe at the entry on the document and Alan nodded. Tait continued.

'So, who the hell is this R. Watson o' Glebe Farm? Whit's more, as far as Ah ken, there's nae Glebe Farm hereabouts, is there?'

'No, Sergeant, I've certainly never heard of it.'

'An' if it wis ootwith oor area, it wid surely have gone tae the nearest goods station an' no' tae Barloch, wid it no?'

'Aye, I would have thought so.'

The door opened; McGinn and Fairbrother returned, a smile playing on the former's lips.

'Well?' asked the inspector. 'Have you turned up anythin'—because we have!'

'Aye' responded Tait. 'We've found a mystery consignment for a—'

McGinn interrupted.

'For an R. Watson at Glebe Farm?'

'Aye, the very one!'

'An' I take it there's no Glebe Farm hereabouts, is there?'

'No, there's no'!'

McGinn gave a chuckle.

'The stationmaster told us the exact same thing. So, what the hell was in the parcel for this R. Watson? I got Oliphant to check back on the last six months' manifests, turns out there's been a few similar consignments during that period. He can't remember what the parcels looked like and this Mr Watson's signature could be anythin', to be honest, but it looks like there's a bogus recipient been pickin' up parcels.'

'Erm, Inspector?'

'Aye, McInnes?'

'The thing is, if this bogus person has already picked up a few parcels, why on earth didn't he just do the same thing this time? Why steal it, set the vans on fire and—well, you know. What d'you think might have happened, what made him act differently and commit a murder?'

They all knew what he meant. McGinn's smile of triumph faded slightly.

'Aye, I take your point...'

Alan continued, his brow furrowed; his thoughts seemed to be coming faster than he could put them into words.

'Y'know, I'm wonderin'...what if someone else found out what was in the parcel an' set out to steal it before this Watson character came to collect it?'

McGinn considered this for a moment.

'Hm, you might actually have a point—otherwise, like you say, why not just collect it as he did before?'

Fairbrother appeared sceptical, however.

'Inspector, don't you think this is just over-complicating the matter. I mean, McInlay—'

'McInnes,' corrected McGinn. The colour rose slightly in the sergeant's cheeks as he continued.

'Erm, yes, of course. Anyway, McInnes may have a point but I do think we're jumping to conclusions here. It said on the manifest that the delivery for this fictitious Watson chap was a small parcel. I think it's most likely that this was consumed in the conflagration and that we appear to be heading off on a wild goose chase here. It seems to me that this was, simply, a petty theft that got out of hand, as we originally thought. Maybe McInnes just has an over-active imagination.'

Once again, Alan could feel his hackles rise at Fairbrother's manner, although McGinn, at least. Appeared to be giving the constable's idea his consideration.

'Aye, you might be right, Fairbrother, maybe we are readin' too much into this, but I think McInnes's idea is worth considerin'...'

The office door opened and, as Bert Oliphant the stationmaster barged in, four pairs of eyes turned to stare at him.

'Erm, aye, listen, Ah've got a bit o' information for ye!'

~~~

Oliphant related his news: the assistant stationmaster had arrived for his shift and, after being quizzed by his superior, he had recalled the previous collection of the parcel for Glebe Farm.

'Aye, it seems the mannie turned up an' said he wis tae collect a parcel for Watson. Davie Kilgour, ma assistant, minded it because he had never heard o' a Glebe Farm hereabouts.'

'Nor had anyone here,' interjected McGinn. 'Sorry—carry on, Mr Oliphant'

'Weel, Kilgour questioned the address but the mannie says he wis frae doon Fairlie way—it's near Largs, that's the terminus, doon on the coast, ye ken.'

'Aye, I know where Fairlie and Largs are, Mr Oliphant,' said McGinn; the stationmaster looked slightly nonplussed.

'Ah daresay—onywey, this mannie says that he had some goods stolen a while back an' he thought it better tae send them here an' collect them rather than risk them goin' astray again.'

'Do you think that likely, Mr Oliphant?'

'Erm, what d'you mean?'

'That goods would be pilfered at the Largs station?'

Oliphant considered the question for a moment.

'Ah ken Jack Halliday the stationmaster doon there; he's a guid man an' Ah widnae hae thought that he'd run a leakin' ship, if ye get ma drift. But Ah suppose ye cannae always tell. Still, Ah wid hae thought it unlikely.'

McGinn rubbed his chin as he considered this fresh information.

'Mr Oliphant, d'you know if there is a Glebe Farm in Largs, or in that vicinity?'

It was Oliphant's turn to pause for thought.

'Ah couldnae really say, Ah dinnae know the area doon there that weel. But Ah could telephone Halliday an' ask, if that wid help?'

'It would, Mr Oliphant. Could you call from here?'

The stationmaster shook his head.

'Sorry, Ah'd need tae go back tae the station fur the number. But Ah'll call here as soon as Ah find out.'

'By the way, was your assistant able to offer any description

77

of this bogus Watson fellow?'

'Weel, it wis a wee bit back, ye ken, but Davie just remembers he wis a big fellow, kinda tough, he said. That's all—we cannae be expected tae remember everyone who collects goods.'

'No, of course not, Mr Oliphant. Look, I really appreciate your help.'

He shook the stationmaster's hand, then Oliphant departed. McGinn lit a cigarette.

'It seems to me that there's somethin' decidedly suspicious goin' on here. We'll wait until Oliphant confirms it but I'd put money on there bein' no Glebe Farm near Fairlie either. In which case, we've got someone who is none too keen on anyone bein' aware o' them pickin' up the parcel—or their identity, for that matter.'

'Can I ask, sir, what do you think might have been in the parcel? I mean, it must have considerable value if it's worth killing someone for.'

McGinn and Fairbrother exchanged a look.

'No need to concern yourself with that at the moment, McInnes,' replied McGinn. 'Let's just concentrate on the matter at hand.'

Sergeant Tait wasn't going to be fobbed off, however.

'Wi' all respect, Inspector McGinn, Ah think we've a right tae know. After all, it's one o' oor ain who's been killed an' it seems tae me that this damned parcel is at the root o' the whole matter. Ah think it's only fair that we hae an idea o' what's goin' on.'

McGinn gave a weary sigh.

'Aye, right enough, Tait, you do have a point.'

Fairbrother interrupted.

'Sir, do you think this is wise, I mean...'

McGinn held up his hand.

'Just you leave this to me, Fairbrother.'

He drew deeply on his cigarette.

'It's like this. Over the last few months we've been aware o' a growin' problem in and around Paisley. The use of illegal substances is, unfortunately, on the rise.'

Alan looked slightly shocked.

'You mean drugs, sir?'

'Aye, that's exactly what I mean. Now, drugs are nothin' new, of course, but a lot of the youngsters are gettin' hooked on smokin' marijuana, or cannabis—they've got a whole lot of names for it but it all boils down to the same thing. The problem is, where there's demand, there's supply. We've been tryin' to catch the main suppliers in the area but we've had no luck so far and, just like every other vice, sooner or later it filters out to the provinces.'

Tait took his pipe out of his mouth, pointing the stem as he spoke.

'Ah'm presumin', then, that ye think this parcel maybe contained drugs?' He turned to Alan. 'McInnes, Ah'm no' aware o' any people in this area that take drugs, are you?'

Alan shook his head.

'No, but how would we know, Sergeant?'

'Exactly,' said McGinn. 'They smoke it—or whatever they do wi' it— in private, or in secret places and I'd put money on there bein' a local dealer or two down here. This shipment clearly wasn't intended for the end users, it was for further distribution. It's just a matter of time before you find out who these local dealers are, but you'll be hard pushed to catch them with any evidence. They're a clever lot and the stakes are high, let me tell you.'

'But we're back to the same question, sir' said Alan. 'Why steal the parcel, why not just collect it as usual? Like I said, d'you not think it might have been someone else?'

Fairbrother and McGinn exchanged another glance, then the sergeant replied.

'Look, McInnes, we don't want to reveal too much, but we think there's maybe a bit of a battle going on between rival factions. If the parcel of drugs was, indeed, taken before the fire, then it's likely that it'll have been taken by a rival gang. It's all about territory, you see —the more territory you control, the more drugs you sell. If the local crowd have lost their supply and their rivals have gained it, it puts the rivals at a decided advantage.'

McGinn stubbed out his cigarette.

'The trouble is, when this kind of thing happens, it can end in violence; we've already seen it in Glasgow. This new breed of criminal, these so-called drug peddlers, are a different kettle of fish altogether.'

The four officers stood in silence for a moment, digesting the information. Finally, Tait asked, 'So d'you hae any idea who micht hae taken the drugs—or who was the intended recipient, fur that matter?'

McGinn shook his head, an embittered expression on his face.

'Not a bloody clue, Tait—an' therein lies the problem.'

~~~

Tait placed the telephone back on the cradle.

'That wis Bert—as expected, there's nae Glebe Farm doon Largs or Fairlie way either an' the local stationmaster has never heard o' anyone ca'd R. Watson. Mind you, the twa places are a fair bit bigger than Barloch, but the local railway men tend tae ken most o' the folk, especially if they get regular deliveries.'

The front door opened and one of the uniformed officers entered.

'Erm, we've carried oot a pretty thorough door-to-door, sir, round all the streets near the goods yard. Naebody saw or heard anythin' or anyone actin' suspicious-like recently. They're a close lot, mind, don't give much away, but I don't think anyone's hidin' anythin. What d'you want us to do now?'

'Away an' get some lunch, lads. I'll have a think but I don't know if there's much more to be done.'

As the officer left, McGinn gave an angry grunt.

'Christ, nobody's seen a thing an' we're no further ahead as to who was meant to be collectin' this parcel. God Almighty, this damned case is goin' nowhere, as far as I can see. Tait, get the kettle on; McInnes, is that wee bakery down the road still open? I could murder a sausage roll.'

Chapter 8

Inspector McGinn was in a decidedly foul mood. The sausage roll had given him heartburn, he had run out of cigarettes and he had just received a call from the Paisley Superintendent, asking for an update on the murder, leaving McGinn in no doubt that an early arrest was expected. He slammed down the telephone, jumped to his feet and strode across Tait's office, which he had commandeered, as previously, as command headquarters. He opened the door and yelled.

'Fairbrother—McGinn, in here, now!'

The two officers duly entered the office to find the inspector seated once more, with a pad and a pencil in front of him on the desk.

'Right, let's get all this down on paper and see if we can make sense o' it.'

He rummaged in his jacket pocket and pulled out a pound note.

'Here, McInnes, do me a favour and nip to the shop, get me twenty Capstan full strength. Oh, and a box of matches as well.'

Alan took the note and exited, feeling rather humbled at being relegated to message-boy. Avoiding Tait's questioning look, he hurried out, determined to miss as little of the meeting as possible.

Five minutes later, he handed McGinn the cigarettes, along with the change, and waited as the inspector lit up. The page before him now had a few rather haphazard notes jotted on it. McGinn exhaled, coughing as the smoke caught his throat.

'Damn—right, now you're back, let's get on. So far we have two burnt-out goods vans, one corpse an' a missin' parcel.'

He drew two squares in the middle of the page, adding the rudimentary shape of a body to one of them, signifying where the unfortunate Combe had been found; Alan gave an involuntary shudder.

'Everythin' in the vans is accounted for, except for this parcel addressed to this fictitious R Watson of the equally fictitious Glebe Farm...'

Alan interrupted.

'And a bottle of whisky, sir.'

McGinn glanced up at him.

'Aye, right enough, a bottle of whisky.'

He drew a rough bottle shape inside the van, with a question mark beside it. He then drew a third box and duly entered the fictitious Watson's information therein; he then drew a line connecting it to the goods van.

'We have a parcel with unspecified contents, possibly drugs, that, as a working theory, we presume was removed before the fire.'

He drew a small square above the goods van, wrote 'drugs' with two question marks then drew another line connecting it to the van. He drew a further box beside it and wrote 'goods depot' before linking it to the parcel. He then drew a circle below the vans and placed a large question mark inside it.

'Right; this is our man. We're pretty sure that he wasn't the intended recipient of the parcel, otherwise he would've just collected it as normal, no questions asked. I'd suggest, then, that we can rule out this fictitious Watson character as our murderer. Do we agree?'

It was Fairbrother who responded.

'It's likely enough, sir, but I don't think we can altogether rule out his involvement.'

McGinn glowered up at the sergeant as he drew on his Cap-stan.

'No, but at the moment I'm goin' with what's most likely. So, the question is—how did our suspect know that there were drugs in the wagon? Did someone tip him off?'

'Again—and with all respect, sir—we don't actually know that there were drugs in the van. We are just hypothesising—it could have been anything, couldn't it?'

McGinn placed the pencil on the desk and leaned back in the chair.

'Look, Fairbrother, we need a workin' theory here. Whatever was in the parcel must've been of enough value to justify killin' the watchman for it. We know there have been several previous deliveries and the fact the recipient chose to falsify his name an' address would suggest that it was contraband o' some sort, wouldn't it?'

Both Fairbrother and Alan nodded their agreement.

'So, what else would be that small and carry that value? As we've stated, the usual recipient had no reason to kill Combe, he'd just have collected the parcel as usual. In which case, our suspect here...'

He picked up the pencil and made a cross at the lower circle.

'...must have known about the delivery and the contents. An' how did he get that information?'

'Have you checked with the Glasgow depot, sir?' asked Alan.

'Aye, and there's damn all joy there. Seems the parcel was originally despatched from a London goods office—the Glasgow depot said they'll check the information on the sender and get back to me, but you can bet your pension that it'll be another false name and address. Anyway, they said that, in general, they're far too busy to remember every person, every parcel, so

I'm no' holdin' out much hope. Another bloody dead end—it doesn't help that nobody in Barloch appears to have seen or heard a damned thing.

He glared down at the page, then added a further circle beside that of the suspect and wrote 'London' inside it. Finally, at the side of the page, he wrote:

No local witnesses

No reliable details of sender (London)

No known local suspects

No proof of parcel contents

No leads

With an expression of disgust, he slammed the pencil back down, causing the point to break off and roll across the notepad. He glowered at it for a moment, then looked back up.

'Hell of a lot of 'no's.' Any ideas—because I'm fresh out o' them.'

Alan looked at the drawings.

'Maybe connect the whisky bottle that was missing to the circle with the suspect, sir?'

'I hardly think that's relevant, McInnes,' retorted Fairbrother; however, the inspector picked up the pencil once more.

'At this stage, Fairbrother, anythin' might be relevant...God Almighty, can someone get me another bloody pencil?'

Alan took his own pencil from his uniform jacket pocket and handed it to the inspector, who duly drew a line connecting the two pieces of information. He handed the pencil back.

'At the moment, there's only one thing for certain—I'm bettin' that this elusive Mr R. Watson is not best pleased!'

~~~

Mr R. Watson was, indeed, not best pleased; he was currently standing in Glasgow Central Station's busy concourse, beside what was known to Glaswegians as The Shell. Although principally a collection box for the Erskine Hospital for war-wounded ex-servicemen, this hollowed-out piece of First World War ordnance was the recognised meeting point for friends, lovers and, in this case, those on more nefarious errands. Although the bustle and anonymity of the busy station should, in theory, have suited Jock Wallace's purpose admirably, it seemed that every fifth person that passed him as he waited was a policeman. He was convinced that they were casting suspicious glances in his direction—this was a very different story from turning up at a quiet country station where, in the space of a few minutes, a parcel could be easily collected with just a plausible false name and address. Glancing up at the clock, he realised that his so-called contact was fifteen minutes late and he decided that he would give it another few minutes then give it up as a bad job. Maybe Brand had changed his mind following the recent debacle; maybe the Londoner had tipped off the police...or maybe his train was late! As beads of perspiration broke out on his forehead, a voice beside him spoke, the accent definitely London.

'Mr Watson?'

Wallace turned.

'Aye, that's me.'

The stranger extended his hand.

'Pleased to meet'cha!'

As they shook his hands, a small slip of paper was passed to Wallace. The stranger engaged in small-talk for a few moments then, with a slight tip of his hat, strode off and disappeared into the Easter Friday crowd. Wallace stepped away in a different direction, heading for the station bar; he needed some fortification before retrieving the delivery from the left-luggage office.

~~~

An hour later, Wallace was seated upstairs on the number 25 tram as it clanked and clattered towards the northern Glasgow suburb of Springburn. He drew heavily on his cigarette, a small, tattered suitcase clutched firmly on his lap. This was unfamiliar territory to the big man but Carlaveri's instructions were clear; he was to make his way along Springburn Road then alight as it crossed Hawthorn Street. He was then to walk along to a small cafe called Verona and await further instructions.

As the tram slowed, he descended the narrow stairs then stepped out on to the cobbled road, still clutching the suitcase. Looking nervously about, he made his way along the street until he reached his destination; an Art Deco sign proclaimed the cafe's name. Casting a final furtive look to each side, he pushed open the glass door and went inside.

A white-jacketed waiter, with slick black hair, approached him with an oily smile.

'Meester Watson?'

'Aye that's me.'

'Ah, bene. Meester Carlaveri said to expect you.'

The waiter extended a hand towards the case.

'If-a you please, Meester Watson.'

Wallace tightened his grip.

'Listen, pal, Ah'm only givin' this tae Mr Carlaveri—an' in exchange fur ma cash.'

The waiter's expression darkened.

'Mr Carlaveri ees-a not in the habit of dealing directly in such matters, I am afraid. He has-a asked that you give me the goods an' he will discuss matters with you in due course. Please, Mr Watson?'

Wallace looked around him; the cafe was quiet, just a few

customers drinking coffee and smoking, but a second, swarthy waiter stood behind the counter, glaring menacingly at him. There was no sign of his new business associate; once again, Wallace felt beads of perspiration break out on his brow. The waiter reached again for the case.

'If you please? Mr Carlaveri will-a be here directly, I can assure you. Please—you can trust me.'

Wallace didn't trust the man in the slightest but felt that he had little choice; with great reluctance, he handed over the case to the waiter. The man smiled ingratiatingly.

'Grazie, Mr Watson, Now, if-a you would please take a seat, I will get someone to bring you a coffee—espresso?'

Wallace nodded and sat down at the nearest table, taking out his handkerchief and mopping his brow. The waiter disappeared into the rear of the premises. A few minutes later, a young woman with black hair and beguiling eyes placed a little glass of dark coffee before him, along with a round, rough-textured biscuit. Wallace stared at it.

'Amaretti di Saronno, Signore. Ees good, you try?'

Once the attractive waitress had taken her leave, Wallace picked up the small, hard biscuit and took a bite; it tasted like marzipan, a flavour he had detested sine he was a child. He picked up the small glass and took a sip of the dark coffee, but the strong espresso seemed only one step better than the biscuit. As he place the glass back on the table, a hand rested on his shoulder.

'Amico mio, how are you?'

Bruno Carlaveri pulled out the chair opposite Wallace; he had barely sat down when an espresso and an amaretti were placed in front of him, He took a bite of the biscuit and smiled.

'Ah, delicious, is it not? You don't-a like?'

'Erm, it's no' really ma thing, tae be honest.'

Carlaveri took a sip of the strong coffee and gave a sigh of gastric contentment.

'Ah, bene, bene. So, Jock, I 'ave the goods—grazie!. And now...'

He reached into the inside pocket of his immaculately-tailored suit jacket.

'...this is for you.'

He handed Wallace a fat envelope; the big man cast a glance inside to see a thick bundle of five-pound notes.

'You can check it if you like, Jock.'

Somehow, Wallace felt that it was prudent not to do so; he slid the envelope inside his own jacket pocket.

'No need, Bruno; like you said, we need tae work wi' people that we can trust. Erm, can Ah ask—an' Ah don't mean tae sound suspicious—but Ah wisnae expectin' tae hand over the goods tae yer man.'

His associate gave an insincere smile and spread his large hands.

'Ah, you were wondering why I was not here in person. Well, you see, as I explained on the telephone, how were you to know that you weren't being followed? I 'ad to make-a sure that the goods were not being...well, let's just say 'observed'. If someone 'ad been following you, well...'

Carlaveri gave a shrug and spread his hands again; the habit irritated Wallace, somehow..

'...but they were-a not—so everything is A-okay!'

He beamed; had Wallace been more observant, he would have noticed that the smile didn't quite reach the Italian's eyes.

'Amico mio, I am so glad you 'ave decided to trust me. It is a good decision—we are partners now, si?'

Wallace smiled.

'Aye, partners, Bruno—we are that! Here's tae a long an' successful business relationship.'

He lifted the espresso glass and the two men toasted each other. Carlaveri's expression became more serious.

'Listen, I 'ave 'eard more of what-a happened to your last consignment. That is most unfortunate, I am-a so sorry.'

Although the Glasgow criminal fraternity was a small and close-knit world, Wallace had hoped that Carlaveri had not discovered the exact details of his recent misfortune.

'Aye, well, these things happen, Bruno; an' God help the thievin' bastart when Ah get hold o' him! Like you said before we need tae show them who's in charge!'

The smile returned to the Italian's face.

'Si, that is the spirit, Jock!'

He drained his espresso, licking his full lips as he placed the glass back on the table.

'So, amico mio, I will 'ave the goods in my vans by this evening.'

'Really—that quick?'

Carlaveri grinned.

'Si! We want to move it as soon as-a possible; it will make no profit sitting in that old suitcase and the longer it is in my personal possession, the greater the risk. No, a quick turnaround is the best way. I 'ave already made the arrangements an' by tomorrow we will 'ave distributed it across my whole network. Glasgow south side, Paisley, Barrhead, Johnstone and the surrounding villages. Everywhere that-a my vans go! Ah, they all love Carlaveri's ice-cream—an' now there is another commodity that I can supply! That is what it is all about, amico mio—supply an' demand. There is a demand—so we supply, si?' I 'ave already set up everything, I am-sure that we will be needing another consignment very soon!'

~~~

Once Wallace had left, Bruno Carlaveri ordered another espresso and sat gazing through the steamed-up window of the small cafe. Although he considered Wallace to be gullible and easily manipulated, the difficult part would be finding out where he sourced his merchandise; that might take time—he would have to play his new-found acquaintance very carefully. Carlaveri supped his coffee and allowed himself a smile; the big man was probably too ignorant to know what was at stake here but he would find out, in due course.

~~~

Wallace had secured a window seat on the tram and stared unseeingly at the drab Glasgow tenements whilst the 'caur' rattled its way back to the city centre. He didn't trust Carlaveri; the man was too smooth by far and Wallace was shrewd enough to disbelieve the Italian's platitudes and proclamations of friendship. Still, he had an envelope full of cash in his pocket—granted, he would have to pay Brand for the lost consignment—but there would be more than enough to treat himself to a pleasurable weekend. He smiled at his reflection in the grimy window; he might give that sexy wee blonde a call; what was her name again...Connie somethin'?

~~~

It was nearly six o'clock before Alan finally arrived home, tired, hungry and just a little bit despondent. The afternoon had brought little, if any, progress and Inspector McGinn had become increasingly ill-tempered as he pored over his meagre notes, making additions, rubbing them out, lighting cigarette after cigarette. He had called the mortuary to discover that Dr Miller was on holiday until Tuesday, meaning that Alex Combe's postmortem wouldn't proceed at least until then. The

Glasgow goods depot had called to advise that, as expected, the address given by the sender in London was bogus. Finally he had dismissed Alan—the truth was that there was little more that they could accomplish and it was with considerable relief that he left the stuffy, smoke-filled office and headed up School Street.

He entered the kitchen and took off his uniform jacket, placing it on the back of his chair as his mother placed a large plate of mince, potatoes and peas before him, along with a glass of milk. She allowed him a few minutes before speaking.

'Hard day, son?'

Between mouthfuls, he replied.

'Aye, it was that, Mother. Y'know, I actually feel sorry for Inspector McGinn—this is his first murder investigation and I think he's findin' it hard. There's virtually nothing to go on.'

Isa appeared unsympathetic.

'Och, he'll just need to get used to taking the knocks as well as the successes. It's Mrs Combe I feel sorry for, the poor woman's in an awful state. I'll go down again over the weekend, make sure she's taking care of herself.'

She watched with a maternal smile as her son devoured his dinner.

'I'm so glad you decided to stay in uniform, son, especially with you and Nancy engaged. Think of the life the poor girl would have had if she'd been married to a detective.'

Alan was inclined to agree.

'Aye, I dare say you're right, Mother. Still, I wish Sergeant Tait would make up his mind whether he's retiring or not. I don't want to wait forever for a promotion.'

'Och, just you let Donny be, he'll leave when he's good and ready; just bide your time, you'll get your three stripes soon enough...more potatoes, son?'

Isa's defensive stance regarding Donny Tait no longer surprised Alan; her astonishing and troubling confession the previous year, that the sergeant was actually his real father, had cast a whole new light on her relationship with Tait, not to mention his own lineage. Even now, he struggled to come to terms with the situation; God only knew how his father, Gilbert, felt.

~~~

The young constable made his weary way up the stairs and into his bedroom. He and his mother had watched a bit of television but he had sat yawning until she had finally ordered him to go to bed and to get some sleep. He smiled—he would always be Isa McInnes's wee boy, he supposed. His mother had promised him a long lie the following morning, which he looked forward to with relish. As he finally lay in the darkness, his mother's statement about not becoming a detective rang in his ears; for the most part he agreed, but there was no denying that he enjoyed the excitement. Still, a long lie *would* be nice!

Chapter 9

Somewhere in his dream there was a strident and persistent noise; it stopped but, as he drifted towards wakefulness, it was replaced by a voice until that, too, stopped. Deep sleep was engulfing him once more when he felt his shoulder being shaken, aware of his mother's voice speaking his name.

'Alan—Alan, son, come on, wake up.'

The curtains had been drawn open, the spring sunshine streaming into the room. He opened an eye and squinted up at the figure leaning over him.

'I thought you were lettin' me have a long lie, Mother,' he complained.

'Och, I know, but that was yon Inspector McGinn on the phone. I might have known!'

Alan was awake now and he sat up.

'The Inspector—what did he want?'

Isa pulled a face.

'He said he needs you.'

'What? What d'you mean, he needs me?'

'That's just what he said, son; apparently there have been developments and he needs you. He said he'd be here to pick you up in about forty-five minutes, so you'd better get a move on. I'll bring you up a cup of tea and a roll while you get yourself ready.'

Despite his earlier-than-anticipated wakening, Alan felt a slight glow of pride at McGinn's comment—it felt good to be needed by the CID Inspector. But, as Isa left her son to make his preparations, her parting comment brought him back to earth.

'Oh, and he said you'd best be in your uniform—have you got a clean shirt or do you need me to iron one for you? I don't want you going out in yesterday's clothes!'

~~~

True to the inspector's word, there was a knock at the door just before eight o'clock. Alan stood up.

'That'll be him, Mother—thanks for the breakfast.'

As he left, he gave her a peck on the cheek, then headed into the hall and opened the door. He noticed the dark circles underneath the inspector's eyes, but McGinn managed a grin.

'Sorry to drag you from your beauty sleep, McInnes, but there's been a pretty important development and I want your local knowledge.'

'That's all right, sir,' replied Alan, as they headed towards the Wolseley. 'Where are we headed.'

'Kilmirrin.'

Alan didn't reply until the powerful car was purring down School Street.

'Erm, Kilmirrin isn't really my area, Inspector. '

'Aye, I'm well aware o' that, McInnes, but it has a direct bearing on this case, so I want you there.'

'Can I ask—what's happened?'

McGinn gave him a sideways glance as he negotiated a sharp bend, narrowly avoiding an oncoming tractor and swearing under his breath.

'We've found a body—at the station.'

'A body?'

'Aye, that's what I said. Look, let's just wait until we get there. To be honest, I know about as much as you do. A farmer was out walkin' his dogs down near the railway and he noticed somethin' on the tracks. He went to the station and told the stationmaster; he had a look and called us. That's all I can tell you at the moment.'

~~~

The narrow, twisting road that ran through the Renfrewshire countryside was quiet and they arrived at Kilmirrin about twenty minutes later. As with all the stations on the Barloch loop line, the platforms were built above ground level, with two bridges running over the road and the single, central island platform accessed by a long ramp. McGinn pulled the Wolseley into the side of the road and the two officers got out. A uniformed constable was standing at the entrance and Alan nodded to him.

'Mornin', Roddy.'

'Alan—this is a bit ootside your territory. What brings you ower this way on a Saturday mornin'?'

McGinn held up his warrant card.

'CID, son. He's wi' me!'

The constable raised an eyebrow at Alan as they passed and headed up the ramp. A rumble overhead indicated the arrival of a train and they arrived on the platform just as a Glasgow-bound green diesel multiple-unit screeched to a halt. A second constable was ushering the early morning passengers down the ramp as they stared curiously along the platform. Once they had been seen off, McGinn showed his identity card again and the constable pointed towards the far end of the station.

'Along there, sir, just past yon goods wagon. Your sergeant's there already.'

Alan noticed McGinn frown but he remained tight-lipped as they made their way along the platform. At the far end, a lone goods van sat on a rather overgrown siding. Checking carefully for any further trains approaching, the two men jumped onto the track and walked towards the van. Another uniformed constable stood on guard as Sergeant Fairbrother walked slowly along the track towards them, head bowed as if searching for something. He looked up.

'Ah, good morning, Inspector; McInnes.'

'You're bright an 'early,' commented McGinn. 'How'd you get here so quickly?'

'Oh, I was in catching up on some paperwork when the call came through, thought I should attend and secure the locus. I knew that you'd be on your way, although I didn't expect McInnes to be joining us'

Once again, his supercilious tone grated on Alan.

'Aye, well, as he was directly involved in the Barloch incident, I thought he should tag along, as by all accounts this is potentially a similar, railway-related crime. I didn't see your car outside.'

'Oh, there's another ramp at this end of the station, I parked at it. A bit quicker.'

As Fairbrother spoke, Alan looked along the track to where the deceased lay spreadeagled on the rails. He swallowed hard but already he was becoming inured to the sight of a body and he was reasonably confident that his stomach would retain its contents. McGinn followed his gaze, then walked towards the corpse.

'So, what've we got?' he snapped.

'Well, sir,' replied Fairbrother. 'Looks to me as if he was trying to break into the wagon but slipped, fell off and cracked his head on the rail. This was lying on the ground beside the door.'

He bent down and, using his handkerchief, lifted a crowbar.'

'If you look at the edge of the wagon, you'll see the mud from his boots.'

McGinn stepped towards the wagon and inspected it, letting out a grunt as Fairbrother continued.

'I haven't had a look in his pockets yet, sir. I thought I'd wait for you.'

'Very thoughtful o' you,' replied McGinn; despite getting a modicum of pleasure at this vague reprimand directed towards the sergeant, Alan was surprised at the inspector's brusque manner. Once again, he got the distinct impression that there was little love lost between McGinn and his new sergeant. He wondered if he would have been treated any differently.

'First of all, I take it no-one recognises him?'

Both Alan and Sergeant Fairbrother shook their heads.

'No, never seen him before, sir,' replied the latter. McInnes voiced his agreement—the man was a complete stranger.

'Right—McInnes, have a look through his pockets, will you? There might be somethin' to identify him.'

Alan gritted his teeth as he bent down beside the body; he reckoned the man was in his early thirties, thick-set, sandy haired and clean-shaven. There was a faint, jagged, scar on his right cheek that could have been made by a broken bottle. He was clad in worn denim trousers and a dark navy double-breast-ed pea-jacket, with a thick navy sweater underneath. His eyes stared heavenwards, although whether that was his destination, no-one would ever know—although not particularly religious, Alan suspected not. As instructed, he checked the contents of, first, the left-hand pocket; a packet of ten Woodbines, half empty, a box of matches and a few pennies and ha'pennies. He put his hand in the other pocket and felt something hard.

'Inspector, there's somethin' in this pocket.'

McGinn knelt beside him, removed his handkerchief and reached into the pocket.

'Well, well, well.'

He withdrew a short, black leather cosh with a loop of thick cord attached to the handle. 'Seems like he came prepared!'

Fairbrother now knelt beside them and looked at the inspector.

'Could this be the murder weapon from Barloch, do you think?'

McGinn hefted the heavy, lead-filled object.

'Aye, I reckon it could—it's certainly got the weight to do serious damage.'

He stood up and looked around, his brow furrowed in thought.

'Do we know what's in the van?'

Alan wasn't sure but he had a good idea.

'I doubt if there's anythin' in it, sir. It's Saturday—just like the ones at Barloch, it'll have probably arrived on Thursday with goods for the Easter weekend and it'll likely have been unloaded yesterday. The Kilmirrin stationmaster'll confirm it, though, but I'm pretty sure it'll have been empty. It'll just be waitin' here for the next pick-up goods to collect it.'

'Perhaps, but would the man have had the intelligence to know that?' commented Fairbrother as he turned to face his superior. 'Sir, it looks to me as if this is our killer—he's got a probable weapon, he appears to have been intent on carrying out the same crime; only difference is he hasn't murdered anyone on this occasion.'

McGinn looked unconvinced.

'Aye, maybe—an' maybe not. We've established that our thief was after this mysterious parcel at Barloch—what the hell was he after here, if the van's empty? Surely to God we're not lookin' at another bogus delivery! McInnes, you away an' ask the stationmaster if there was anythin' of value in the van; and see if he maybe recognises the deceased.'

As Alan headed back along the track he could hear Fairbrother arguing his case in his superior manner; he only wished that he could hear McGinn's retort.

~~~

Having confirmed that the van was, indeed, empty, he was about to head back along the platform when a tall figure stepped from under the ramp canopy, wearing green boots and carrying a brown leather bag. Alan stopped and waited.

'Good morning, Dr Miller.'

'Ah, good morning—McInnes, isn't it? Bloody nuisance, this, I was supposed to be making up a four-ball at Elderslie golf club this morning. Still, duty calls, I suppose. I might manage back in time if we can get a move on. So what have you got for me today?'

As they walked, Alan outlined the details of their grim discovery; once they arrived at the scene, the doctor wasted no time in kneeling beside the deceased, having given the other officers a peremptory nod.

'Morning all. Right, let's have a look.'

He made a visual examination then gently rolled the head to one side to reveal a bloody indentation at the rear of the cranium.

'Hm, yes, I'd say it's likely that he fell backwards, probably from a height consistent with that of the wagon. Striking the metal of the rail at that velocity would certainly cause a wound consistent with this one and I would think that death would have been instantaneous.'

'Any ideas as to when, Doctor?' asked McGinn.

The doctor considered the question for a moment.

'I'd be inclined to say not before midnight, given the current temperature. Rigor mortis is just beginning to pass—it'll have been prolonged by the drop in temperature overnight. As I said, unlikely to have been much before then but probably not later than about three in the morning. I can't be any more precise than that, I'm afraid.'

'I can check when the last train went through, sir,' said Alan. 'See if we can track down any passengers who could have witnessed something. The stationmaster might have been on duty, or his assistant. They'd have noticed a stranger hanging about.'

'What did the stationmaster have to say about the van?'

'Empty, sir, like I suspected. Oh, and he had a quick look at the body earlier; hasn't seen him before.'

'Aye, as expected. Right, away an' see what they have to say about the trains.'

As he clambered back on to the platform once more, two ambulance men appeared at the head of the ramp, closely followed by a shabby little man wearing a brown coat that flapped as he walked, a disreputable soft hat pushed back on his head and a cigarette clamped between his thin lips. He carried a press-style camera and he nodded as he passed. Alan smiled to himself; it appeared that he was becoming known at murder scenes, although he wasn't entirely sure if that was necessarily a good thing.

~~~

Having spoken to the stationmaster for a second time, Alan returned to the siding.

'Well?' asked McGinn.

Alan shook his head.

'He was on duty last night—last train for Glasgow passed through about eleven-fifteen and he knew all four passengers who alighted. The station was locked up by eleven-thirty and he's certain there was no-one hangin' about.'

'Hm,' grunted McGinn. 'Not much help. What's your thoughts, McInnes—d'you think this could be our man?'

Alan looked down at the corpse, the eyes now closed. The photographer had done his job and the ambulance men had laid their stretcher next to the body in preparation for its removal. Fairbrother was giving him a scrutinising stare and he chose his words carefully.

'I'm not sure, sir. I think we might be jumping to conclusions if we assume him to be the murderer, but he does seem to fit the bill. It's the same type of crime, he's carrying a cosh and we think that poor Mr Combe was coshed before...well, you know.'

'So what's your reservation?'

Alan wasn't sure; was it just that it all seemed too simple? There was some vague, niggling doubt in the back of his mind and he wondered if, maybe, it was just that it seemed a rather anti-climactic ending. Surely that wasn't a reason to discount the man's guilt? He shrugged.

'I suppose I don't really have a specific reservation, sir, it just seems very...'

'...convenient?'

Alan nodded.

'Aye, sir. Exactly that.'

'I agree—and yet, as you said, he certainly fits the bill. We'll see what Dr Miller has to say after Combe's postmortem. If he can possibly identify the cosh as the likely weapon, then I think we can safely say that this is the murderer.'

The ambulance men made off with their grim burden and the three officers followed.

'There's not much else we can do until Tuesday—the doc said that he'd carry out Combe's postmortem first thing an' let us know. C'mon, I'll drive you home, McInnes.'

He stopped to light a cigarette, leaning against the platform edge.

'I think we can safely have the weekend off, anyway. Not much more we can accomplish until we hear from Dr Miller.'

He grinned, appearing considerably more relaxed.

'Might even to get to roll the Easter eggs with the wee fellow on Sunday after all! You got any plans, McInnes?

'Erm, no, nothing sir. '

'Not seeing your ladyfriend?'

'She's away to Edinburgh with her parents—visiting family friends. The school's are off, you see.'

'Aye, of course. What about you, Fairbrother—anything planned?'

There was a brief hesitation.

'Erm, I'll be heading down to my local, sir, for a pint or two. Just a quiet weekend, really.'

'An' where's your local?'

Again, that fractional pause.

'My local? Oh, it's the Bird in Hand, in Elderslie.'

'Oh aye, I know it—just on the main road, isn't it?'

'That's the one, sir. I'm in digs just up the hill from there, it's pretty handy. I go there most weekends.'

'Well, see an' enjoy yourselves, both of you. It's been a tough couple of days, you deserve a break.'

He threw away his cigarette-end and stood up.

'Right, McInnes, let's get movin'. Fairbrother, can you tell the stationmaster to make sure that the wagon remains here, just in case. I don't want any of our evidence being shunted off.'

'I will do, sir. See you next week. '

As Alan and McGinn headed along the platform, the vague niggling doubt was still in the constable's mind. He was also surprised at the change in the inspector's demeanour—presumably his bad mood resulted from the stress of leading a murder enquiry. Once again, he silently commended himself on having made the correct decision regarding his future.

Once back in Barloch, McGinn slowed the Wolseley, ready to turn up School Street, when he spotted a young man at the kerbside.

'Is that not your fellow constable—Brodie, isn't it?'

'Aye, it is, sir, he was away for the week. Could you just drop me off here? I'll away and have a wee blether with him.'

'Aye, that's fine. Right, you see an' relax, McInnes, you've been a big help.'

As Alan stepped out of the car, McGinn called after him.

'An' you'd have made a bloody good CID man, if you ask me!'

The Wolseley drew away, leaving Alan standing with a silly grin on his face. Kerr Brodie crossed the road and extended his hand, receiving the customary response.

'Hob-nobbin' wi' the CID again, Alan? Ah hear you've had an' excitin' week?'

'You can say that again!'

'Where've you been wi' McGinn?'

'Another body turned up, at Kilmirrin station. He asked me to go along to help him!'

'Really?'

Alan grinned again; the single word carried the obvious question.

'No, Kerr, no regrets. God, the stress that McGinn has been under the last few days, I definitely wouldn't want to go through that on a regular basis—he was like a bear with a burnt paw! He really took it out on thon new sergeant too.'

'Here, I saw him wi' a ginger-headed bloke yesterday, when Ah wis comin' up frae the station—is that him?'

'Aye, Sergeant Fairbrother's his name.'

'Fairbrother? Rings a bell; mind you, there wis somethin'

vaguely familiar aboot him, couldnae place him, mind. Listen, Alan, Ah need tae be headin' up tae Paisley tae 'try an 'get a haircut. Are you seein' Nancy tonight?'

'No, she's away through to Edinburgh.'

'Well, d'you fancy meetin' for a couple o' pints an' a natter?'

'Aye, that'd be grand, Kerr. About seven?'

'See you then.'

~~~

The two young men ensconced themselves at a corner table in the lounge of The Gables. Of the three public houses in Barloch, this was considered the most genteel, being favoured by couples, local businessmen and those who considered themselves a cut above the working men of the village, most of whom drank in the Hole in the Wa. While Alan and Kerr didn't particularly consider themselves to be of this upper class, the quieter environment suited their purposes. Alan had bought two pints of heavy and was already sitting at a small table when his friend entered; Alan grinned as he approached.

'I thought you were gettin' a haircut?'

Kerr pulled a face.

'Damned barber was closed for the Easter weekend. No' much Ah can dae until Ah'm next off, hope Tait doesnae notice.'

Alan smiled.

'Not much chance o' that!'

The two men took a deep draught of the rich, dark beer.

'Aah, jist the job. So, tell me, Alan, whit's been goin' on in ma absence!'

Alan related the week's events to his friend, the two supping their pints as the story unfolded. Finally, Kerr placed his empty glass on the table.

'Bloody hell, seems like Ah've missed a lot o' excitement! Poor auld Combe though, that's a real shame, so it is. He wis a decent enough wee man.'

'Aye, he was, Kerr. His widow's fair cut up about it. My mother's been down to see her a couple o' times—you know what she's like, always wantin' to take care o' somebody! Still, hopefully it's all over an' done with now.'

'An' d'you think that the body you found today really is the killer, then?'

Alan hesitated. Did he?

'Well, McGinn and Fairbrother seem to think so, so I suppose they're the ones makin' the decision. Another pint?'

'Aye, but it's my round.'

Kerr crossed to the bar and ordered two more pints He took the glasses back to the table and Alan nodded his thanks.

'Cheers, Kerr.'

'Cheers! Here, speakin' o' Fairbrother, Ah wis chattin' to ma old man—he wis a sergeant doon in Greenock, mind.'

Alan nodded as he took a long draught of the refreshing brew. Kerr went on.

'So, he says that, before he retired. There wis a chief inspector called Fairbrother doon there.'

'Really—d'you think that the sergeant is a relation, then?'

'Aye, definitely; the super is his uncle! Ma faither says that this Niven bloke o' yours started on the beat in Greenock, worked for a couple o' years afore ma old man retired. Apparently he wisnae liked, seemed tae be a right uppity piece o' work. Ma faither says that the chief inspector wis jist the same—they went tae a fancy school doon there, had a right high opinion o' themselves. You know what it's like, too—there was talk that he just got promoted tae sergeant on account o' his uncle.'

Alan nodded.

'Aye, that certainly fits with the sergeant—he's fair full o' himself right enough! Even Inspector McGinn doesn't seem to like him—he's always nipping away at him.'

Brodie grinned.

'He's probably just wishin' it wis you, Alan!'

'Och, away with yourself!'

'No, seriously, Ah'm surprised you didnae ask McGinn aboot joinin' the CID— Ah'm pretty sure he'd wid have had you in a minute.'

Alan supped his pint before replying—he hadn't told anyone about McGinn's offer the previous year.

'Actually , he did ask me to join but I turned him down.'

Brodie looked at his friend in astonishment.

'Whit? You turned it doon—God, are ye daft, man? Whit an opportunity! I'd be happy tae get away from Barloch—Ah mean, stolen bikes, broken windaes, Ah could dae wi ' a bit more excitement!'

Alan laughed.

'Excitement? An' what about the two murders last year—not to mention poor old Combe! Is that not excitement enough?' He shook his head. 'No, it's definitely not for me, Kerr. McGinn has been up to high doh this week with this investigation; I couldn't be doin' with all that carry on, especially now that I'm engaged. Speaking of which, how are things with you and Jeanette?'

Kerr grinned.

'Aye, grand, Alan, jist grand. We had a few days awa' at Butlins, doon at Heads o' Ayr. It wis great, dancin' every nicht, cheap booze—aye, we had a rare time!'

Alan felt a slight pang of envy—somehow, he and Nancy didn't seem to experience such simple delights. His friend continued.

'Speakin' o' that, mind Ah said Ah thought Ah'd seen thon sergeant Fairbrother before?'

'Aye?'

'Weel, Ah remembered where it wis; ye ken that Jeanette lives doon in Glensherrie?'

'Aye, I do.'

'Ye see, often, on a Saturday, we go tae the Masonic Arms, it's a nice wee pub down the Main Street. Ah like it 'cos naebody there kens Ah'm a polisman.'

Alan smiled his understanding—his entrance to the local hostelry often caused a slightly awkward silence to ensue.

'So, there's been a couple o' times that we've been in an' Ah've noticed this red-headed, freckly bloke sittin' at a table. He usually sits in a corner, as if he's tryin tae keep oot the way.'

'Really! An' you think it's him, Kerr?'

Brodie nodded.

'Oh aye, nae doubt aboot it—there's nae missin' that red hair! Thing is, each time he's been in, he meets up wi' a sleekit wee man wi' dark hair an' a wee moustache. The two o' them seem as thick as thieves, leanin' across the table, low voices, ye ken whit Ah mean. But the last time we were in, Ah'm sure Ah saw the redhead handin' the other an envelope an' the sleekit bloke handed him a wee packet o' somethin'. Ah never thought much aboot it until Ah saw him here an' you telt me who he wis.'

Alan took another sip of beer as he considered what Kerr had related.

'So what d'you think was going on?'

'Nae idea! As Ah said, Ah never gave it much thought until you told me he wis the new CID man. It does seem a bit odd, though; ach, likely as no' it's nothin,' Ah widnae worry aboot it. Here, d'ye fancy some peanuts?'

~~~

Four pints and a bag of chips on the way home had induced

a decidedly mellow mood as Alan made his way homeward. His parents were in bed and, as quietly as he could manage, he made his way upstairs. Hanging over his door was his smartest casual attire and he remembered that he had promised to attend the Easter service with his mother the following morning; he was glad that he had called it a night after four pints! Once undressed, he put on his pyjamas and clambered into bed, but as he lay on his back, hands clasped behind his head, his mind was occupied with thoughts of Sergeant Fairbrother and his apparent shortcomings. Brodie's information had troubled him somewhat and, just before the blanket of sleep finally enfolded him, he realised that his feelings of dislike for the CID man were turning to feelings of mistrust.

Chapter 10

The Easter service had, for the most part, been cheerful and uplifting; the Minister's short but heartfelt tribute to the late Alex Combe had been accompanied by Mrs Combe's quiet, yet dignified, sobbing. However, the enthusiastic singing of the gaily dressed children had brought a smile to everyone's face and, following the customary tea and biscuits in the adjacent hall, the congregation were now mostly gathered outside in the glorious spring sunshine, exchanging pleasantries and gossip in equal measures. The children, meanwhile, were restless, anxious to make their way up to the slopes behind the village to roll their painstakingly painted, hard-boiled Easter eggs.

Alan wasn't a regular church-goer but had agreed to accompany his mother to the Easter service, on account of his father's staunch atheism. There was no doubting Isa McInnes's pride in being seen with her tall, handsome son, immaculately turned out in his smart checked sports jacket, crisp white shirt, perfectly-knotted tie and well-pressed flannels. However, he noticed his mother's gaze stray occasionally down the street to where the nearby Free Church was now disgorging its occupants; he suspected the reason and was proved correct when she spoke.

'Oh, there's Donny—I'll away and have a wee word with him; are you coming, son?'

Alan nodded and accompanied his mother down Church Street and under the railway bridges until they reached the entrance to the Free Church. Alan noted that the congregation seemed to be more sombre in their dress, reflecting the rather more austere doctrine of their Church. Donny Tait smiled and approached.

'Mornin', McInnes. Isa, how nice tae see you, my you're lookin' very spring-like!'

Isa had worn a pretty floral-patterned frock and her good dark navy woollen coat; her matching hat, adorned with a small sprig of flowers, she now held in her hands. As Alan turned to look at her, her eyes sparkling, the sun shining on her greying hair and a smile on her full lips, he caught a tantalising glimpse of how she must have appeared as a young woman; smart, pretty, clever, strong-willed...in that same brief moment, he wondered why she had married Gilbert McInnes and not Donny Tait. He would probably never know—nor did he really want to. As they made small talk, a movement at the ramp leading up to the goods yard caught his eye; two people were walking down the slope. His mother followed his look.

'Here, is that the Benson lad?'

'Aye, it is, Mother.'

'Is he stepping out with the Seaton girl now?'

Alan shrugged; the previous year, Benson had initially been implicated in the murder of Mary Campbell, his then girlfriend. Although cleared, the fact that the unfortunate young woman had been expecting his baby must have come as a shock to the rather slow-witted young man and it was to his credit that he had both retained his job on McGeoch's coal lorry and found himself another young woman to court. However, Alan was curious as to why they appeared to have been up at the goods yard.

'I'm goin' to have a wee word with Benson, see what they were up to.'

'Och, Alan, leave the poor laddie alone, surely he's had enough grief without you pestering him!'

'I won't pester him, Mother, I just want to have a quick chat, that's all—he's got no reason to be up at the goods yard on a Sunday. You go on up the road without me, I won't be long.'

As Alan walked briskly away, Sergeant Tait smiled at Isa.

'Aye, he's keen, richt enough.'

Isa gave a sigh of resignation before she resumed her conversation with Tait, her son's absence allowing a very slightly more intimate level of discourse.

~~~

Billy Benson and Alma Seaton were sauntering down Kirk Street, arm-in-arm, and it didn't take Alan long to catch up with them.

'Benson!'

The couple turned, the colour immediately rising in the young woman's cheeks; she looked at Alan with a rather sullen expression as Benson responded.

'Hullo, Mr McInnes.'

'What were you doing up at the goods yard, Benson?'

It was Benson's turn to blush.

'Erm, we wisnae dae'in' nothin', Mr McInnes, Ah wis just showin' Alma whit had happened, like.'

The scarlet-faced young woman was staring at her shoes and Alan tried not to smile; he had little doubt what had been going on, well away from prying local eyes.

'Aye, well, remember it's still a crime scene, Benson, an' you shouldn't really be there unless in connection with your work.'

He was about to take his leave but something made him pause and ask, 'By the way, Benson, you're quite sure that you didn't see anything suspicious, no strangers hanging about before the incident?'

Benson gave him a blank look.

'What d'ye mean, Mr McInnes?'

'Oh, for goodness sake, Sergeant Fairbrother asked everybody if they had seen anyone or anything suspicious in the weeks leading up to the fire.'

Something in Benson's expression prompted him to add, 'Did you see anythin', Benson?'

Billy Benson scratched his stubbled chin.

'Aye, weel, I micht have, Ah'm no' sure.'

Alan could feel his impatience rising.

'What d'you mean, you might have? Did you or didn't you? And if you did, why didn't you tell Sergeant Fairbrother?'

"Cos he never asked me, like.'

'Rubbish! The sergeant interviewed everybody last Thursday.'

'But Ah wis off on holiday fur the week, Mr McInnes, Ah wisnae there!'

This stopped Alan in his tracks—surely the sergeant would have made sure that all employees were accounted for when carrying out his questioning?

'You were off work?'

'Aye, Mrs McGeoch said that the weather wis tae be fine an' there'd be less demand, so she said tae tak' a week's holiday.' He beamed suddenly. 'Me an' Alma went tae Rothesay, didn't we, hen?'

Alma managed a smile, although her face remained scarlet.

'Very nice, Benson; but what is it you think that you might have seen? It could be important.'

The thought of being important seemed to appeal to the coalman.

'Weel, it wis wan evenin' aboot twa weeks ago, me an' Alma wis...weel, we wis up at the yard, like, just fur a wee bit privacy, if ye understand?'

He gave Alan what could best be described as a conspiratorial wink.

'Yes, I get the picture.'

'So, we wis jist ahent the coal office when Ah heard footsteps—Ah keeked oot an' sees a man comin' up the ramp. He looked a bit shifty-like, lookin' this way an' that. We kept oot o' sicht but Ah managed tae keep an eye on him. He wis jist peerin' aboot, as if he wis...'

He looked at Alma.

'Whit is it the Yanks say in the picters, hen?'

She gazed back at him, her expression instantly softening; Alan was slightly touched at her obvious affection for her rather uncouth young man.

'They say they's casin' the joint, Billy.'

'Aye, that's it, Mr McInnes, he looked as if he wis casin' the joint. He waited a minute or twa then went back doon the ramp.'

'Did you see where he went afterwards?'

'Weel, Ah kinda sneaked alang an' had another keek—there wis a van sat at the foot o' the wee brae, Ah thocht it looked like wan o' they Post Office vans, it wis red, like, but the sign wis worn off, or faded awa', mebbe. There wis another mannie sat in the driver's seat wi' the engine runnin'. The first wan got in an' they drove aff.'

'Could you describe the man you saw?'

Benson scratched his chin again.

'Aye, weel, he wis kinda wee, like, no' a lot bigger than Alma, but he was richt weel put together, if ye ken whit Ah mean. Like a wrestler, broad shouldered, powerful-lookin'. He had black hair, cut richt short, looked a wee bit older than me. Oh, an' wan eye wis goin' for sweeties, the ither was comin' back, if ye ken whit Ah mean?'

'He had a squint?'

Benson frowned.

'Eh?'

'A squint—och, skelly-eyed, if you like.'

Benson smiled.

'Aye, richt enough, that's whit ye cry it, Mr McInnes; a wee skelly-eyed mannie wi' dark hair.'

'And there was definitely two of them?'

'Aye, like Ah said, the ither was already in the van, waitin' tae drive aff. Ah never got a look at him, him bein' inside the van, like.'

'Right, Benson, I'm going to need you to come into the office tomorrow and make a statement. I take it you're still off?'

'Aye, it's Easter Monday—here, could Ah no' leave it 'til Tuesday maybe?'

Alan smiled—no doubt this would allow Benson some additional time off work.

'Oh all right, I'll square it with Mrs McGeoch. Be at the office for ten o'clock.'

'Aye, Ah will, Mr McInnes, cheerio.'

The couple turned and continued their perambulation down Church Street, still arm-in-arm; however, Alan noticed that there was now a definite swagger to Benson's stride.

~~~

As he walked through The Cross and back up School Street, he felt a frisson of excitement at this fresh discovery. This was partly due to his desire to impress Inspector McGinn, despite his decision to remain in uniform. However, he also harboured a rather irrational desire to show up Sergeant Fairbrother, not only because the man had effectively taken Alan's position in the CID but also because he was a decidedly arrogant and supercilious individual who appeared to wish to humiliate the young constable, not to mention his fellow villagers. In Alan's opinion, the sergeant had made a rather glaring error in not ascertaining that every employee of McGeoch's had been interviewed. He had also been very quick to apportion the blame for Combe's murder to the as yet unidentified deceased. He smiled to himself; to Alan's mind, Fairbrother was another Inspector Nisbet in the making and could do with being taken down a peg or two.

Although anxious to impart this latest piece of information, he decided to leave telephoning McGinn until the morning. As he made his way up the hill towards his house, however, the faint niggling doubt about the body found in Kilmirrin wormed its way back into his mind. What was it that had appeared wrong? He couldn't for the life of him think what it was.

His reverie was broken by a nearby discordant jangling sound; it was a tune that he remembered from his schooldays—Greensleeves—although it sounded as if it was being played on an out-of-tune music box. Recently the sound had become a rather unwelcome feature of village life, heralding the daily arrival of a new ice-cream van. Alan was used to visiting the village's cafe whenever he wanted sweeties or an ice-cream, but the van seemed to have quickly become a local attraction, welcomed by children and adults alike. As well as sweets and ice-cream, cigarettes and matches were available, effectively providing the services of a small travelling confectioner's shop to the local community. Progress, he supposed, but the noise, at least, was unwelcome. As he continued towards his home, he noticed two crows pecking at something on the pavement; they cak-cakked at his approach, reluctant to leave their repast. As they flapped off across the street, he realised that it was an ice-cream cone on which they had been feasting. He remembered the childhood trauma of the dropped treat, the tears, the pleading for a replacement. The ice-cream was already beginning to melt and the lower half of the cone was missing, presumably taken by the crows. He walked on, leaving the birds to return to their snack.

As he opened the door, his nostrils detected the smell of a traditional Sunday roast. He smiled—his theories and thoughts could wait until the next day.

~~~

That night he lay in his bed, relaxed and content; the family meal had been delicious, the conversation surprisingly stimulating. Gilbert had been in unusually good form, possibly due to the several bottles of beer he had consumed during their Easter feast. His mother had been particularly animated too and, briefly, he wondered if it had been due to the prolonged conversation with Donny Tait that afternoon. He pushed the thought out of his head but, as he did so, it was replaced by his misgivings regarding the body found at Kilmirrin the previous day.

His eyes were beginning to close when, suddenly, he was startled back to wakefulness; in a flash of inspiration he knew exactly what had been troubling him about the body and, in that same moment, he resolved what he would do about it. As Alan McInnes drifted off to sleep, there was a smile of self-satisfaction playing on his lips.

Chapter 11

The morning sky was becoming overcast and the temperature was dropping as Alan made his way up the ramp to Barloch station; he hoped that the deputy stationmaster might be on duty but, as he walked along the platform, Bert Oliphant came out of his office to meet him.

'Mornin', Alan—you're up bricht an early the morn!'

'Aye, Mr Oliphant, just wanted to get on with things. How are you?'

Oliphant gave a half-hearted smile and replied that he was 'no' too bad' but Alan noticed that he was wearing a black armband over the sleeve of his jacket and both men's gazes were inexorably drawn to the goods yard, where the burnt-out wagons had been covered by dirty grey tarpaulins. Oliphant shook his head sadly.

'Aye, an' awfy affair—jist awfy.'

'It is indeed, Mr Oliphant, I'm very sorry.'

'Aye, weel, be thankful, son, it could jist as easily been...'

He broke off, not wishing to upset the young man. They both understood what he meant.

'An' Ah hear there's been anither body found at Kilmirrin?'

'Yes, there has.'

Oliphant gave Alan a questioning stare.

'Ah'm wonderin' if there's a connection?'

'I can't really say, I'm sorry. It's an ongoing investigation, you know how it is.'

'Aye, Ah daresay. Anyroads, ye're no' here tae pass the time o' day, Ah'm thinkin'. Whit can Ah dae for you?'

This was the question that Alan had hoped to avoid.

'Erm, I'd like a return to Kilmirrin, please.'

Oliphant's stare lasted longer this time.

'Kilmirrin, is it? Official business?'

Alan had prepared his response.

'Och, it's just that the inspector wants me to make sure the wagon isn't moved, that's all.'

'It's a holiday, son, the wagon'll no' be moved afore tomorrow. Ye should ken that.'

'Aye, but you know what he's like, wants to make sure.'

'Look, Alan, Ah can save ye the time an' the cost o' yer ticket; Ah'll phone through an' make sure the wagon stays where it is—the railway has plenty o' wagons, it'll no' miss that yin.'

'I appreciate that, Mr Oliphant, but Inspector McGinn was adamant that I go myself, just to make sure.'

The stationmaster gave Alan yet another long stare until, finally, he turned towards the office.

'Aye, weel, if that's whit ye want, come ye on then; but it's a limited service the day, whit wi' it bein' the holiday, so there's only wan train an hour. Next yin's no' due for...'

He consulted his pocket watch.

'Thirty-eight minutes, so ye've got a bit o' a wait. '

'That's fine, Mr Oliphant, I'll just have a wee seat outside.'

He didn't want any further interrogation by the now highly suspicious stationmaster.

~~~

It was just after nine-thirty when Alan stepped off the near-deserted diesel multiple unit on to the Kilmirrin platform. As it rumbled off across the bridge, Alan handed his ticket to the stationmaster, who gave him a nod of recognition. Alan thought it best to explain his intent.

'Erm, I'm not leaving, actually, I just wanted a wee look about in case we've missed anything.'

The stationmaster seemed as curious as Bert Oliphant.

'Ah don't see what ye can have missed, that other plain-clothes mannie had a damned good look aboot yesterday before you an' the inspector turned up.'

Alan remembered that Sergeant Fairbrother had been scrutinising the track when he and McGinn had arrived. The stationmaster continued

'Here, has this got anythin' tae dae wi poor old Combe's murder, by any chance?'

'I can't say at present, sir, it's an ongoing investigation... look, if it's okay, I'll just step on to the track an' have a look beside the wagon.'

'Aye, weel, watch yersel'—even though it's a holiday there'll be the odd train passin' through an' Ah don't want another damned body in ma station.'

~~~

Alan walked along the platform then, after a precautionary look in either direction, he jumped on to the main up-running line. The goods van was further along in one of the two adjacent sidings but he remained on the main track; he was facing oncoming trains and, as it would be an hour before the next passenger service passed through, he felt reasonably safe. He walked slowly, inspecting the ballast, looking along the platform edge, until he drew level with the wagon. He walked past it and along the line for about thirty yards, then turned and walked back along the siding until he reached the wagon. Nothing caught his eye and he stepped on to the outer siding and walked back towards the station, still scanning right and left. He was past the platform and approaching the sets of points from which the sidings diverged when he noticed something in the 'six foot' between the tracks. At first he thought it was a coin but closer inspection showed it to be exactly what he had hoped to find. He took out his handkerchief and bent down to retrieve the object when there was a shout from the stationmaster.

'Here, get yersel' aff the line, there's a train o' empty coal wagons comin' up frae Glensherrie!'

As the man spoke, Alan heard the shrill whistle of the approaching locomotive; he stepped to the side of the tracks and, a few minutes later, a soot-begrimed steam locomotive clanked and snorted its way past, its wagons click-clacking behind it. As it rumbled away across the bridge, the stationmaster called across to him.

'Right, all clear, ye're fine for a wee while yet. '

Alan crossed the tracks and made his way back to the platform.

'Actually, I've got what I came for—when's the next train for Barloch?'

'Should be here in a few minutes, other side o' the island.'

Alan clambered back on to the platform and crossed to a wooden bench. With a smile of triumph, he sat down, the small object safe in his pocket. But, as he enjoyed the peace for a few moments, the intrusive and discordant jangling of Greensleeves in the nearby village of Kilmirrin brought a frown to his face.

~~~

It was just past eleven o'clock when Alan alighted at Barloch. After managing to avoid answering any more of Oliphant's questions he walked briskly up the road and turned into the police office. The front area was empty but the reek of Sergeant

Tait's pipe indicated that he was in his office. The sergeant appeared, uttering a gruff, 'Aye, can Ah help...oh, it's yersel', McInnes! What brings you doon here on yer day aff?'

Alan smiled.

'Well, I've been across to Kilmirrin and I've managed to dig up a bit more evidence for Inspector McGinn.'

Tait looked sceptical.

'Have ye indeed? An' Ah take it ye remember whit happened last time ye went galivantin' on yer own an' 'dug up a bit more evidence?"

Alan was undaunted.

'Och, that was different, Sergeant. This time it's all above board, I've not done anything that I'll get in to trouble for.'

'Weel, Ah hope not—so whit are ye goin' tae dae aboot it?'

'Well, I was going to phone the inspector—I'm pretty sure he'll be keen to hear what I've found out.'

'Aye, weel, on ye go, Ah'll awa' back tae ma paperwork. Mind, it's still the Easter holiday, he micht no' be best pleased tae hear from ye!'

Tait ambled back to his office, his pipe billowing smoke much like the train that had passed through Kilmirrin. Alan lifted the phone, consulted the office directory then dialled the number for the Paisley CID office.

'Hello. Erm, it's Constable McInnes from the Barloch office... no, McInnes! Yes, that's correct. Can I speak to Inspector McGinn please?'

He waited a few moments.

'Oh, I see, yes, that's all right, I'll call back tomorrow.'

Tait came back out from his office.

'Weel?'

Alan looked a bit disheartened.

'Och, he's off today and he's left word that he's not to be disturbed under any circumstances—unless another body turns up!'

~~~

Jock Wallace could feel beads of sweat trickling down the back of his thick neck as he held the telephone receiver to his ear. Dicky Brand's 'hail fellow, well met' tones had been replaced by a hard-edged monotone that carried more than a hint of menace.

'...that's all very well, Jock, but there's still the small matter of the lost shipment.'

'Aye, Ah know that, Dicky, but give me a couple o' months an' Ah'll make it good. Ah've already passed on the latest shipment, Ah just need a bit more time.'

The pause was ominous; Brand finally went on.

'Yeah, but you remember our agreement, Jocky-boy; you get the goods, I give you a week to get the funds together, I send my man up to collect.'

'Aye, Ah know that Dicky, but how can Ah get the funds when the goods has gone missin'? The latest shipment isnae enough.'

This wasn't strictly true and Wallace suspected that Brand knew it. Wallace continued in a pleading tone.

'Ah mean, Ah lost a whole load o' sales wi' whit happened. Ah didnae have anythin' tae sell, did Ah? Ah'm only just catchin' up now.'

The pause was longer this time; Wallace could hear the static crackling ominously on the long-distance call. When Brand finally spoke, there was now definitely menace in his voice.

'See, fing is, Jocky-boy, how do I know I can trust you?'

Wallace could feel his temper rising.

'An' what the hell's that suppose tae mean?'

'Look at it from my point of view, me old son. You're tellin' me that the shipment was nicked—how the hell do I know it ain't all just a pack o' lies? Maybe you decided t'do a little bit on the side; maybe you fink I'm stupid, Jocky-boy—an' let me tell you, that would be a grave mistake. Just because I'm down in the smoke don't mean I ain't got...well, let's just call it 'authority', if you get my drift. Glasgow's only a train journey away, after all.'

Wallace was angry now; he also felt very slightly intimidated, but he decided to bluff it out.

'Listen tae me, Brand, Ah'm tellin' ye straight—some bastart knew aboot the shipment, they broke intae the van an' lifted it. Aye, an' they bloody killed the night watchman intae the bargain! D'ye think Ah'm goin' tae make all that up just tae steal the package? An' d'ye think Ah'm stupid enough tae murder someone?'

He took a deep breath, trying to calm himself.

'Look, Dicky, we've got a good thing goin' here, let's no' fall oot ower this.'

'All very well for you to say, Jocky-boy, but it's me that's carryin' the loss at the moment.'

'Aye, an' Ah've telt ye that Ah'll make it good, just gie me a bit o' time.'

Brand sighed.

'Yeah, okay, I'll give you the benefit o' the doubt—this time! But for Gawd's sake don't let it 'appen again!'

'It won't, Dicky, Ah've already changed the method o' distribution. It's workin' like clockwork noo—in fact, the way things are goin', Ah'll be needin' another shipment very soon.'

'So what's your new method, Jock?' asked Brand, his tone seemingly innocent; Wallace wasn't fooled, however.

'Hah, never you mind, Dicky, that's between me an' the lamppost! Ah'll be in touch—have Ah let ye doon yet?'

Brand didn't reply.

Wallace hung up the receiver, wiped his brow and poured himself another glass of whisky. He had developed a strong dislike for Dicky Brand; and a considerable fear.

Chapter 12

'You're up bricht an' early the day!'

Sergeant Tait had entered the police office looking as if he had just fallen out of his bed; his grizzled grey hair stuck up in tufts and his tie was askew but, despite his early-morning dishevelment, he had found time to light his pipe. Alan was busy with his pencil and his notebook.

'Och, I'm just thinking over my ideas and what I'm going to say to the inspector; here, I'll go and put the kettle on.'

'Good idea, lad. Mind that Brodie's back today.'

'Aye, it'll be good to have an extra body.'

As he went through to the rear office and switched on the kettle, he could hear Tait mumbling something about having had enough of extra bodies!

~~~

Kerr Brodie arrived at eight-thirty on the dot, Tait giving him a long stare.

'Are ye plannin' on becomin' one o thae—whit is it they ca' them—oh aye, 'rockers', Brodie?'

'Sorry, Sergeant, Ah went tae get it cut on Saturday but the barber wis shut for Easter—Ah'll get it done as soon as Ah'm off again.'

Alan handed Kerr a mug of tea, then looked at the clock; Tait noticed.

'Ach, for goodness sake, awa' an' try him, pit us all oot o' our misery.'

'What's the matter?' asked Brodie.

'Och, he's dug up some more evidence on Combe's murder an' he's jist burstin' tae tell the inspector.'

Brodie grinned.

"See, Alan, Ah told ye, ye should have joined the CID."

'Och, away with you; is that okay, Sergeant?'

'Aye, on ye go.'

Alan entered the small back office and closed the door. He sat at the rather cluttered desk, lifted the phone and dialled the number; he knew it off by heart now.

'Hello, is Inspector McGinn available please...yes, it's Constable McInnes from Barloch...thanks.'

The phone crackled for a few moments, then McGinn came on.

'McGinn here.'

'Erm, good morning, Inspector, it's PC McInnes from Barloch speakin'.'

Alan heard the striking of a match and could almost smell the Capstan full strength.

'Aye, so they told me. What can I do for you, McInnes?' He chuckled. 'I hope there's not been another murder down your way?'

Alan was encouraged by McGinn's apparent good mood.

'No, sir, but I've found some evidence that I think might be important.'

There was a pause.

'Have you now? Off doin' your own thing again, were you?'

The inspector's tone had changed subtly.

'Well, sort of, sir; you see, I was at the Easter service and when we came out, I saw Billy Benson coming down from the goods yard.'

'Benson? Oh aye, the lad that worked on McGeoch's coal lorry—the poor bugger's lassie was murdered last year. So what's he been up to now?'

'Oh, nothing, sir, he seems to be doing okay. He's still working with McGeoch and he's got another young woman in tow.'

'Good for him, but I presume you're no' phonin' to tell me about Benson's love-life?'

'No; well, I was just asking what he'd been doing up at the yard with the lassie and...er...'

McGinn chuckled.

'I get your point—go on.'

'Well, I decided to ask him again if he had noticed anything suspicious and he said that he had.'

There was another pause.

'Look, McInnes, Sergeant Fairbrother questioned all Mc-Geoch's employees.'

'Yes, he did, sir, but it turns out Benson was on holiday for the week and didn't realise that the sergeant had been interviewing the staff.'

The ensuing pause told Alan that he'd surprised the inspector.

'Was he indeed? So, what did he have to say for himself?'

'Well, he and Alma Seaton—that's his new girlfriend—had been up at the yard one evening the previous week and he saw a man come up, said he was snooping about—'

McGinn interrupted.

'Have you taken a formal statement from him?'

'No, not yet, sir, I've asked him to come in today at ten.'

'Good—right, I'm on my way. Keep him there an' don't take his statement until I arrive. Got it?'

'Yes, sir. '

With a smile on his face, Alan hung up the phone then realised that he hadn't told McGinn about the second piece of evidence that he'd found. It would just have to wait.

~~~

Just before ten, the office door opened and McGinn entered.

'Is Benson here yet?'

'No, sir,' replied Alan. 'But he should be here any minute.'

'Good. Tait, can I use your office?'

'Aye, of course, Ah've cleared the desk a bit.'

'Good man.'

The door opened again and Billy Benson entered. Although his clothes seemed permanently stained with coal-dust, his hands and face had been cleaned—no doubt by Mrs McGeoch, thought Alan.

'Ah, Benson,' said McGinn. 'Just come in with me. McInnes, can you come and take down Benson's statement?'

Pleased to comply, Alan followed the pair into Tait's cramped office, where McGinn sat behind the desk and gestured for Benson to sit opposite him. The young man was obviously nervous, no doubt remembering his interrogation at the hands of Inspector Nisbet the previous year. McGinn sensed his discomfiture.

'There's no need to worry, son, we're only takin' your statement regardin' the person you saw in the coal yard. You're no' in trouble, no need to be scared.'

Benson cast an apprehensive glance at Alan, who smiled.

'The Inspector's telling the truth, Billy, all you need to do is tell him what you told me the other day, I'll write it down and then you can sign it. Okay?'

Benson's face started to redden and Alan realised that he was probably illiterate.

'Or you can just make your mark—don't worry, it'll be fine.'

Benson appeared to relax again as McGinn spoke.

'So, Billy, can you tell me what you told the constable?'

Benson scratched his chin.

'Aye, weel, it wis like this...'

~~~

Benson finished his rather hesitant, rambling narrative. Alan
noticed that there were a few unnecessary embellishments
since he had heard the story the previous Sunday: Benson had,
presumably, been giving his statement some thought. Alan had
omitted those which he considered to be of little relevance; the
statement didn't require to know what Alma Seaton had been
wearing on the night in question.

'Right, Benson, that's all, you've done very well,' said McGinn,
kindly. He looked up at Alan.

'McInnes, can you get this typed up so that Benson can sign
it?'

Alan hesitated; his skills on the ageing Remington typewriter
left a lot to be desired but he was keen not to let the inspector
down.

'Yes sir, I'll do it right away.'

He left the two men and returned to the front office, where
Tait was chatting to the Minister while engaged in lighting his
pipe.

'Weel?'

'Aye, Benson did fine, Sergeant. Good morning, Minister.'

'Good morning, Alan—it was nice to see you and your mother
on Sunday. A lovely service, I thought. '

'Aye, it was. Sergeant, the inspector had asked me to type up
Benson's statement, so I'd best get on with it.'

He entered the back office and sat down, placing a sheet of
paper in the machine. It took about fifteen minutes, plus several
sheets of paper, before the statement was prepared. Finally, he
pulled it out of the machine and returned to the office, handing
it to McGinn.

'Good man. Right, Benson, if you can just sign—or make your mark—at the bottom there.'

Benson took the pen that McGinn had proffered then looked at the document; he frowned.

'Here, whit is it Ah'm signin'?'

Alan took the sheet of paper.

'I'll read it out, Billy, just to make sure.'

He read Benson's statement then handed the page back.

'Is that what you want to say?'

Benson nodded.

'Aye, that's aw' right—thanks, Mr McInnes.'

He put the pen to the paper and left a vague squiggle that might have read 'Billy'. Alan felt a pang of sympathy for the man, counting his blessings for his own education as McGinn took the sheet.

'There, that wasn't too bad, was it, Benson? Right, we really appreciate your help, you can get back to work now.'

As Benson stood up, McGinn extended his hand. The younger man looked at it for a moment, then shook it, a smile of pleasure on his unshaven face. Once he had left the office, Alan commented, 'I think you've made his day, Inspector.'

McGinn pulled a face, but Alan could see him trying to suppress a smile.

'Aye, an' he might just have ruined ours—this casts a whole new damned light on things. Accordin' to Benson's statement, it looks as if our killer probably wasn't acting alone, in which case we're now looking for his accomplice.'

Alan suddenly recalled the other piece of evidence he had uncovered.

'Oh, I forgot, Inspector—there was something else.'

McGinn raised an eyebrow.

'Was there now—an' what might that be?'

Alan swallowed hard; McGinn's scrutinising gaze was making him nervous.

'Well, you see, on Saturday, when we went to Kilmirrin and I saw the body, I had the feeling that there was something not quite right about it, if you know what I mean?'

'No, I don't, McInnes—look, just spit it out, man, whatever it is.'

Despite all his rehearsals, the words spilled out in a rush.

'So, you see, it was only afterwards when I'd thought about it... the deceased was wearing a dark jacket, the kind that sailors wear.'

'Aye, a pea-jacket—common enough, What of it, McInnes?'

'Well, when I thought about it, I realised what was wrong— there were a couple of buttons missing.'

McGinn frowned.

'But it was an old jacket, I can't see what—'

'Aye, but these jackets are pretty well made, sir, and I'd imagine that the buttons are well-enough sewn on. You might lose a single button but there's three sets of two buttons and both the middle ones were missing, It would take a pretty strong tug on the jacket to pull off both buttons and that's what got me thinking. On Monday I went over to have another wee look about at Kilmirrin...'

He reached into his pocket and took out the handkerchief that was folded carefully around the object he had found. He handed it to McGinn.

'...and I found this. It was along at the other end o' the station, just where the points come off for the siding.'

McGinn unwrapped the handkerchief; inside was a shiny black button, with a few strands of dark thread attached.

'I reckon that's from the deceased's jacket, sir.'

McGinn stared at the button, then looked up at McInnes.

'So what, exactly, are you suggestin', McInnes?'

Alan hesitated; what he was suggesting was pure conjecture, yet it seemed to make sense—to him, at least.

'Erm, well, it crossed my mind that, if there were two of them involved then, maybe, there was an altercation...'

McGinn held up his hand.

'Right—let me think about this for a minute, will you?'

A silence ensued as the inspector continued to stare at the button.

'Okay, McInnes—am I correct in sayin' that you think our victim may have been in a fight with this other man, the dark-haired one that Benson claims that he saw?'

'Erm, yes, sir. '

'And then, presumably, this other person may have pulled our victim along by the jacket, causing the button—or buttons, maybe—to get pulled off his jacket?'

'Well, obviously, I don't know...'

McGinn raised his voice a notch.

'Aye, you don't know, McInnes, that's the thing.'

He reached into his jacket pocket, took out his cigarettes and lit up, exhaling a cloud of blue smoke.

'Christ, McInnes, you an' your damned theories! Just when we've got the whole thing tied up nice an' neat, the Super's delighted that we've got an early result, then you go off on your own an' come up with a couple o' spanners to throw into the works...'

He stopped and shook his head.

'...but God help us, you might just be right.'

He paused for a few moments, deep in thought; Alan waited, feeling slightly guilty at being the cause of the inspector's obvious dilemma. Finally, he spoke.

'Right, if there's the faintest suggestion that this person was assaulted—or worse—before he fell on to the railway tracks, then we need to let Dr Miller know. After all, we already have a pretty good idea of what happened to poor old Combe an', if this poor bugger is also a murder victim, then we need to know pretty damned quickly.'

He lifted the telephone.

'I'll phone the mortuary now an' ask him to do our second corpse first, see if he can find anythin' to indicate that it wasn't an accident. Then you an' me are goin' across to Kilmirrin; I want to see where you found this damned button!'

~~~

As they exited the station, Kerr Brodie was coming in from his rounds; he gave Alan a knowing look.

'Off investigatin' again, eh, Alan?'

Alan smiled as he followed McGinn to the Wolseley; working with the CID Inspector certainly engendered a feeling of importance!

~~~

Half an hour later, they were standing once more on the platform of Kilmirrin Station, having made the stationmaster aware of their intent. Checking for any oncoming trains, they jumped down on to the track and headed to where Alan had found the button.

'Over there, sir, just next to the points. I put a mark on the sleeper to show where I found it.'

McGinn nodded approvingly as they crunched their way over the ballast.

'There, sir, that's the mark.'

They stopped and McGinn looked down at the tracks.

'Hm—nothin' to suggest any altercation here, mind you.'

He looked over at the fence.

'Looks like the fence-wire's been pulled down there, though. What d'you reckon, McInnes?'

'Aye, it does right enough, sir. '

They crossed to the fence, beside which ran a rough farm track.

'So, if they came along the farm track here, in their van, I suppose someone could have dragged the body over the fence and along to where the wagon was sittin'.'

'Maybe, sir, but they'd have needed to be pretty strong, wouldn't they?'

'Aye—but remember what Benson said, this other man was well-built, like a wrestler. Might not have been too much of a problem for someone like that.'

'No, I suppose not. '

They clambered over the fence and on to the muddy farm road. There were a few vehicle tracks but none that were discernible as having come from a light van.

'Nothin' much to show that a van came along here. There's probably been tractors comin' an 'goin' since Friday.'

Alan didn't reply; he was walking slowly along the track, gazing intently down at the muddy surface, when something caught his eye..

'Inspector!'

McInnes strode over and followed the constable's gaze, his face breaking into a smile as he bent down and lifted the small object.

'Well spotted, McInnes. Looks like we've found the other button!'

Chapter 13

Inspector McGinn had finally left the Barloch police office, taking with him Billy Benson's statement and the two jacket buttons. Despite their small size, it might be possible to find viable fingerprints on them and the inspector hoped that, if detected, they would help to put a name to this second, unidentified, party. Dr Miller, having reluctantly agreed to carry out the unidentified corpse's postmortem before Alex Combe's, had advised the inspector that he would give him the results as soon as they were available. McGinn, in turn, had assured Alan and Sergeant Tait that he would let them know the outcome. What had appeared to be a relatively clear-cut case now seemed to have been turned upside-down but Alan couldn't help but feel a sense of excitement and anticipation—and, indeed, pride. As the door closed behind the CID man, Kerr Brodie winked at his colleague.

'Aye, ye're well in there, Alan.'

Sergeant Tait nodded.

'For once, Ah agree—ye've definitely made an impression, McInnes, weel done, Ah'm proud o' ye!'

Alan felt himself redden at Tait's rare words of praise.

'Och it was nothin' much, really...'

'Weel, Inspector McGinn seems tae think it wis plenty; Ah had a wee chat wi' him an', whilst he's havin' tae go back tae the drawin' board as far as Combe's murder is concerned, you've certainly given him somethin' tae think aboot. Anyway, Brodie—awa' an' get the kettle on an' we'll drink a toast tae oor ain detective!'

Alan tried to appear nonchalant but his pleasure was obvious; he couldn't wait to tell both Nancy and his mother.

~~~

Naturally, Isa was first to hear the news; she smiled proudly at her son.

'Oh, you're a clever laddie right enough—do you really have no regrets about turning the inspector down?'

Alan shook his head.

'No, Mother, as much as I've enjoyed doin' a bit of investigating, I really couldn't be bothered with all the responsibility. I mean, the inspector can be called out at all hours—'

Isa interrupted.

'And what about you, with those fires in the village—weren't you called out at all hours? Not to mention the—well, you know what I'm talking about.'

She was correct, of course, and Alan smiled—his mother was an astute woman.

'Och, well, that's just the occasional incident; I mean, if you're investigating a murder, if you're having to deal with serious crime on a day-to-day basis, it's a different story altogether.'

'Yes, I daresay it is. Right, sit you down and I'll get your tea out—it's a shepherds' pie tonight, I hope that's all right?'

'Aye, Mother, that's just grand.'

Really, there was nothing that Isa McInnes could place in front of her son that wasn't 'all right'.

~~~

By Thursday morning Alan's excitement had abated somewhat; there had been no word from Inspector McGinn and, once more, he was engaged in the rather dull routine of a village police station. Having investigated a broken window, more likely to have been youngsters with a ball than an attempted burglary, he headed back to the office. The weather had taken a turn for the worse and the precipitation from a fine, west of Scotland drizzle lay on his police-issue greatcoat as he opened the door to the office. Tait nodded, taking his pipe from his mouth.

'The inspector's been on.'

Alan felt excitement rise once more.

'Oh! Has he any news, Sergeant?'

Tait smiled benevolently.

'Aye, indeed he has.'

Tait called over his shoulder..

'Brodie, bring us some tea, yer fellow-constable's lookin' a bit drookit.'

As Brodie called out an affirmative, Alan could hardly hide his impatience. He took off his damp coat and hung it up.

'Em, so what did the inspector have to say?'

'Weel, seems they've managed tae identify the body.'

'Really—my, that was quick work. Did he say who it was?'

'No, he didnae. Oh, an' that's no' all; there's another piece o' information for ye.'

Alan grinned; he realised the sergeant's game.

'And are you goin' to tell me, Sergeant?'

'Aye, maybe—Dr Miller's carried oot the postmortem on the body an' all's not what it seems.'

'Not what it seems...what's that supposed to mean?'

The door opened behind him, a draught of cool air sweeping into the office.

'Ye can ask him yersel'—here's Inspector McGinn noo.'

~~~

The inspector was leaning against the office bar, mug in one hand, cigarette in the other. The other three officers stood expectantly.

'Ahh, that's just what the doctor ordered; aye, as I was sayin', we sent out a description o' the deceased. I made the assumption that he'd be reasonably local—probably Glasgow at the furthest. Turns out he's from the opposite direction.'

He took another slug of tea.

'We think that our anonymous corpse is a petty thief from Greenock; the name I've been given is Frank Kilbride, aged thirty-four. Got a fair bit of form, mostly assault, breakin' an' enterin', never anythin' involvin' this level of violence, mind you. He did a stretch in Barlinnie about two years ago, seems to have been keepin' his head down since then. Until now, that is.'

'So at least we've got a name for the bugger,' said Tait, with some vehemence.

'Aye maybe, although we still need to check the prints, see if they're a match—that'll give us the final confirmation. Don't forget, though, that thanks to our friend McInnes here, we believe that there's a second party involved. So, in actual fact, Kilbride may or may not have been Combe's killer.'

He drained the mug and placed it on the counter.

'However, the plot thickens, as they say. Again, thanks to the efforts of McInnes, we formed a suspicion that Kilbride may have been knocked unconscious then dragged along to where his body was found. You see, as I mentioned earlier to Sergeant Tait, the postmortem didn't exactly show what we originally expected. Although Kilbride did die as a result of striking his head, the doctor also discovered a second contusion, consistent with being struck on the back of his head, quite possibly with the very cosh we found in the deceased's pocket. Dr Miller is inclined to think that the first blow wasn't fatal—apparently there was slight bleeding from the second blow, which wouldn't have happened if the first blow had been the fatal one. I've sent the cosh for analysis and possible prints but I suspect it'll have been wiped clean if someone else used it.'

This statement elicited a surprised silence.

'So ye're sayin' ye don't think that it wis the blow from the cosh that killed him?' asked Tait.

McGinn shook his head.

'No, the Doc doesn't think so; there's some bruising an' he thinks it likely that the blow merely rendered him unconscious; that would also fit in with the torn buttons McInnes found. If Kilbride was knocked out elsewhere, he could have been dragged along the track, put in a position consistent with him falling, then his head cracked off the rail. The killer would have hoped that the latter blow would have concealed the first one...'

He turned and smiled at Alan.

'...and if it hadn't been for the persistence o' young McInnes, we might never have found the buttons off Kilbride's jacket. We wouldn't then have known to look for a possible lesser injury and we'd all have made the assumption that Frank Kilbride was Combe's killer and that he died as a result of an accident. Nice an' tidy.'

'So now we're looking for this other person?' asked Alan.

'Aye, we most certainly are; we've got Benson's description but that on its own isn't a lot of help.'

He turned to Tait.

'Can I borrow McInnes for the afternoon, Sergeant? I want to head down to Greenock and have a chat with the inspector who identified Kilbride. Our man might have family down there, or he might have had known associates.'

'Aye, that's all right, Inspector; we'll manage—is yer sergeant no' available today?'

McGinn shook his head.

'There was an armed robbery at a post office in Paisley yesterday, a couple of hoodlums on motorcycles held the staff up with a shotgun. They're still on the loose so Fairbrother's in charge of that and my other two detective constables are helpin' him out. The public don't like people bein' threatened with firearms, especially in the local post office, an' the Super's breathin' down my neck for a quick result—as usual! So, if it's all right, we'll head down to Greenock right away.'

Alan grabbed his coat and followed McGinn out of the office. Tait gave Brodie a knowing look.

'Ah reckon it's only a matter of time before young McInnes changes his mind; he's fair got the investigatin' bug!'

Brodie pulled a face..

'Ah'm no' so sure, Sergeant—don't think the hours would suit him, tae be honest!'

~~~

McGinn didn't spare the powerful police Wolseley as he negotiated the twisting back roads of Renfrewshire. Fortunately, Alan was seated beside him in the front—the last time he had accompanied the inspector on this particular journey, he had arrived decidedly green about the gills, being unused to travelling in the back seat of a fast-moving police vehicle. Soon, they were coasting down Port Glasgow's steep Clune Brae, the long stretch of shipyards and docks, backed by the broad sweep of the Clyde Estuary, forming an impressive panorama before them.

They drove along the main road through Port Glasgow, flanked by tenements, public houses, cranes and engineering works, until they arrived in Greenock, the tall tower of the municipal buildings, in which was housed the headquarters of Greenock Burgh Police, marking their destination. The car rattled along Dalrymple Street until McGinn finally pulled over, reaching over to the back seat and lifting a brown foolscap envelope. As they got out, he gazed up at the grandiose Victorian edifice.

'They've been talkin' about a new headquarters for a few years, might even get round to buildin' it one o' these days.'

They walked along the cobbled Drummers Close, climbed the stone steps then entered the building and crossed to the main desk; the building had a decidedly institutional feel, with green-painted walls and a pervading smell of disinfectant and stale tobacco smoke. McGinn showed his warrant card and asked for Inspector Melville. After a short wait, a tall and rather cadaverous-looking officer with a bald, shiny head, strode along the corridor.

'McGinn? Duncan Melville.'

The two men shook hands. McGinn introduced Alan and handed the envelope to Inspector Melville.

'That's the details we've got on our corpse—fingerprints plus a description.'

Melville slid the piece of paper out of the envelope and read the rather sparse details.

'Hm, like I said on the phone, your description certainly sounds like our man.'

A door beside him opened and a young, uniformed female constable came out; Melville stopped her and handed her the file.

'Ah, Helen, take this along to Mr McNeil in fingerprints, will you, we're lookin' for a match. Oh, an' tell him it's urgent—you may as well wait an' bring it straight along to my office once he's done.'

The young woman smiled.

'Certainly, Inspector.'

As she turned to go, Melville patted her rather shapely rear. 'Good girl.'

Although Alan was aware that such behaviour took place, it didn't sit at all comfortably with him. Seeing his expression of distaste, McGinn caught his his eye and shook his head slightly. As they followed the inspector along the corridor, Alan felt sympathy for the young woman, as well as a distinct lack of respect for the senior officer.

They entered Melville's cramped office, the inspector indicating that they should sit; he offered them cigarettes, one of which McGinn gratefully accepted. A large, cast-iron radiator was blasting out heat, making the room uncomfortably warm and Alan briefly wondered if this was, perhaps, used as part of his interrogation technique. He had heard rumours of prisoners being handcuffed to radiators until they confessed to their crimes and he certainly wouldn't now put such behaviour past Inspector Melville.

Once the other two had lit up, Melville asked, 'An' you think Frank Kilbride's met a sticky end? Well, if we get a positive ID, that is. McNeil's a good man, he won't take long, but from what you've told me I'd put money on the body bein' that o' Kilbride. So what happened?'

'Well,' replied McGinn, 'you heard about the incident at Barloch?'

Melville nodded.

'A few days later, we got a call to say a body had been found at Kilmirrin, the next station along the line. At first we thought he'd just had an accident in the course of tryin' to break into a goods van but McInnes here managed to turn up some further evidence. This suggests another party might have been involved and it's now lookin' likely that we've got two murders on our hands. What can you tell us about this man Kilbride?'

Melville exhaled a huge cloud of smoke before coughing violently.

'Christ...excuse me.'

He pulled out a grubby handkerchief and, to Alan's disgust, cleared his throat and spat into it before placing it back in his jacket pocket.

'Anyway— Frank Kilbride; well, I cannae really tell you a great deal an' it's a story that ye'll have heard many times before. Came from a broken home, the father left when he was just a bairn. Started young, petty thievin' an' the like—he left school early, worked in the docks for a bit, got sacked for pilferin'. He was known to take a drink, after which he tended to become violent an' he got a couple o' years for grievous bodily harm. We've no' seen him since then—I assumed he'd moved away.'

'Any family?'

'Aye, as far as I know his mother still lives in Lynedoch Street, up across from the entrance to the station an' the goods yard —there's a row o' tenements due for demolition but that was Kilbride's last known address—I've written it doon for you, it's no' too hard to find but I've put directions.'

He handed McGinn a sheet of paper, which the latter folded, placing it in his jacket pocket.

'Thanks. Did he have any known associates?'

Melville gave a grimace, revealing nicotine-stained teeth.

'Aye, he did—a right nasty bugger by the name o' John Scanlon. He was a wee bit older—to be honest, I always got the impression that Kilbride was a bit soft in the head an' was influenced by Scanlon.'

'Could you describe this man Scanlon?' asked Alan.

Melville furrowed his brows.

'Scanlon's a right wee ruffian, not very tall but well-built an' broad-shouldered—looked a bit like a wrestler. Very dark hair, from what I remember...oh, an' he had a bad squint too!'

McGinn and Alan looked at each other.

'Thanks, sir,' said Alan. 'That's the description I got from a witness who claims to have seen him.'

Melville frowned.

'I'd hoped we'd seen the last o' Scanlon; he got a four year stretch for assault. A right vicious piece o' work, didn't hesitate to lash out, didn't discriminate between men or women. I'm sorry he's turned up on your patch, won't surprise me in the slightest if it turns oot he's your killer.'

Once again, Alan felt that there was something vaguely niggling in the back of his mind; this time, he had an idea what it was.

'Can I ask, Inspector, would you say these men were well-known in the Greenock area?'

McGinn gave him an odd look as Melville answered.

'Oh aye, without a doubt—just like you probably know most of the local ne'er-do-weels in Barloch, we tend to know most of our felons down here! Even now, most officers would still have a good idea of what these two looked like. If a crime's committed and a description's given, it's always useful to have an idea of who you're lookin' for. Isn't that right, McGinn?'

McGinn nodded, still giving Alan a sideways glance.

They exchanged police small-talk for a few minutes more until there was a knock at the door. The WPC put her head round.

'Here's the report from Mr McNeil, Inspector.'

'Ah, good girl. McInnes, could you...?'

Alan stood up and took the report, giving the young woman what he felt to be his most sympathetic smile as she left. He handed it to Melville, who peered at it for a moment.

'Aye, right enough, the fingerprints show that it's a positive

145

identification. So, we can take Kilbride off our list of active felons now, I suppose.'

McGinn and Alan rose to take their leave and shook hands with Melville, although Alan's was considerably less warm than when he had arrived. As they exited the building, McGinn asked, 'What was that about, McInnes? Why ask if those two were well known?'

Alan chose his words carefully.

'Och, I was just wantin' to make sure we had reliable descriptions—especially of this John Scanlon. After all, he's the one we're after now, isn't he?'

'Well, he's the one I'm after, McInnes—it's not really your concern. Oh, an' take no notice of Melville's behaviour towards that young woman constable—it's just his way.'

Alan felt his hackles rise slightly.

'I just thought it wasn't very nice, sir, he'd no right to—well, you know. '

'You've never worked in a bigger station with female officers, have you?'

'No sir, but—'

'Well, maybe you should—it's just the way o' things, McInnes, like it or not. Melville's nearing retirement age and if he pats the occasional female posterior, then so be it. Don't go reading anything into it and, for God's sake, don't even think about making trouble for a senior officer. That's a sure-fire way of killin' your chances o' promotion stone dead! Anyway, the WPC didn't look particularly upset, did she?'

'Well, no, I suppose not.'

'Exactly—so just forget about it, all right?'

Alan nodded; he was slightly surprised at McGinn's acceptance of Inspector Melville's behaviour but McGinn continued as if nothing had happened.

'Anyway, let's go an' pay a visit to Lynedoch Street, see if there's anyone there. Hopefully it's not been demolished!'

~~~

Following Melville's directions, it wasn't long before they arrived outside the dilapidated tenement that was the last known address of Frank Kilbride. A few of the ground floor windows had been smashed and were boarded up, but the upper floors had net curtains in their windows, presumably an indication of occupation. As they exited the car, they could hear the clanking of railway wagons and the occasional short crow of a whistle as the shunting engines carried out their duties in the extensive goods yard across the street.

'Hell of a noisy place to live,' observed McGinn, as they walked to the entrance to the tenement close. Surprisingly it was reasonably clean and smelled of disinfectant.

'Okay, first floor, on the right—says his mother's name is Marion.'

They climbed the stairs and reached the faded door, on which was a small plate bearing the name D. Kilbride.

'Wonder how long that's been there, if the father left when Kilbride was young?'

McGinn knocked on the door and they waited, the noise from the adjacent goods yard still clearly audible through the open stair window. They heard the turn of a key before the door opened a crack.

'If it's the rent ye're efter, ye're oot o luck. It's no' due yet, Ah've no' got it an' Ah'll no' have it 'til the morn!'

'It's the police, Mrs Kilbride' stated McGinn, holding his warrant card up to the narrow opening. 'Can we have a word, please—it's about Frank.'

They heard the woman sigh as she opened the door wide.

'Ye'd best come awa' in— whit's the silly bugger gone an' done noo?'

~~~

The furniture was old, the carpet frayed and threadbare, but it was clear that Mrs Kilbride kept a tidy house. In the grate, a meagre fire, seeming to consist mostly of dross, burned in a rather desultory manner. In front of it stood a clothes horse, on which was an array of ladies' undergarments. Mrs Kilbride cleared her knitting from the couch and indicated that they should sit.

'Ah'm sorry aboot, the mess, it's washday, ye'll just have tae excuse me.'

She dropped her small frame into the sagging armchair.

'So whit's that daft boy o' mine been up tae this time?'

McGinn cleared his throat.

'Mrs Kilbride, I'm afraid I have bad news. I'm very sorry to have to tell you that Frank is dead.'

Mrs Kilbride's already hollow cheeks seemed to collapse, her eyes seemed to dull before they filled with tears. She started to sob gently, pulling a dainty lace handkerchief from the front pocket of her apron. McGinn leaned over and whispered to Alan.

'Away through to the kitchen an' see if you can rustle her up a cup of tea; us too, if you can—we might be here for a wee while.'

Chapter 14

Having put the kettle on the stove, Alan had hunted for tea, milk and sugar. The caddy had enough leaves for a pot but there was only a small jug with little milk and he couldn't find any sugar. After a few minutes, he had given up and crossed the landing, where he elicited the help of a large, blowsy woman who had introduced herself simply as Elsie. On hearing of Marion Kilbride's loss, she had immediately adopted a mother hen response similar to that of Isa McInnes, promising to bring tea and to offer comfort to Mrs Kilbride once Alan and his superior had departed. Alan suspected that this was motivated as much by curiosity as by altruism. He returned to the lounge, where Mrs Kilbride now appeared to be tearfully pouring her heart out to an impatient-looking Inspector McGinn.

'...wisnae a bad boy, really, he jist got in wi' the wrang crowd, if ye ken whit Ah mean. An' efter his da' left—weel, it wisnae easy...he wis aye a big lump o' a laddie, Ah could hardly keep him fed...'

'Mrs Kilbride, can I ask...?'

'...an' then he got in tow wi' that bad lot—whit wis his name—oh aye, Johnny somethin'-or-other...'

'Johnny Scanlon?'

The woman nodded.

'Aye, that wis him, a richt bad yin. He had some kind o' influence over poor Frank...'

Alan managed to stem the flow.

'Mrs Kilbride, your neighbour Elsie's bringin' us a cup of tea an' she says she'll stay with you for a wee while.'

Mrs Kilbride dabbed her eyes then blew her nose.

'Och, she's a good sort, is Elsie. Hell o' a gossip, mind, but she's aw richt.'

McGinn asked, 'Could we have a look at Frank's room, Mrs Kilbride?'

She looked across at him with red-rimmed eyes.

'Aye, that's aw right, but he's no' stayed here since he came oot o' the jail.'

McGinn immediately became alert.

'Oh? Where was he stayin', d'you know?'

'Och, he'd moved in tae digs up in Johnstone. Ah've got his address somewhere.'

She got to her feet as Elsie entered, carrying a tray. Mrs Kilbride burst into a fresh paroxysm of grief and Elsie, placing the tray on the stained table, gathered the grieving mother into her ample arms.

'Aw, hen, Ah'm that sorry.'

McGinn glared across at Alan and spoke in a low voice.

'We'll be here all bloody day at this rate. McInnes, you go an' have a look around his room, I'll try an' find out where our man was stayin'. We could be on to somethin' here—if she calms down long enough to find the bloody address!'

~~~

Over half an hour later, they took their leave. Marion Kilbride had been left in the tender care of Elsie, who had promised to take care of her bereaved neighbour. Alan's search of Frank Kilbride's room had elicited nothing of note; some old clothes, a near empty Brylcreem tub and a few coppers in change. McGinn, however, was clutching a scrap of paper with the deceased's address in Johnstone.

'Got anythin' on tonight, McInnes?' he asked, as he started up the Wolseley.

'Erm, no sir.'

'Good. We'll head up to Johnstone then, see if we can turn up anythin' of interest there.'

He grinned.

'Join the CID an' see the world, eh!'

~~~

The journey was arduous; the main Glasgow road followed the southern bank of the River Clyde and the Greenock and Port Glasgow conurbation before passing through the small village of Langbank, all with their 30 mph speed restrictions. Their journey had been further hindered by a grindingly-slow Walker's tanker carrying bulk sugar grinding its way up the steep Hatton Brae but, eventually, they arrived at the village of Bishopton, where they had taken the road to Paisley. Finally, they reached the adjoining town of Johnstone and McGinn pulled over, consulting the scrap of paper given to him by Mrs Kilbride.

'Right—Armour Street—aye, it's just off the Thorn Brae, if I recall. Not far now.'

They pulled up outside a red sandstone tenement and exited the Wolseley, observed by a group of scruffy-looking youths who offered a few stage-whispered and derogatory comments about 'the polis'; McGinn took care to lock the car doors. They entered the tenement close, which smelled considerably less sanitised that the one in Greenock.

'Right, all we've got is the name—Forbes; see if there's anythin' on any o' the doors.'

There wasn't. Of all six flats on the three floors, only one bore a name: Mason. McGinn knocked and waited.

'Who is it?' came a frail, tremulous voice.

'Police—is that Mrs Mason?'

'Mr Mason, if ye please.'

The door opened to reveal an elderly gent, clad in vest, braces and shapeless grey trousers; stains on the front of his garments indicated a recent meal consisting of egg.

'Aye, whit d'ye want? Ah've no' done nothin' afore ye ask, too bloody old for ony capers!'

He chuckled, favouring them with a toothless grin.

'Mr Mason' said McGinn 'we're lookin' for a Mrs Forbes, can you tell me which flat she lives in?'

'Huh, so it's the widow Forbes ye're lookin' for eh? Whit's she been up tae—or is it wan o' her bloody lodgers that ye're efter?'

'As a matter o' fact, it is. Can you tell me anythin' about any o' them?'

'Och, no muckle really, but Ah watch their comin's an' goin's. This latest ane—weel, he's a bit o' a layabout, never seems tae be workin'. Keeps strange hours an' sometimes he comes alang wi' a richt hard ticket o' a man.'

'I see—can you describe this other man, Mr Mason?'

The old man scratched the stubble on his chin.

'Hm, weel, he wisnae a big lad, ye ken, but he's weel built, wi' long erms—looked a bit like a monkey!'

He chuckled again at his unflattering description.

'Did you see his hair colour?'

'Dark—mind, it's no' that well lit in the close. Ah think he had kind o' skelly eyes tae, from whit Ah could mak' oot.'

McGinn and Alan exchanged yet another meaningful glance; the description was a recurring one.

'Thanks, Mr Mason. Now, can you tell me, which flat does Mrs Forbes live in?'

Mason grinned once more.

'That yin across the landin'—an' she's standin' ahent ye listenin' tae every bloody word!'

~~~

The two officers entered the opposite flat, Mason still chuckling behind them and Mrs Forbes standing in silence as they passed, her hair set tight in curlers and her arms folded across her ample bosom. Once inside, she closed the door, with more force than was necessary.

'Whit's a' this then? Ye're askin' aboot Frank Kilbride?'

'Yes, Mrs Forbes.'

'Well, he's caused me nae trouble, his rent's paid up tae the end o' the month, so Ah've nae complaints.'

'When did you last see him?' asked Alan.

Mrs Forbes frowned.

'Weel, let's see, he kind o' comes an' goes, if ye ken whit Ah mean, but he wis here last Friday—aye, that'd be the last time Ah seen him. He spoke o' his mother doon in Greenock, mind ye —maybe he's awa' visitin' her.'

'How did he seem? Did you notice anythin' unusual about him, or his behaviour?' asked McGinn.

She gave them a suspicious look.

'He disnae say much at the best o' times, but he maybe seemed a wee bit agitated. Why're askin' aboot the laddie?'

'Mrs Forbes, I'm afraid Mr Kilbride is dead,' said McGinn. The colour drained from the woman's face as she lifted her hands to her mouth.

'Deid? Oh dear God! Deid? Whit happened?'

'I'm afraid I can't say,' replied McGinn. 'It's an ongoin' investigation. Can I ask—was he with anyone last time he visited?'

Mrs Forbes took out a grubby lace handkerchief and blew her nose.

'Aye, he wis with his pal, thon wee dark-haired fellow. Ah dinnae like him, ye ken, he looks at ye richt funny wi' thae skelly eyes o' his.'

'Scanlon again, by the sounds o' it,' muttered McGinn.

'Eh?'

'Nothing, Mrs Forbes, never mind. Could we have a look at his room, please?'

Her belligerence having evaporated, Mrs Forbes opened a door and turned on the light.

'This wis Frank's room—mind ye there's precious little tae see. Ah'll leave ye tae it—Ah'll be ben the livin' room.'

The two men searched the untidy and sparsely-furnished bedroom but, once again, found little of interest. The wardrobe contained some well-worn clothes and a couple of pairs of shoes. However, in a jacket pocket, Alan found a roll of sixteen one-pound notes; he handed them to the inspector.

'Fair bit o' money for someone' not long out of jail and not workin', eh, McInnes? I wonder where that came from?'

Nothing further came to light and, their search concluded, they crossed to the living room, where a television was blaring. McGinn knocked on the door; there were some heavy footsteps before it was opened by Mrs Forbes, her face flushed. Alan saw McGinn raise an eyebrow—the reek of whisky was immediately apparent.

'Right, Mrs Forbes, that's us finished, but I'll have to ask you not to touch Frank's room in the meantime, we'll probably get the fingerprint boys over in the next day or so.'

Alan, however, was looking past the woman; sitting on a small bureau beside the television set was a near-empty bottle of whisky and a glass tumbler. He nudged McGinn and pointed.

'Erm, look at that whisky, Inspector.'

Mrs Forbes also turned.

'Here, whit's wrang wi' a wummin' hae'in' a wee drink—Ah've had a hell o' a shock, you comin' here an' tellin' me...'

McGinn interrupted; any hint of sympathy had disappeared from his voice.

'Mrs Forbes, I must ask where you got that bottle from.'

'Whit d'ye mean—Ah cannae quite mind.'

'Did you get it from Kilbride's room, by any chance?'

'Erm, eh, here, whit're ye sayin'?'

The inspector's tone hardened.

'I'm askin' you a question—did you take that bottle from Frank Kilbride's room?'

After a bit of bluster, Mrs Forbes finally admitted that she had.

'Ah mean, he'd been awa' for near a week, Ah wisnae sure when he'd be back...it wis just sittin' there, there wisnae much left...'

'We'll need to take it as evidence, Mrs Forbes; and we'll also need your fingerprints.'

The woman looked affronted.

'Whit? Whit the hell d'ye need ma fingerprints for?'

'Just to rule them out, Mrs Forbes, since you've handled the bottle. You will need to attend the Paisley headquarters tomorrow—I'll make sure they know you're coming.'

He crossed the room and, using his handkerchief, carefully lifted the bottle of VAT 69 whisky; Mrs Forbes appeared close to tears.

'Erm, listen, could ye no jist pour oot that wee drop that's left?'

~~~

Mr Mason's door was still ajar as they left Mrs Forbes' flat and Alan suspected that the old man was listening behind it, no doubt grinning toothlessly at his neighbour's discomfiture. As they exited the tenement, McGinn turned to Alan.

'That was a damned good bit of work there, McInnes. I always said you were an observant bugger.'

'Och, thanks, Inspector, it was the upside-down label that caught my eye.'

McGinn opened the car door, handing the bottle to Alan; its contents remained inside, much to Mrs Forbes' chagrin.

'Aye, a bottle designed for the gantry in a pub; well, if the prints match up, then that'll finally place Kilbride at the Barloch robbery—it's the same brand as that label you found in the burnt-out van an' it'll account for the missing bottle. Good work—aye, good work indeed, McInnes.

~~~

McGinn drove Alan back to Barloch, dropping him at the Cross and, as he walked up School Street, he barely noticed the persistent drizzling rain; he was still glowing with pride at Inspector McGinn's words of praise. He opened the door of his house, his nostrils detecting the aroma of liver and bacon, one of his favourites. He hung his damp coat on the peg and entered the kitchen; his mother smiled.

'My, you're late, son. Don't worry, Donny called to say you were out with the inspector. Sit down, I'll get your tea.'

Alan barely registered Isa's familiar term for his superior officer.

'Hello Mother—wait 'til I tell you what happened...'

Chapter 15

Alan couldn't help but feel disappointed, when Saturday came, that he had heard nothing further regarding what he now privately referred to as the Kilbride Case. He had hoped that, by the weekend, Inspector McGinn might have matched the fingerprints on the whisky bottle; he had also hoped that he would be kept informed, one way or another, although he realised that, in truth, he was simply a village constable and not part of Paisley's CID. Maybe McGinn had just forgotten; or maybe he felt there was no obligation to keep Alan apprised of any developments.

So it was that, with a lingering feeling of self-doubt, he made his way to Barloch Station to meet Nancy Wright, his fiancé, who was due to arrive just after midday. The weather had improved and he had the day well planned. A visit to Janetti's cafe, a pleasant stroll around the village before high tea at his home; he had left his mother busy baking what she called teabread—scones, pancakes and fruit-loaf—which would be preceded by bacon and eggs, or possibly kippers. His mother still had a tendency to feel that she had something to live up to where Nancy was concerned, although his young woman had never been anything but charming to Isa. He smiled—he would maybe press her for a wedding date today, if it seemed appropriate; and, just maybe, she would agree at least to taking a look at the vacant police house that he had been so diligently renovating. He felt a slight pang of guilt—work commitments had conspired to curtail these renovations and he had hoped that he might have made more progress before Nancy's visit.

His thoughts were interrupted by a distant whistle; the train was approaching and he quickened his step, his arrival on the platform coinciding with the arrival of the hissing steam engine and its two grimy coaches. A few passengers alighted but he only had eyes for one; clad in a pretty, navy-blue frock, a red coat and matching hat, Nancy Wright's smile at his approach immediately lifted his spirits. He walked towards her and kissed her powdered cheek.

'Hello, Nancy—you look lovely!'

'Hello yourself,' she trilled. 'My, you look smart too—very handsome!'

His heart soared.

~~~

They sat in the warmth of a cafe drinking hot, milky coffee; cappuccino, Nancy had informed him. Alan had first sipped the cooler froth before taking a mouthful and scalding his palate, much to Nancy's amusement.

'Oh, you silly thing, didn't you realise that the coffee would be so hot?'

'No, I didn't— I've never had this before; it's nice though.'

He felt very adult, sitting in the cafe, drinking exotic coffee with this beautiful young woman to whom he just happened to be engaged. Mrs Janetti, the proprietress, made her way over, a smile on her round, homely face.

'So, Alan, ees this-a your fiancé?'

He felt his chest swell with pride; already, a few of the local youths had cast envious glances in their direction.

'Yes, Mrs Janetti, this is Nancy.'

"Ello, my dear, 'ow nice to meet you—you are a lucky man, Alan, what a beautiful young lady that-a you 'av. Bella, bella.'

Nancy smiled at the compliment; Alan beamed.

'Thank you, Mrs Janetti—yes, she is, isn't she. Anyway, how are you—you seem to be a bit quieter today.'

Mrs Janetti's smile turned to a scowl.

'Si, it is this damnable ice-a-cream van that is-a coming round. We are a small village—you know that—and there is not—'ow you say—not room for us both. They take away my business, people do not-a want to walk here to get sweeties, ice-cream an' cigarettes. But what can we do, what can we do?'

'I'm sorry, Mrs Janetti, that's a shame.'

Mrs Janetti wasn't finished, however.

'And-a that racket that they make, like a broken music box... ohhh!'

She pulled a face of both rage and frustration.

'Anyway, I'd better go—we 'ave a customer. It is lovely to meet you, Nancy. Ciao.'

Nancy smiled at the woman then looked across at Alan.

'She's a nice lady—but what was all that about?'

'Och, there's been an ice-cream van coming around for a few weeks now, playing some horrible tune—Greensleeves, I think it is. We used to sing it at school.'

'We still do,' said Nancy, smiling, 'and it probably sounds every bit as bad as your ice-cream van! Still, that's a shame if it's affecting her business. Is there nothing you can do?'

Alan shook his head.

'I'm afraid that's outwith our jurisdiction, Nancy and, yes, it is a shame. The thing is, Mrs Janetti's right, we are just a small village and I can't see how an ice-cream van makes enough money to make it worth their while. I mean, the cafe's open until about eight o'clock, the ice-cream van just comes and does its rounds once a day—well, maybe twice at weekends—so they can't have a lot of trade. Doesn't seem to make sense, really.'

The conversation moved on, Alan paid for the coffee and they headed outside; as they did so, they heard the distant, discordant chimes. Nancy laughed.

'Right on cue!'

'Aye, right on cue, right enough!'

But, as Nancy took his arm, all thoughts of the ice-cream van were immediately banished.

~~~

Following a pleasant stroll around Barloch, the couple finally made their way up School Street towards Alan's house. They heard the chimes on several occasion, laughing, as lovers do, at the jarring rendition of Greensleeves. Half way up the hill, it sounded again, closer this time. A few minutes later, a leather-jacketed youth crossed the road a few yards ahead of them; Nancy stopped momentarily.

'Here, is that not Hamish Calder?'

Alan smiled; it seemed that teachers invariably remembered each and every pupil that had passed through their care.

'Aye, it is. Last time I saw him he'd just bought a motorbike.'

The young man was carrying an ice-cream cone, which he suddenly threw to the ground as he walked on up the hill. Although it would, undoubtedly, be quickly devoured by the numerous crows nesting in the adjacent trees, nonetheless Alan felt that such a blatant disregard for the tidiness of the village should not go unchecked. He called out.

'Here—Hamish—Hamish Calder!'

Nancy squeezed his arm.

'Oh, leave him, Alan, it was just a wee accident—didn't you ever drop your cone?

'No, it wasn't an accident, Nancy, he threw it on the ground—you saw him. Why buy a cone then just throw it away?'

160

The young man had ignored Alan's shout and they had now reached the dropped cone; Alan peered at it with surprise—as before, the lower half of the cone was missing but, on this occasion, its absence could not be blamed on avian intervention. He called again.

'Hoy, Calder—I want a word with you.'

The young man turned briefly then started to run; Alan was about to give chase but Nancy tightened her grip on his arm.

'Alan, you're off duty, in case you'd forgotten, and your mother's expecting us; after all, it's only a cone. Come on, we don't want to be late.'

Nancy was right, of course but, as they walked the last few yards to his house, his mind was puzzling over the fact that he had now seen a couple of dropped ice cones recently—each with their lower portion missing. Something seemed to be telling him that that wasn't normal.

~~~

The high tea went splendidly; Isa had, indeed, pushed the boat out considerably, serving delicious grilled lemon sole with fried potatoes and peas—there was even a lemon wedge as garnish, not a common accompaniment in the McInnes household! This had been followed by a mouth-watering selection of home baking, the crowning glory being a wonderfully light Victoria sponge. Nancy had been highly complimentary of Isa's cooking and baking, eliciting an 'och, it was nothing special' from the smiling woman. Even Gilbert McInnes had been on his best behaviour and some judicious teasing from Nancy had elicited a rare smile from the normally taciturn man. Once the customary thanks and goodbyes had been said, Alan and Nancy made their way, arm-in-arm, back down to the station.

'Now, Alan, there's really no need for you to get the train

to Paisley with me—I'm perfectly capable of making my own way home.'

Alan, however, wouldn't hear of it and, soon, they were sitting beside one another in the dingy carriage compartment, gazing out into the inky-black night that was dotted with the lights of the various farms and villages en route to Paisley. If truth be told, his main motivation for accompanying his fiancé home was to prolong the time spent in her company.

~~~

It was after eleven when Alan alighted once more at Barloch station; he had walked Nancy to the end of her street in the exclusive Paisley suburb of Ralston, then made a dash for the ten-fifteen train that would take him back to Barloch. He had been torn between an extended goodnight and an hour's wait for the next train but, in the end, it was Nancy's common sense that prevailed. He smiled to himself—no doubt such female guidance was an indicator of things to come.

He spent a few minutes chatting to Bert Oliphant, who was still wearing a black armband in memory of Alex Combe. The stationmaster advised him that Combe's funeral was due to be held the following Friday afternoon and Alan fully intended to be present. He walked down the ramp on to Kirk Street but, as he turned for home, he was aware of a figure walking somewhat unsteadily towards him, hands in pockets and head down. Alan backed slowly into the station entrance until the figure was level with him, then stepped out.

'Hamish Calder, I want a word with you.'

The young man made to run but Alan grabbed his arm.

'Not so fast, sonny boy.'

Calder looked at Alan; even in the dull gas light of the station entrance, the policeman could see the glazed look, the dilated pupils. Calder gave an imbecilic grin.

'Whit're ye wantin', Mister Polis?'

'You know damned well—I shouted for you to stop earlier but you ran.'

'Aye, ye cannae catch me, Ah'm the gingerbread man!'

The young man gave a silly giggle.

'Shut up. What's this nonsense with you throwin' away your ice-cream cone?'

The smile widened.

'Didnae fancy it—too bloody cold.'

'In that case, why did you buy it?'

Calder shrugged.

'Dinnae ken. Let me go, Ah wan't tae go home, Ah'm needin' a pee. '

Alan tightened his grip, sensing another escape attempt.

'It's not the first cone I've seen that's been dropped—or thrown away. What's goin' on, Calder?'

The youth shook his head.

'Search me, Pee-Cee!'

He giggled again at his own crude humour.

'I will bloody search you, if you don't answer my question. In fact, maybe a night in the cells would put a stop to your bloody cheek.'

Hamish Calder's grin vanished and was replaced by a look of alarm.

'Here, ye cannae just—'

He was interrupted by a shout from further up the street.

'Alan—everythin' okay doon there?'

A uniformed Kerr Brodie was striding towards them, no doubt on his nightly round. For a moment, Alan was distracted and that was all the opportunity that Calder needed. He wriggled out of Alan's grasp and made off down the street, like

163

a hare being chased by a pack of hounds. Brodie drew level with his colleague.

'What the hell wis goin' on there?'

Alan shook his head.

'No idea, Kerr. It's Hamish Calder—he seems to be away with the fairies—didn't seem to be drunk, just...well, sort of stupid, if you know what I mean, talkin' rubbish. It's funny, I saw him earlier when I was out with Nancy—he'd bought an ice-cream cone but he just threw it away. The odd thing is, the end was broken off and I'd seen another one recently that was the exact same.'

Brodie frowned.

'Y'know, I saw one the other day, just like you said. Thought nothin' of it at the time but now that you mention it, the end was missin'. What d'you reckon it's all aboot?'

'No idea, Kerr, but I think it has to be something to do with that damned ice-cream van that's been going around. Here, are you heading back up the road now?'

'Aye, just finished my rounds, Ah'll head back to the station, grab a cuppa an' settle down for the night. Hopefully all the excitement's over for the time bein'!'

~~~

Alan went into the station and had a cup of tea with his colleague, chatting about recent events; after some internal debate, he decided to discuss his latest concerns with his friend.

'Kerr, y'know that CID sergeant—Fairbrother?'

'Aye, the ginger one! '

'Well, something strange came up the other day when we were down in Greenock. Remember you said that Fairbrother had started down there and that his uncle was Superintendent?'

'Aye, that's right.'

'And you know that we've identified the body found in Kilmirrin? Turns out he was a Greenock man as well.'

Kerr yawned.

'Aye, Kilbride, wasn't it—what of it?'

'See, the thing is, I asked the inspector down there if this Kilbride chap would be well known to the police in Greenock and he said that he would.'

Kerr grinned.

'Ye tak' a long way for a short cut, Alan—but most local men will have a good idea what their felons look like. What's your point?'

Alan paused; what was his point? What was he actually implying—and should he voice his concern to Brodie? He decided that he had come this far.

'Well, surely if Fairbrother had been on the beat in Greenock, he would have been familiar with Frank Kilbride—he seems to have been reasonably notorious in the area. Yet, when we found the body, he showed no sign of recognition at all, even when McGinn asked.'

Brodie sat forward in his chair.

'Alan, the man was dead—surely that would have changed his appearance?'

'Maybe, but remember that Inspector Melville recognised him only from the description that McGinn circulated. Surely Fairbrother would have recognised him if he saw him in the flesh?'

Brodie pondered this for a moment.

'Maybe aye an' maybe no'. So what are ye sayin', Alan—are ye implyin' that Fairbrother deliberately failed to identify Kilbride?'

Alan hesitated once more—that was exactly what he was implying but to hear it put into words was rather alarming.

'Well, I'm not quite sure I'd go that far, Kerr...'

His friend cut him off.

'Look, if you think Fairbrother should've recognised this Kilbride fellow, but claimed he didn't, then surely ye are sayin' he did it deliberately. That's a hell o' an accusation, man, ye need tae be careful what ye're sayin' about senior officers!'

'Aye, I know that, Kerr. Listen, just keep this to yourself, if you don't mind. It's just a daft theory o' mine but it seemed a bit odd that he failed to recognise a criminal that seems to be well-known on his home turf. Och, just forget it—listen, I'd best be away up the road. I hope you have an uneventful shift—I'll see you on Monday.'

Chapter 16

There was a spring in the young constable's step as he strode down School Street on Monday morning; his weekend had exceeded all his expectations, apart for the facts that there had been insufficient time for Nancy to view the vacant police house and that a date for their wedding somehow still hadn't been finalised. As he looked down the street, bathed in bright April sunshine once more, he noticed the police Wolseley parked outside the office. He smiled optmistically; it seemed that Inspector McGinn hadn't forgotten him after all.

He entered the office to find the inspector leaning on the bar, chatting to Sergeant Tait, mug in one hand and the inevitable cigarette in the other.

'Mornin' McInnes. Good weekend?'

'Yes sir, very good, thanks.'

'Good stuff. Right, I didn't get a chance to tell you sooner, Friday turned out to be a hell of a day. Anyway, I got the results of the fingerprints back, it seems that our friend Scanlon was drinking whisky along with Kilbride. Both men's prints—as well as Mrs Forbes', of course—are all over the bottle.'

'So that places him at the scene of Combe's murder?'

McGinn shook his head as he stubbed out his cigarette.

'No, it doesn't, unfortunately. All it proves is that the two men were drinkin' the stolen whisky together, most likely in Kilbride's digs, but it doesn't specifically place both Scanlon an' Kilbride at the original crime scene. Either man could have taken the bottle then shared it with the other on a later occasion.'

He took out another Capstan and lit up.

'However, we've had a bit o' luck—the fingerprint boys have managed to get a partial thumbprint from one o' the buttons that you found. Now, it probably wouldn't stand up in a court of law, but it's a fair certainty that the print belongs to our friend Scanlon. In which case, this would seem to place him at the scene o' Kilbride's murder.'

Tait took his pipe from his mouth.

'So Ah'm reckonin' that ye're now huntin' for this man Scanlon?'

'Aye, we certainly are. Not an easy task, mind, an' it's possible that he's already moved on, especially if he's committed one, or maybe two, murders. But the hunt is on an' we've circulated a description to all offices in the west of Scotland, as well as to the railway stations, as well as any ports where he might catch a ferry; mind you, if he was doing a runner he's probably already gone by now. Still, it's worth a try; needless to say, if you hear anything, anything at all, get in touch. It's highly unlikely that he'll turn up down here, but on the off-chance that he does, bear in mind that he's a right violent bugger so be very careful.'

The Inspector stubbed out his second cigarette and made to leave.

'I'll be off—McInnes, I must thank you for your assistance—you've been a great help.'

He extended his hand and the customary handshake took place; this was repeated with Tait, after which McGinn headed to the door. As he opened it, he turned back, a mischievous smile playing on his lips..

'An' if you do happen to change your mind, McInnes, I could easily find a place for you. Cheerio.'

Tait smiled benevolently.

'Aye, lad, ye've really scored a hit there, right enough. Ah cannae quite fathom why ye didnae take the opportunity in the first place. Ah mean, why wid ye chose tae stay doon here, in this wee backwater?'

Alan just smiled; how many hints did Tait need that he was hoping, in the near future, to take his place as sergeant? He was saved by the ringing of the phone, which Tait answered.

'Hello, Barloch Police...aye...aye...richt, Ah'll send a constable along richt awa'. Cheerio.'

He placed the receiver down.

'It's auld Miss Dean, she thinks someone tried tae get in her back door last nicht—again.'

Alan smiled.

'Och, she's a poor old soul—I'll away along an' see her, put her mind at rest.'

Tait nodded

'Ah think she's headin' for her second childhood, it's a damned shame. Off ye go, then, maybe ye'll be regrettin' no' joinin' the CID in aboot an hour or so!'

Alan headed out of the office, hoping that Tait's words wouldn't prove to be accurate!

~~~

True to the sergeant's prediction, Alan spent almost an hour comforting and calming the elderly Miss Dean, assuring her that her back door hadn't been tampered with. He felt sorry for the poor old lady; she had no family to care for her and relied on the assistance of neighbours to make sure she was reasonably well looked after. He finally managed to take his leave, refusing a third cup of tea, and made his way along Main Street and down Factory Street towards the Bar Loch. He walked past the factory, an empty and dilapidated building that had once serviced and maintained hand-looms for the few local weavers left in the village and its surrounds. Yet another industry that seemed to be faltering, he thought, as a grimy steam engine clattered across the bridge, slowing down as it approached the goods yard. A small crane, a few flat trucks and a guards van trundled behind it and he wondered if this was the recovery train for the burnt-out wagons. He hoped so—their presence was an unpleasant reminder of recent events.

~~~

His perambulation around the village was uneventful; he engaged in a few conversations with several locals, he walked up to the goods yard where a number of railway personnel were engaged in salvage operations, then he headed up to the Cross and into the baker's shop. The distant sounding of the school bell told him he was just in time to miss the deluge of hungry schoolchildren. He purchased three hot bridies and three iced buns before crossing the road, just as the tide of ravenous youngsters swept down the hill. Kerr Brodie arrived at the office just before him, ready to start his shift. He sniffed then grinned appreciatively at his colleague.

'Is that bridies—good man!'

Alan smiled back—Kerr Brodie was perpetually hungry.

'Did you no' have lunch at home, Kerr?'

'Och, Ah just had a sandwich—c'mon, let's get in an' get the kettle on.'

~~~

The three officers had finished their tasty lunch and were drinking their second cup of tea when the phone rang.

'A busy wee day, richt enough,' commented Sergeant Tait as he picked up the receiver.

'Hello, Barloch Police...aye...'

He looked across at Alan.

'Ah see...hmm...richt,' Ah'll send him up richt away... aye, it'll be Constable McInnes himsel'...cheerio.'

He hung up the phone.

'That wis Miss Shaw, the headmistress up at the school; there's been an incident.'

Alan had a pang of unease as he and Kerr stared at the sergeant.

'An incident? What does she mean by that?'

Tait shook his head.

'She didnae say—but she's asked for you personally. Best get yersel' up there richt awa', ye dinnae want tae keep Miss Shaw waitin'!'

Alan stood up, wiping crumbs from his trousers. Miss Shaw had been the headmistress for as long as he could remember and Sergeant Tait was quite correct; she was a woman who didn't like to be kept waiting.

~~~

As he entered the familiar playground of Barloch School he experienced a pang of nostalgia, tainted slightly by the charred remains of the janitor's shed in the far corner. This reminded him that his enquiries into the recent spate of fires remained unsolved, overtaken by more serious events. He climbed the few steps and entered the red sandstone building, the smell inside immediately familiar and somehow comforting. The lady in the office looked up and smiled.

'Och, it's yourself, Alan, good afternoon—just go on through, I'm sure you remember the way!'

Alan smiled back.

'Aye, indeed I do, Mrs Murdoch.'

As he turned the corner towards the headmistress's' office,

however, his heart began to beat faster; although he had not been a troublesome child, nonetheless he had had to pay the occasional visit to Miss Shaw's office. Despite her small stature, she could be a formidable lady.

Standing in front of the small waiting area was the school janitor, an older man wearing a shapeless black uniform jacket and trousers, as well as a peaked cap. He smiled and gave a salute before extending his hand; they exchanged the customary handshake.

'Hello, Mr Purdie; still here, I see—how are you?'

'Ach, I'm all right, lad. Yersel'?'

'Och, I'm fine, thanks. I hear there's been what Miss Shaw said was 'an incident'?'

Purdie cast a glance over his shoulder; two young girls were seated in the waiting area, heads down, hands in their laps. One had been crying but the other looked up at Alan with a sullen expression.

'Aye—they two got up to a bit o' mischief durin' lunch break. I'll let Miss Shaw explain, though—just awa' through.'

Alan knocked on the door and a sharp, familiar voice called, 'Come in.' He opened the door and, to his surprise, Nancy was seated beside Miss Shaw's desk. The headmistress smiled.

'Ah, Constable McInnes, I appreciate you coming so promptly. Of course, you and Miss Wright are acquainted—congratulations on your engagement.'

'Thanks, Miss Shaw.'

Nancy stifled a smile—Alan's unease was all too apparent.

'Anyway, have a seat and I'll explain what has happened. No doubt you observed the two girls outside?'

Alan sat down at the desk.

'Yes, I did. What have they been up to?'

Miss Shaw leaned forward, placing her tweed-clad elbows

on the desk and steepling her fingers. Her expression became rather more severe.

'At the end of lunch break, Mr Purdie noticed the pair sneaking off behind the ruins of his shed; this, of course, is out of bounds for pupils, it's both dirty and dangerous. He followed them and watched for a moment, then caught them setting light to an object.'

She leaned back and reached below the desk.

'This is what they were attempting to burn.'

Alan looked at the object and noticed Miss Shaw's face redden with anger; the partly-charred item was a crudely fashioned doll-like figure but what shocked him more was the scrap of paper pinned to the front, on which was scrawled 'Miss Shaw.' He took the offending object, which still carried the faint reek of paraffin, from her hands.

'This is quite shocking, Miss Shaw, I'm very sorry. What did they have to say for themselves?'

'Not a great deal. Their names are Gwen Meldrum and Ann McSween. Gwen's not the brightest of children, unfortunately, and the McSween girl seems to hold sway over her. I suspect it was she who was the perpetrator of this...'

She struggled to find the appropriate word.

'...this outrage! Oh, Mr Purdie also found this—in the McSween girl's possession.'

She handed Alan a dark blue-ribbed bottle, carrying the legend Milk of Magnesia. He opened the stopper and sniffed the contents.

'Paraffin? I wonder where she got hold of that?'

'I'd imagine that many of the poorer households use paraffin heaters to heat their homes; it shouldn't be too difficult to get hold of. However, perhaps it would be best if you spoke to the girls themselves. I'll get Mr Purdie to bring them in.'

She rose but Alan held up his hand.

'Actually, if what you say regarding their relationship is correct, I think it might be best to speak to them individually. I think we should begin with Gwen—Meldrum, did you say?'

Miss Shaw gave him a grim smile.

'Very well, Constable, I dare say you know best.'

Somehow, Alan doubted the sincerity of Miss Shaw's words!

~~~

Miss Shaw returned with a still-weeping Gwen Meldrum, ushering her across to where Nancy was seated; she held out her small hand as if for re-assurance and Nancy took it. Alan sat down once more and smiled at the trembling girl. He reckoned she would be about ten years old, wearing a worn but reasonably clean floral frock and a grey cardigan with patched elbows. He leaned towards her, noticing her flinch, and wondered if the girl had been the victim of violence in her home.

'Now, Gwen, I only want to ask you a few questions; do you understand?'

The girl nodded, continuing to grasp Nancy's hand tightly.

'Good girl—you know that what you did was wrong, don't you?'

She nodded again.

'So, first of all, whose idea was it to make the doll and set it on fire?'

This time the girl shook her head fervently.

'Now, Gwen, you must answer me. Was it your idea, or was it Ann's idea? Don't be afraid, nothing will happen as long as you tell me the truth.'

The girl sobbed then spoke in a faltering voice.

'It—it wisnae ma idea, it wis Annie's, she said it'd be richt guid

174

fun tae set the wee dolly on fire. But she'll kill me if she kens Ah telt ye, so she will.'

'No she won't, I'll make sure of that. So it was Ann—Annie's—idea, I see. Now, where did you get hold of the paraffin?'

The girl was visibly shaking now and Alan felt great pity for the child.

'It wis...weel...ye see, Annie's big brother had some, he keeps it...'

She clammed up suddenly, placing her free hand over her mouth.

'Come on, now, Gwen, where does he keep it?'

The girl broke down altogether and Nancy put her arm around the frail, heaving shoulders, drawing the girl close to her.

'He'll kill me, so he will, he's horrid.'

'Gwen, you need to tell me—where does he keep it? This is very important, you know.'

'In...in a shed roon' the back o' his hoose. He...he's got loads o' the stuff, Annie says he widnae miss a wee drop. She got the bottle oot o' the midden. Ah didnae mean ony harm, Mister, honest Ah didnae.'

She burst into a fresh paroxysm of tears and Alan sat back. Miss Shaw leaned across the desk.

'I think she's had enough, Constable. I doubt if she can tell you much more.'

Alan agreed and Nancy led her away to the main office, into the care of Mrs Murdoch; once she had returned, Ann McSween was brought into the room. Alan realised immediately that he was dealing with a very different young girl; her face was set in a scowl and, although placed next to Nancy, just as Gwen had been, her arms remained resolutely folded in front of her. Alan leaned towards her.

'Now, Ann—can I call you Annie?'

The girl just stared at him.

'Annie, then. Now, you know that what you did was wrong, don't you?'

There was no response.

'So I'm going to ask you a question; was it your idea to set fire to the doll?'

Again, his question elicited no response and he decided to adopt a firmer tone.

'Annie, you are in quite a bit of trouble; we know that you obtained the paraffin from your brother and we know that it was your idea to—'

Annie McSween screamed in his face.

'Naw ye dinnae—an' if that stupid wee bit bitch Meldrum telt ye that, then she's a bloody wee liar; an' just wait 'til Ah get ma haunds on her...'

Miss Shaw was on her feet; she spoke in a stentorian tone that even sent a shiver down Alan's spine!

'Ann McSween—don't you DARE use language like that in here! I will not have it. You are in big trouble, my girl—if you're not careful, then you'll be heading the same way as your brother.'

Alan looked questioningly at Nancy, but she shook her head. Ann McSween's jaw had dropped and her face had turned white. Despite the situation, Alan had to stifle a smile as, clearly, Miss Shaw's authority far outweighed his own. He continued his questioning.

'Look, Annie, you may as well tell me. Was it your idea?'

The girl snuffled and Alan waited for the tears, although they didn't materialise. The girl shrugged.

'Micht've been, Ah cannae mind.'

'And did you get the paraffin from your brother?'

Another shrug.

'Micht've.'

Alan stood up.

'I don't think there's much point in continuing, Miss Shaw.'

'No, I agree. Nancy, could you accompany Ann to the office until I decide what to do about this?'

'Certainly, Miss Shaw.'

She rose and extended a hand to Annie but the girl kept her arms folded. Nancy gave Alan a brief smile before they left and Miss Shaw leaned back in her chair.

'Well, what do you make of that, Constable—may I call you Alan?'

'Yes, of course, Miss Shaw. Can I ask, what were you referring to when you mentioned Annie's brother?'

'Hm, I thought you might have remembered but it was probably after you had left school and I'm not sure if you'd started with the police. Douglas McSween—every bit as sullen and stubborn as his sister. He must be about eighteen now, I'd think, we can check his school record. He'd always been a bit of a rogue, even at school, but on this occasion he'd deliberately thrown a stone and broken a window, somewhere up in the housing scheme, as I recall. When the householder reported him, he responded by setting fire to their garden shed. Fortunately the damage was confined to the shed but it could have been a lot worse. He was sent to borstal for his efforts and, fortunately, I haven't come across his since. Not a pleasant youth, I'm afraid.'

She paused for a moment, then gave Alan a hard stare.

'It had crossed my mind that McSween may have been responsible for the fire in the playground. I'd imagine that you've already spoken to him?'

'Erm, no, we haven't as yet.'

Despite the veiled criticism, Alan felt a thrill of excitement. Was Miss Shaw correct? Could Douglas McSween have been responsible for the recent spate of arson attacks in the village? He was surprised that Sergeant Tait hadn't made the connection but he would certainly be following this line of enquiry now.

'Miss Shaw, I'm going to look into this matter further—can you keep both girls here in the meantime please? We'll be paying a visit to the McSween house and I don't want Annie McSween warning her brother—if he's there, that is. Do you have an address for her—also for the Meldrum girl, although I think she's more of a bystander.'

'Yes, I would tend to agree; I'll get you both girls' particulars and they will be kept here until school finishes, which will be...'

She consulted her watch.

'...in just over an hour. Will that be sufficient? I could keep them in later as punishment, if you need more time?'

'Would that be all right? I don't want to inconvenience any of your staff.'

The headmistress gave a grim smile.

'I'm usually here until five o'clock so I will be supervising them personally. A hundred lines each will hopefully drum some common sense into them. Had it been boys, I would have given them six of the strap but I do draw the line at girls.'

Alan shuddered; although he had never personally experienced Miss Shaw's corporal punishment, her strength and the pain that her Lochgelly leather strap inflicted had been notorious.

'Well, if you really don't mind, that'll give us sufficient time to pay him an unheralded visit. Many thanks, Miss Shaw, I appreciate your help and it's been nice to see you again, despite the unfortunate circumstances.'

The headmistress stood up and extended a bony hand.

'Yes, it was nice to see you too, Alan. As I recall your last visit was following the burning of Mr Purdie's shed so let's hope we don't meet again under similar circumstances!'

As he turned to leave, she added, 'You were always a good pupil, Alan McInnes—and I'm very proud of how you've turned out.'

He felt his face redden, although his smile stretched from ear to ear!

Chapter 17

With a growing sense of excitement, Alan made his way quickly back down School Street, barging into the office, causing Sergeant Tait to look up from his newspaper, his spectacles perched precariously on his nose.

'Aye-aye, ye're in a richt hurry, lad. Where's the fire?'

'You might be closer to the mark than you think, Sergeant!'

Alan explained what had happened at the school as Tait puffed on his pipe, a frown on his craggy features.

'Hm, now ye come tae mention it, Ah do mind o' the trouble with the McSween laddie. It wis a guid few years back, though, an Ah'd forgotten all aboot it. Weel, Ah suppose ye better get up an' have a chat wi' him afore the schools get oot.'

'Miss Shaw said she'd keep the girls in until five, so we should be all right. Is Kerr not here?'

Tait shook his head.

'Och, there's been a wee accident wi' a car, it seems auld man Wylie took the corner at the Cross a bit too fast an' collided wi' a van. From whit Ah can gather, naebody's been hurt but Brodie's awa' takin' details. D'ye think ye'll need him—McSween's just a youngster, efter all'

'Aye, I know, but I think it'd probably be best—I'll get Kerr to guard the rear o' the property, just in case he tries to sneak out the back door.'

Tait smiled.

'Aye, but ye'll remember whit happened last year when ye sent Brodie tae guard the rear o' a property—he micht no' be so keen this time!'

~~~

It was almost four-thirty before his colleague returned to the office, and Alan was becoming increasingly impatient. He quickly brought Kerr up to date and as predicted, the constable was none too keen on guarding the rear.

'Here, Ah got a jeely nose for ma trouble last time, Alan, so Ah think it's your turn—Ah'll take the front door, if ye don't mind.'

Alan reluctantly agreed; he felt that, having identified the possible arsonist, it should be him announcing their arrival, but he realised that Kerr had a fair point. The two officers set off up the hill at a brisk pace, turning right into Glenhead Street. Soon they reached Cruicksfield Oval, where Alan noticed that the former Campbell household now sported fresh net curtains, a new gate and a neatly trimmed hedge. As they turned into Cruicks Crescent, he was aware of the upstairs curtains twitching slightly.

'I see old man Plunkett's still keeping watch.'

Kerr chuckled.

'Some things never change—oh, by the way, I saw oor friend Fairbrother again on Saturday.'

'What—in the Masonic?'

'Aye, we were a bit later goin' an' the funny wee man wi' the moustache wis just leavin'. I'm presumin' he wis talkin' tae Fairbrother though, he wis sittin' at a table by himself an' he left a few minutes later.'

'Did he recognise you?'

Brodie grinned.

'Don't think the bugger knows I exist—he just walked past withoot a glance. Right, there's number seven.'

They stopped for a moment to confer about their tactics, but

Brodie's news about Fairbrother and his seemingly clandestine liaison grumbled at the back of Alan's mind; he tried to concentrate on the matter at hand.

'Kerr, you give me a minute to get round to the back door before you announce our arrival. If I need help, I'll give you a shout.'

'Right you are, Ah'll be listenin.'

The two constables walked up the concrete steps as stealthily as their police boots would allow; like many of the adjacent gardens, the grass was uncut and the garden untidy. Alan headed towards the side path, where an old pram beside a rusty dustbin barred his way; he moved it on to the grass and made his way around to the rear of the house. He was about to stand guard beside the back door when he noticed the wooden shed at the far end of the garden; the door was open and he halted—was someone inside?

He walked slowly over the untended grass and was approaching the shed when he heard Kerr Brodie banging loudly on the front door, accompanied by his authoritative announcement.

'Police; open up. '

Alan froze; the call was repeated and, suddenly, a figure came charging out of the shed. A young man, with longish greasy fair hair and the same eyes as his sister Ann.

'Douglas McSween...'

The youth lowered his head and charged at Alan, but the constable deftly stepped aside and lifted his foot, sending McSween sprawling on to the grass. Alan managed to call out 'Kerr— round the back!' before pouncing on his quarry, but McSween was already on his knees and lashed out at Alan. The blow caught the side of his head and he grabbed McSween's wrist, twisting his arm up his back and eliciting a yelp of pain. He pushed the youth face-first on to the grass.

'Douglas McSween, you're under arrest on suspicion of arson.'

McSween unleashed a string of expletives as Kerr arrived, handcuffs at the ready. Once the youth was safely secured, Alan pulled him to his feet.

'Right, down to the station with you, sonny Jim. Kerr, you hold him a minute, I'll just have a wee look in the shed.'

The expression on McSween's face told Alan that this action was unwelcome and the constable turned towards their captive.

'Am I going to find something of interest in there, McSween? A stock of paraffin, from what I hear.'

McSween spat viciously in Alan's face, prompting Kerr to punch him in the small of his back; the youth collapsed to his knees, moaning in pain. Kerr grabbed McSween's hair and pulled his head back.

'Less o' that, you wee bugger, or we'll charge you wi' assaultin' a police officer intae the bargain. Right, Ah've got him, Alan, on ye go.'

Wiping his face with his handkerchief, Alan made his way to the shed, noticing that, despite its dilapidated condition, a stout padlock hung from the hasp. The solitary window had been boarded over and the inside was dark, with a strong smell of paraffin and dampness. He stood for a moment, allowing his eyes to adapt, then looked about; sure enough, on the floor were several dozen gallon cans of Esso Blue paraffin. A rickety table stood at one end, on which were piled various boxes, some of which appeared to contain canned foods; below the table were some crates of beer and a few bottles of brandy. It appeared that Douglas McSween, or one of his associates, was running a rather successful black-market business from his decrepit premises. Alan crossed to the table and peered behind the boxes; he lifted a grubby blanket that seemed to be concealing something and, underneath, found a smaller parcel, wrapped in brown paper and securely tied with string. He lifted it up, surprised at how light it was, then took it over to the door. He gasped in astonishment as he read the label, on which was neatly printed:

Mr R Watson, Glebe Farm. Via British Railways. To Be collected. Barloch Goods Station, Renfrewshire.

~~~

The two officers made their way back down Glenhead Street; Kerr had a firm grasp on Douglas McSween's arm, while his hands remained securely cuffed behind his back. As they turned into School Street, they almost bumped into a hard-faced woman, cigarette in one hand and half-dragging the sullen-faced Ann McSween with the other. She halted, her mouth agape, but she quickly found her tongue.

'Here, whit the hell's goin' on—whit are ye daein' wi' ma boy?'

'He's under arrest, Mrs McSween.'

The woman dropped her cigarette, but her hold on her daughter remained firm. She shook her free fist in Alan's face.

'Aye, just because he got sent tae the approved school, Ah always knew ye'd never leave the poor lad alane. Ah can tell ye this—there's a lot worse in this village that ye should be arrestin'—'

Kerr interrupted.

'Mrs McSween, we've found gallons o' paraffin in your son's possession, not to mention other stolen goods. '

'An' can ye prove that? How d'ye know they're stolen, eh—answer me that?'

Alan held up the brown parcel.

'Can you explain this, then, Mrs McSween? It was in the shed—as far as I am aware, there is no Mr R Watson living at your address.'

Mrs McSween's mouth opened and shut a few times as her

son squirmed in Kerr's firm grasp. Suddenly an idea seemed to pop into her mind.

'Here, did ye ha'e a search warrant fur that shed?'

'We didn't need one,' replied Alan. 'The door was open and your son raised no objection to us looking inside.'

'Aye, that's right, isn't it?' added Kerr, twisting McSween's arm.

'Go tae hell, copper, Ah'm sayin noth...aaargh...'

With a stream of expletives, Mrs McSween went for Kerr but Alan managed to restrain her.

'If you don't stop that, Mrs McSween, we'll be arresting you for obstruction and assaulting a police officer. D'you hear?'

Douglas McSween turned and glared at his sister.

'Wis it you that clyped on me?'

She looked at him with a terrified expression.

'Wh...whit...naw, it wis that wee cow Grace Meldrum—honest, Duggie, ye ken ah widnae tell on ye.'

'Aye, weel, jist wait til' Ah get ma hands oan the wee bitch... aargh!'

'Cut that out, McSween,' hissed Brodie. 'Go near any bairns in this village an' ye'll have me tae deal with—got it?'

He twisted Duggie McSween's arm further up his back until the youth, howling with pain, eventually nodded. His mother's face was like thunder and she looked as if she might attempt a further attack, but a warning look from Alan stopped her in her tracks and she backed off. Ann finally started to cry; her mother seemed to remember the child's presence and turned towards her daughter.

'It's awright, pet, Duggie'll be home soon...'

'Ma, Ah'm hungry, Ah want ma denner!'

Alan and Kerr exchanged a glance; it seemed that the daughter's priority certainly wasn't her brother's release. With a snort of disgust and a few more foul-mouthed insults, Mrs McSween grabbed her daughter's hand once more and marched round the corner. Kerr pushed their prisoner forward.

'Nice to see your family's got your wellbeing in mind, McSween. Right, down the road. We've got a comfy bed in one o' the cells all ready for you.'

~~~

Sergeant Tait was in his office when they arrived; he ambled out to meet them.

'Ye were some time up the road...'

He stopped mid-sentence, his bushy eyebrows rising in surprise.

'Well, well, what've we got here?'

'Douglas McSween, Sergeant,' said Alan proudly. 'We've arrested him on suspicion of arson—an' we found this in his shed.'

He placed the parcel on the counter, having been careful to carry it by the string. Tait peered at the label then looked up at the constable.

'Good God Almighty!'

They stood in silence for a few minutes, then Tait seemed to be galvanized into action.

'Richt, get yer man intae the first cell. Belt an' shoelaces aff, just in case, make sure he's no' carryin' anythin' sharp—ye ken the drill.'

As Kerr pushed the sullen, subdued McSween towards the corridor leading to the cells, Tait looked at Alan.

'An' ye ken who ye need tae phone—richt away. Ye might just catch him.'

~~~

'McGinn here.'

'Inspector—it's Constable McInnes at Barloch.

186

Alan heard the faintest of sighs above the static on the line.

'Aye, McInnes, what is it now? I was just headin' home.'

'I'm sorry, Inspector—the thing is, I was called to the school today, there was an incident involving two children—'

'Cut to the chase, McInnes, I don't have all day—trouble at your school is no concern of the CID.'

The reprimand stopped Alan in his tracks.

'Erm, yes, sorry, Inspector. The thing is, we went to interview a suspect and we found the missing parcel—the one addressed to R Watson.'

There was a short silence.

'You're sure o' this?'

'Absolutely, sir, it's sitting here in front of me. R. Watson, Glebe Farm. Via British Rail.'

'Aye, that's good enough. What about this suspect?'

'He's in the cells, sir. Young man by the name o' Douglas McSween—I haven't interviewed him yet, I thought I'd be best to phone you first.'

McGinn's tone softened.

'Aye, you did the right thing, McInnes. Look, just let me get home, grab a bite to eat, an' I'll be down in about an hour and a half—can you hang on that long?'

Alan smiled.

'Of course, sir. I'll call my mother and I'm sure she'll bring us something to keep us going.'

'Aye, I don't doubt it! I'll see you soon—an' don't let that bloody parcel out of your sight!'

As McGinn hung up the phone, he swore, then smiled; if Donny Tait was there, he had little doubt that Isa McInnes would ensure that they were adequately fed and refreshed.

~~~

As predicted, following a phone call from her son, Isa McInnes arrived half an hour later with a basket containing a substantial quantity of cold mutton sandwiches and half a dozen scones, as well as a pat of butter and a pot of homemade raspberry jam. There was also a small parcel wrapped in greaseproof paper which Alan suspected was his mother's delicious tablet. As Kerr Brodie's eyes lit up, Donny Tait couldn't resist making a comment.

'That's awfy kind o' ye, Isa, but how many folk d'ye think ye're feedin'? There's only the three o' us.'

She smiled at him; rather fondly, Alan noticed.

'Four, Donny—you've got the McSween boy here too, have you not?'

'Aye, but...'

Her tone became firmer.

'But nothing, Donald Tait. He's another human being, he'll be cold, frightened and hungry. Anyway, am I not right in thinking that the prisoner is innocent until proven guilty?'

Donny Tait shook his head; arguing with Isa McInnes was always a futile pursuit.

'Aye, of course, you are right, Isa, an' ye're a richt guid-hearted soul. Thank ye kindly. Brodie, awa' an' get the kettle on.'

As Kerr left, Isa called after him.

'Don't forget to make a cup for your prisoner.'

Tait frowned.

'Hm, we cannae give him a cup though.'

'Why ever not?' queried Isa.

'Because it's china, Mother,' replied Alan. 'He could smash it and...well...'

Isa's eyes widened.

'You surely don't mean he'd try and harm himself?'

Tait nodded as he helped himself to a sandwich.

'Ah'm afraid he's richt, Isa—it wouldnae be the first time a prisoner has tried—or succeeded, for that matter—tae commit.'

The stricken look on Isa's face halted him.

'Sorry, Isa, but ye ken whit Ah mean.'

She nodded silently; her life was usually sheltered from the harsh realities of incarceration. Her practicality returned quickly, however.

'Have you a flask? You could give him the metal cup from the top.'

Alan smiled; his mother was one of the most caring—and practical—people that he knew.

~~~

'Man, that was richt tasty,' remarked Sergeant Tait, wiping mutton fat from his mouth. 'Ah'll let that go doon then we can hae a scone.'

The office door opened and Inspector McGinn entered, clad in a tweed jacket and a pair of corduroy trousers; Alan had never seen him in such casual attire. Catching sight of their repast, he grinned.

'So I was right enough, McInnes?'

'Aye, you were, sir.'

'An' what about the prisoner?'

'He's had his share,' said Tait.

'Good; we don't want accusations about starvin' our suspects do we? Right, let's hear the whole story.'

Between them, Kerr and Alan related the afternoon's events as McGinn stood puffing on a Capstan; once they had finished, he exhaled a stream of smoke.

'It seems to me we've had a right bit o' luck here, lads. It looks like you've probably caught your arsonist, but we now have the matter of this missing package that's mysteriously turned up in McSween's shed. D'you think the boy's capable of murder, though?'

Alan shook his head.

'No, I don't, sir. He's a right wee hardcase and there's no doubt that he's crooked, but I don't think he's a murderer.'

Kerr Brodie nodded in agreement as McGinn continued.

'Well, let's accept what you say, in which case it begs the question—if he didn't steal it from the goods van, what the hell was the parcel doin' in McSween's shed? By the way, where is it? I take it you've not opened it?'

Alan shook his head as Tait went into his office; he returned with the parcel, carrying it once more by the string, and handed it to McGinn.

'We've been richt careful with it in case there's fingerprints.'

'Good—right, let's see if we can get it open without causing too much damage.'

He undid the string and painstakingly began to unwrap the brown paper; there seemed to be rather a lot of it and, once removed, whatever the parcel contained was wrapped in what appeared to be part of an old cotton sheet. Finally, the contents were revealed—a considerable number of small cotton bags, their contents filling the room with a pungent, herby aroma. Even before McGinn opened one of the bags, he said, 'It's marijuana—can you smell it?'

Alan nodded.

'Aye, it's an odd smell, I thought it would be unpleasant but it's not—not really.'

'Probably no more unpleasant than tobacco, but the effects are quite different.'

McGinn opened a bag and pulled out a handful of the dried leaves, rubbing it between his fingers. It looked similar to pipe tobacco.

'Aye, it's marijuana right enough; a fair bit too, by the looks o' it. '

He reached for one of several smaller packages that were sitting amidst the cotton bags, wrapped in waxed paper. McGinn lifted it and unwrapped the packaging; inside was a lump of what looked like brown clay. He sniffed it.

'Cannabis resin—you grind it up an' put it in a roll-up. Aye this here's a fair haul o' illegal drugs. Worth a good bob or two, I'd say.'

He grinned at Alan and Kerr.

'Well done, you two, quite a haul here—that's a damned good day's work.'

'Like you said, Inspector, it was luck, mostly,' said Brodie. 'If the two lassies hadnae tried to set fire tae that wee dolly, well, we'd never have gone after McSween.'

'It's often luck that gets the result, Brodie,'said McGinn, 'but it's what we do with the luck we're dealt that counts. No, I reckon we've put a hefty dent in someone's finances here and they'll no' be happy. The question is, whose?'

Carefully, McGinn wrapped the parcel back up and handed it to Tait.

'Keep this safe for the time being; I'll not be heading back to the office tonight so I don't want anythin' happenin' to it.'

He lit a fresh cigarette.

'Right, we know what we've got, we know where it was found; time to have a word with our friend. Tait, can I use your office?'

Chapter 18

Kerr Brodie stood with his back to the office door, while Alan had been invited to sit next to Inspector McGinn, his pencil and notebook at the ready. McGinn was seated opposite Douglas McSween, elbows on the desk, staring intently at the few random jottings in his own notebook. The only noise in the room was the ticking of the clock on the wall. A minute passed in silence; McSween chewed nervously at his thumbnail, his narrowed eyes looking alternately at the floor, the desk and the inspector.

Another minute passed; McGinn fussily turned a page.

By the end of the third minute of silence, even Alan was becoming uneasy. Beads of perspiration had broken out on McSween's forehead and Kerr Brodie shifted restlessly from foot to foot. Finally, McGinn looked up at the prisoner.

'You know, they still hang folk for murder.'

The sentence hung in the air for a moment; a look of terror passed across McSween's face.

'Whit? Wait—Ah never...here, ye cannae pin Combe's murder on me, Ah didnae...'

McGinn gave an evil leer.

'Who said anythin' about accusin' you o' Combe's murder? I was just statin' a fact.'

'Eh? B-but...'

McGinn leaned forward and lowered his voice; his tone conspiratorial, friendly even. He gave the captive a knowing wink.

'Look son, it's very simple. Combe was murdered, the goods

van was set alight with his body inside. Personally, I don't think you killed him, but a parcel was taken from the van—we know that from the paperwork—an' it mysteriously turns up in your shed. The parcel happens to contain a substantial quantity o' illegal drugs.'

He leaned back, an insincere smile on his face as he spread his hands.

'So, either you stole the drugs an' killed Combe to cover your tracks, or somebody else did an' gave you the parcel for safe-keepin'. Which is it?'

McSween glanced nervously from side to side.

'Ah dinnae know nothin' aboot ony parcel...'

In a flash, McGinn had leaned forward, banging his fists on the desk and causing even Alan to jump. He screamed across at McSween, spittle flying from his mouth.

'DON'T BLOODY LIE TO ME, BOY!'

McSween trembled, mouth agape. The inspector sat back once more.

'Let's ask that again. Did you kill Combe? Or did someone else kill him and give you the parcel?'

The clock continued to tick off the seconds of silence.

'Well?'

Alan looked at McSween; the youth appeared to be on the verge of breaking down. Finally, he muttered something.

'What was that?' demanded McGinn.

'Ah dinnae know anythin' aboot a parcel.'

McGinn took a deep breath then exhaled slowly.

'Fine. McInnes, make sure you take this down.'

Alan poised his pencil; McGinn spoke in a clear, officious tone.

'Douglas McSween, you stand accused that, on the morning of the seventh of April, nineteen sixty, you did enter the goods yard at Barloch Station, you did assault the night watchman, Alexander John Combe and you did murder him...'

McSween jumped up from his chair; Brodie crossed the room in an instant and forcibly pushed him back down as he protested.

'Ah telt ye, Ah never killed naebody—please, ye have tae believe me. For God's sake...'

McGinn leaned forward once more; all traces of friendliness had vanished as he hissed

'Then bloody well tell me who did.'

McSween broke down completely. .

'Ah...Ah cannae, he'll kill me, so he will...'

'Who'll kill you. TELL ME?'

McSween shook his head vehemently.

'Fine; so you'd rather hang. Where were we—oh aye ...Alexander John Combe and that you did murder him. Douglas McSween, I am charging you with...'

McSween jumped up again, only to be pushed down once more, with considerably more force.

'Naw, naw!' he wailed ' Ah never, Ah never killed Combe, he just gave me the stuff tae keep, Ah wisnae there. Please, Ah didnae kill Combe, please...'

He started to sob; Alan was almost beginning to feel sorry for the youth but McGinn's interrogation was relentless. He yelled across at the prisoner.

'Who gave you the parcel, McSween? Tell me, for Christ's sake, tell me who did or I'll make sure you bloody hang for this. D'you hear me, McSween? If you don't tell me, I'm charging you with Combe's murder—last chance.'

McSween snivelled for a few moments, then mumbled almost incoherently; Alan struggled to make out what he was saying.

'Speak up,' demanded McGinn.

'It wis a bloke ca'd Johnny; Ah dinnae ken his second name. Ah've done a few—weel, a few wee jobs fur him, an' he asked me tae look efter thon parcel. Ah didnae ken whit wis in it, honest, Ah swear tae God, Ah never knew it wis drugs.'

McGinn leaned back once more.

'What does this Johnny look like?'

McSween snivelled some more.

'Weel, he's kinda wee, heavy built like, wi' black hair; an' there's somethin' wrang wi' his eyes.'

'What's wrong with his eyes?'

McSween shook his head and shrugged.

'Ah'm no' sure—they're kinda skelly-like.'

'Does he have a squint?' asked Alan.

Another shrug.

'Ah dinnae ken—they jist look skelly-like.'

McGinn exchanged a glance with Alan.

'So he gave you the parcel to keep?'

McSween nodded.

'Aye.'

'For how long?'

Another shrug.

'Dinnae ken—he said Ah wis tae keep it until aw the fuss died doon. Said he'd let me know.'

McGinn frowned.

'How's he goin' to let you know?'

McSween continued to snuffle and Alan noticed a drip at the end of his nose; the youth wiped it off on the back of his grubby sleeve.

'Ah sometimes keep stuff fur him, Ah wait at the telephone box alang frae the hoose.'

'An' how the hell d'you know when he's goin' to call?' demanded McGinn.

'He tells me tae wait every Sunday evenin' at eight o'clock. Sometimes he calls, sometimes he disnae. Ah just wait fur aboot ten minutes.'

'Has he made any arrangement to collect this parcel?'

Again, McSween shook his head.

'Naw.'

McGinn raised his voice once more.

'You'd better be tellin' me the truth, McSween.'

'Honest, he hasnae called fur a while, no' since he gie'd me it. Ah dinnae ken when he wants tae collect it an' Ah didnae know whit was in it, honest Ah didnae. Please, mister, ye have tae believe me, Ah wis only keepin' it for him, Ah swear!'

McGinn paused, then turned to Alan.

'Have you got all that, McInnes?'

'Yes sir. It's all here.'

'Good. Right, Brodie. Take him back to the cell.'

McSween looked stricken.

'Whit—am Ah no' gettin' hame?'

McGinn gave a wry laugh.

'Home? You'll be bloody lucky if you see your home before next Christmas. Take him away, Brodie.'

~~~

'What d'you think, McInnes?'

'What—me, sir?'

'Aye, you. McInnes. There's no-one else here.'

Alan thought for a moment.

'Well, I think he's telling the truth; he's terrified, although I think he's almost as much afraid of this Johnny character— Scanlon, presumably— as he is of the police. But, yes, I do think he's telling the truth.'

McGinn lit a cigarette, inhaled deeply then coughed violently.

'Damn—need to bloody cut down! Aye, I'm inclined to agree, McInnes. Overall, though, I think he's more afraid o' bein' hanged than he is o' this Scanlon bugger.'

'Would they really hang him if he was found guilty of murder, sir?'

McGinn considered this.

'They might; if he was found guilty of murder, the judge would likely take his age into consideration when passin' sentence. There's a lot of them nowadays that prefer to hand out a life sentence an' I think it'll only be a matter of time before they do away with capital punishment altogether. Still, it puts the fear o' God into them and it tends to make them a bit more truthful.'

Alan wasn't sure how he felt about such shock tactics and it must have showed in his expression. McGinn grinned.

'Don't lose sleep over it, McInnes, at the end of the day we have to use whatever mean we have. The fear o' being hanged is a powerful tool, as no doubt you've gathered. Especially when dealing with the likes of McSween—he'd have no compunction about lying to us otherwise.'

He took another draw on his Capstan.

'What we have to do now is think how we can use this information to our advantage. I have a feeling that we may just be closing in on this bugger Scanlon but we'll have to play it carefully.'

He stubbed out his cigarette and stood up.

'Let's leave it at that. Give McSween a night in the cells an' I'll come back down in the morning to have another chat with him, see if we can figure out some way o' catching John Scanlon.'

He grinned.

'An' we haven't even touched on your arson cases yet—maybe you'd like to question him on that account?'

The suggestion caught Alan off guard; he opened and shut

his mouth as if to speak, but was pre-empted by a still-grinning McGinn.

'Well, you can think on it overnight. Off you go an' get some sleep—it's been an exciting evening all told.'

As Alan was about to leave, McGinn added, 'That was good work today, McInnes, I appreciate it. Don't let it go to your head, mind.'

~~~

Bruno Carlaveri hung up the phone, subconsciously wiping his hands on his suit trousers as if they had, somehow, been sullied by the caller; even on the phone, speaking to Jock Wallace always made the Italian feel grubby. On this occasion, Wallace had phoned to give Carlaveri some snivelling excuse about a delayed delivery, due to some misunderstanding with his supplier. Carlaveri knew only too well that Wallace was in debt to the unknown supplier and he also knew why. At some point in the near future, he hoped to bypass Wallace and deal directly with the unknown dealer in illicit substances, but he had to play that hand very carefully.

He thought for a moment, then reached a decision. Although it might cause Jock Wallace to ask some difficult questions, it was time to call on his reserve supply. He lifted the phone once more, dialled a number, then spoke in fluent Italian to the person on the other end. There were a few matters to be taken care of before he could proceed; Jock Wallace, however, wasn't one of them.

Not yet, at any rate.

Chapter 19

Isa McInnes smiled as her somewhat tousle-haired son entered the kitchen.

'My, you look you've been tossing and turning, Alan; is there something on your mind?'

There was and, mostly, it was guilt; guilt that he hadn't told his mother that the prisoner had spent the night in the cells, knowing that she would immediately have felt that it was her duty to provide breakfast for both Sergeant Tait and Douglas McSween. He decided that he should confess.

'Och, nothing really, Mother, it's just that we detained the McSween boy last night, we think he might have been involved in those cases of arson...'

Her expression changed.

'What? You mean you left poor Donny all on his own, in charge of that poor lad? For goodness sake, Alan, why didn't you tell me? I'd have taken them something else to eat. How on earth do you expect Donny to provide for the McSween boy's breakfast?'

'Mother, it's not your responsibility! Look, I know it's really kind of you, but you don't have to—'

'And who do you think is going to do it, Alan McInnes? Donny struggles to feed himself, from what I can see, so how on earth is he expected to feed the McSween boy? He's entitled to eat, no matter what he may or may not have done. All I took down last night were some cold meat sandwiches—I could easily have taken something hot if I'd only known he was being kept in the cells.'

'I know, but—'

'But nothing!'

Isa immediately started fussing about with the frying pan, taking some sausages and bacon from the larder.

'You get yourself ready and I'll give you this away with you— they'll both need a decent breakfast!'

As Alan went back upstairs to finish dressing, he realised that his own breakfast appeared to have been overlooked!

~~~

Sergeant Tait looked harassed as Alan entered the office but the smell of freshly cooked bacon and sausage quickly put a smile on his grizzled features. He took two rolls to the prisoner, then returned.

'Och, she's a grand woman, is your mother, just make sure ye remember an' thank her.'

'Aye, I will,' mumbled Alan as he masticated a bacon roll; his mother hadn't forgotten him after all.

The office door opened, bringing a gust of fresh air and heralding the arrival of Inspector McGinn, accompanied by Sergeant Fairbrother. The latter sniffed rather disdainfully.

'Hm, do you not have your breakfast before you come on duty, McInnes?'

As Alan felt his hackles rise, Tait glared at his fellow sergeant.

'If ye must know, Fairbrother, McInnes's mother made breakfast for the prisoner an' the constable brocht it doon as soon as he could. Ah think he's every richt—'

McGinn interjected, glaring at his assistant.

'Drop it, will you; Tait's quite right, the prisoner has a right to be fed and I'd imagine that McInnes brought his own breakfast down early to ensure that this was done—am I correct?'

Tait gave a sly wink to McGinn.

'Aye, you're quite richt, Inspector.'

Fairbrother pursed his lips but seemed to think better of a reply; McGinn lit a cigarette, then asked.

'Any chance of a fly cuppa then? Here, is that roll going a' begging...?'

~~~

Suitably refreshed, McGinn took his place behind the desk in Tait's office; Alan was seated beside him once more, ready to take notes, Fairbrother having been tasked with bringing in McSween and guarding the door. The young man was unshaven and bleary-eyed, although he managed to glance malevolently at each of the three officers in turn. Once again, McGinn took his time in speaking, Alan noting that the tactic appeared to be effective. Finally, the inspector looked across at the apprehensive and nervous young man.

'So, McSween, I hope you had a good night's sleep and that you've come to your senses?'

The young man bit his lip as he glowered across at his inquisitor.

'Eh? Whit d'you mean?'

McGinn smiled.

'Well, by now, I'd have thought you'd have realised just how much trouble you're in. Y'know, borstal's one thing, but a stretch in Barlinnie, or even just the Paisley Gaol, well...'

He leaned back in Tait's chair, which creaked alarmingly.

'I've sent down a lot of hard men in my day. I've sat in the police van, once the sentence has been passed, an' I've listened to all the bravado, all the boasts. 'Two years—ach, Ah can dae that staunin' oan ma heid!' Or 'Aye, a decent Christmas denner this year.' Trust me, McSween, I've heard it all; but, once you're through that outer gate, once those grim, dark Victorian walls are towering over you, it suddenly goes quiet—very quiet. No matter how hard you think you are, no matter how easy you think it'll be...well, there's always someone harder, someone tougher than you. Some of these old lags, they go...what is it the Yanks call it? Oh aye, 'stir crazy'. Say the wrong thing, look at them the wrong way and, before you know it, they've sharpened up a spoon an' they're jabbing it into your kidneys! Aye, it's no' for the faint-hearted, is the gaol, especially the big Bar-L.'

Alan shuddered at this bleak description of Glasgow's infamous prison. He glanced across at McSween, who was visibly shaking.

'B-but Ah've no' done anythin' tae get me in the Big Hoose, whit d'ye mean?'

McGinn leaned forward once more, pointing an accusatory finger at the prisoner.

'See, I think you have; we've not even touched on these local arson cases yet, although I'm sure Constable McInnes will be wanting a word with you about those. No, I'm talking about being in possession of a supply of illegal drugs.'

McSween was half out of his chair before Fairbrother pushed him back down.

'Whit? Whit' d'ye mean—Ah telt ye, Ah had nothin' tae dae wi' they drugs, whit're ye talkin' aboot?'

'You know damned fine, McSween; that parcel you were keeping for this Johnny bloke, a man that you seem to know so little about. It was found in your possession so you're implicated—carries a hefty sentence.'

'But Ah telt ye the truth, mister, Ah did'nae ken it wis drugs! He just asked me tae keep hold o' the parcel, Ah never kent whit wis in it—honest, Ah swear!'

McGinn remained silent; Alan was, once again, aware of the

clock ticking. McSween was perspiring now, his eyes darting right and left as if seeking his escape, but there was none. Finally, McGinn continued.

'But you can help yourself, you know. You can help us too, McSween—help us to catch this acquaintance o' yours.'

The young man stared wide-eyed at McGinn.

'But...but...Ah telt ye, he's a mad bastart, he'd kill me!'

'Listen to me, son; if you help us catch this Johnny fellow, then, for a start, you'll be safe from him; and I'm pretty sure that, if you do help us to catch him, the sheriff will take it into account when he sentences you.'

McSween's eyebrows shot up.

'Sentences me?'

'Oh aye, there's no doubt that you're lookin' at a stretch inside, McSween. But if you choose to help us, I'm sure the sheriff'll be lenient. Maybe even just a few months, as opposed to a couple of years.'

Alan could see tears filling the young man's eyes.

'Years? But...b...but...'

McGinn leaned back once more, clasping his hands over his stomach

'Aye, that's what you'll be lookin' at, McSween. Arson, handling drugs, not to mention all that other stuff in your shed—I'm pretty sure it's stolen. I'd reckon a couple o' years—what d'you think, Sergeant?'

Fairbrother nodded his agreement.

'Oh, at least, sir, maybe more. After all, there was quite a quantity of illegal substances in that parcel.'

McSween had turned to look at Fairbrother, before his eyes swivelled to Alan.

'Here, you tell him, Mister McInnes, Ah didnae know anythin'. Please!'

Alan wasn't sure how to respond; it was clear that McSween was being pressurised into something, but he had no idea what. He looked at McGinn but the inspector ignored him, leaning forward once more.

'Right, McSween, I'm goin' to make you an offer; if you take it, then I can make sure things go as smoothly as they can. If you don't, then...'

He shrugged and spread his hands.

'I'll be straight with you, son. You're a small fish, you're of no real interest to us. Let's say you're the foot-soldier; we want the general, the man who sits in the background sending the likes o' you to do their dirty work. We want this Johnny friend of yours; and you're going to help us catch him, aren't you, McSween?'

The young man chewed on his lip again; the silence seemed interminable. Suddenly, McGinn slammed his palms on the desk.

'AREN'T YOU, McSween—or d'you want to spend the next couple o' years lookin' over your shoulder, wonderin' which nutter you've upset, frightened to go for a shit in case someone knifes you...'

'AYE!'

'Aye what, McSween?'

Douglas McSween snivelled for a moment then wiped his nose on his sleeve.

'Aye, Ah'll bloody help ye, just dinnae send me tae the Big Hoose, please—Ah'll dae whatever ye want.'

McGinn leaned back once more in the creaking chair, smiling almost beatifically.

'Good; right, here's what you're goin' to do...'

~~~

McSween having been secured once more, the three officers

joined Sergeant Tait in the front office and explained the plan. Tait fiddled with his pipe as he considered the matter.

'Hm, it micht work but Ah think ye're takin' a hell o' a risk, letting this character go. Ah mean, whit guarantee d'ye have that he'll no' just bugger off somewhere?'

'It's a calculated risk, Tait,' said McGinn. 'You're quite right, there's always that possibility, but I've made it abundantly clear to him that, if he decides to go AWOL, then we'll be after him for murder.'

Fairbrother interrupted, eliciting a scowl from his superior.

'With respect, sir, I don't honestly think we could convict him on the meagre evidence in our possession. The Fiscal would never bring a charge of murder to court.'

'But d'you think that McSween knows that? Use your eyes, man—of course he bloody doesn't! You saw him, we put the fear of God into the boy. No, I'm pretty certain that he'll stay put; God help him if he doesn't.'

Alan glanced across at the detective sergeant; it was hard to read his expression but it didn't appear to be one of humility. Not for the first time he wondered at the curious relationship between Fairbrother and McGinn but his thoughts were interrupted as the latter spoke to Sergeant Tait.

'Might be worth havin' a word with your friend Oliphant, mind, just in case the wee bugger does try to get a train somewhere. What about the local buses?'

'We can speak tae them at the depot in Johnstone,' replied Tait. 'There's a couple o' regular conductors on the route, Ah daresay they can keep a look oot for him if he tries tae get awa.'

'Good. Well, in that case, all we need to do is let him out and wait for a development. He's said that the normal procedure is that he waits for a call on a Sunday so I doubt anything'll happen before then. Fairbrother, go an' fetch him, we'll have another word with him before we let him go—with the four o' us here, I honestly don't think we'll have a problem!'

~~~

McGinn's prediction was correct—McSween positively cowered as the four officers surrounded him, the inspector speaking in his most official and intimidating tone.

'Right, sonny boy, you listen to me an' listen very carefully. If we let you out, d'you understand exactly what you've to do?

The youth nodded energetically.

'Aye, mister, as soon as Ah hear anythin' frae Johnny, Ah've tae come doon here an' let youse know.'

'Good. Once we know when he's coming to collect the stuff, we'll make the arrangements. All you have to do is behave normally and let him in to the shed. We'll do the rest. Understand?'

McSween nodded again; McGinn took a step closer, causing the youth to try to step backwards, but Fairbrother was immediately behind him. The inspector leaned down and jabbed his finger into the terrified young man's chest, emphasising his words.

'Now, if you decide to run off, or if we think you've informed this Johnny character that we're waiting for him, then the game will be well and truly up; unless we can catch your pal Johnny, I'll be charging you with the murder of Alex Combe and you'll be sent to Barlinnie on remand before you've got time to shout for yer mammy. D'you understand me, McSween?'

Tears were welling up in McSween's eyes once more.

'Aye, mister, Ah promise Ah'll no' run awa'—an' Ah promise Ah'll no' say anythin' tae him.'

He wiped his nose on his sleeve for the umpteenth time, then mumbled, 'You'll no let him get hold o' me, will ye?'

McGinn stepped back.

'If you help us, son, your friend Johnny won't be seeing the light of day for a very long time—if ever; you have my word. But remember this—if he gets away an' if he thinks you've informed on him, then you'll have more than us to worry about! Right, escort him out, McInnes.'

As Alan left, the inspector gave him a wink; this was all part of the plan.

~~~

'Thanks, Mister McInnes, Ah'll no' let ye doon, Ah swear.'

'You'd better not, Duggie. The Inspector means every word he said and if you help us then we'll do our best for you, so don't worry about this Johnny fellow—once we get him, you'll be safe from him. Right, off you go, and you make sure you let us know as soon as you hear anything.'

With that, McSween set of up School Street, hands in pockets, shoulders slumped. Alan felt an enormous pang of pity for the dejected youth, knowing fine well that a spell in Barlinnie was more likely to hone his criminal skills than to offer rehabilitation. He went back into the office—such matters were outwith his control.

Chapter 20

By Wednesday morning, Barloch Police Station had returned to its customary humdrum normality. Kerr Brodie was out on the beat and Alan was sitting in the office, half-heartedly writing his report while Sergeant Tait puffed on his pipe. He looked over at the young constable, who appeared distracted..

'Somethin' on yer mind, McInnes?'

Alan hesitated; there most definitely was, but despite his thoughts and despite the complexities of his relationship with Donny Tait, there was still a distinct protocol in place regarding what he wanted to say. He remained silent for a moment.

'Aye, Sergeant, there is, but I'm not sure if I should discuss it. It's just—well, a feeling, I suppose.'

Tait nodded but said nothing.

'You see, it's about Sergeant Fairbrother.'

The older man raised an enquiring eyebrow as he took his pipe out of his mouth.

'Is it, now? An' whit aboot the guid sergeant?'

'Erm, the thing is, I don't want to get into bother by saying anything about a senior officer.'

Tait leaned towards Alan.

'Look, son, there's just the twa o' us here. Whatever it is, it'll no' go any further an' it'll no' be held agin' ye. Go on, whit were ye wantin' tae say?'

'Well, there just seem to be a few things about him that don't add up. You know that he started his career in Greenock?'

'No, Ah didnae—Ah knew he'd transferred frae Gasgow an'

Ah just assumed that wis where he'd started.'

'It was Kerr that told me—his father worked with a Superintendent Fairbrother and it turns out the sergeant is his nephew.'

'Is he indeed? Hm, that's interestin'. Go on.'

'You see, it stuck me that, if Sergeant Fairbrother was a beat constable in Greenock, I'd have thought that he'd have recognised Frank Kilbride. When Inspector McGinn and I were down there, I asked Inspector Melville if Kilbride would have been well-known in the area and he said that he would.'

'Aye, but Kilbride had been deid for a wee while—he might no' have been that recognisable; anyway, it's probably been a guid few years since Fairbrother was on the beat doon there, the man Kilbride micht have changed, for a' we know. '

'Yes, I appreciate that, Sergeant, but he'd only been dead for about ten hours or so, it was a cool night and Inspector Melville recognised him from Inspector McGinn's written description alone—surely the sergeant would have recognised him in the flesh? The other thing is he seemed very quick to suggest that, when we found Kilbride on the tracks at Kilmirrin, the case was closed and that Kilbride alone was Alex Combe's killer. Surely he'd have known about the association between Kilbride and Scanlon? If I hadn't found the buttons off Kilbride's jacket, we probably wouldn't be looking for Scanlon at all—would we?'

Tait pondered this for a moment, nodding sagely.

'Maybe aye an' maybe no'—again, it must've been a guid few years since the sergeant worked doon the watter, maybe it was before the twa men got in cahoots wi' each other. We cannae just go jumpin' tae conclusions. Mind, Ah suppose ye do have a point, richt enough, although Ah don't know whit tae make o' it. Is that all?'

'No, it's not; erm...'

'Spit it oot, lad.'

Alan was beginning to regret having told Tait.

'Well, there's been a couple of times when the sergeant has said that he was going for a pint at his local.'

'Nothin' wrong in that, surely?'

'No. But on Saturday he distinctly told the inspector that he was going to the Bird in Hand in Elderslie—I heard him say so myself, but Kerr Brodie saw him that night in the Masonic Arms in Glensherrie.'

Tait frowned.

'Wait—Ah hope ye've no' been gettin' Brodie tae spy on the sergeant?'

'No—no, not at all. It just came up in conversation. Kerr's seen Sergeant Fairbrother a couple of times in the Arms—he's always seems to meet with another man an' he's witnessed them exchanging somethin', although Kerr's not sure what it is. But it just seems odd when he said that he'd be at his local in Elderslie. It's a fair drive down to Glensherrie for a pint.'

Now that he'd said it, however, Alan felt that it all sounded rather feeble. Tait puffed on his pipe for a few moments before responding; when he did, his tone was stern.

'Now listen tae me, son. Ye cannae just go aboot surmisin' things an' makin' unfounded accusations against a senior officer—especially one in the CID. Ah'm quite sure that there's a legitimate reason for what Fairbrother is doin' an', to be quite honest, it's nane o' your damned business. My advice to you, Alan, is to keep oot o' it—let him get on with whatever he's doin' an' if there's anythin' amiss, it's up tae Inspector McGinn tae deal wi' it. Is that clear?'

Alan felt deflated; was his theory simply based on the fact that he disliked Fairbrother? And did that dislike stem from the fact that the sergeant had effectively taken what could have been Alan's position had he chosen to join the CID? He mumbled an apology and Tait smiled benevolently.

'That's a' richt, son, we'll say nae mair aboot it, but if ye've any plans tae go further in the police then the last thing ye should be doin' is castin' suspicions on a senior officer...ah, here's Brodie back—awa' an get the kettle on.'

~~~

The rest of the day passed without incident until finally, and somewhat dispiritedly, Alan made his way home. As he entered the kitchen, Isa smiled at him.

'Sit yourself down, son, your tea's nearly ready. It's just sausages and fried potatoes, I hope that's all right?'

'Of course it is, Mother'

He noticed that only two places were set at the table.

'Where's Father?'

'Och, he's away up to Glasgow for a trade union meeting.'

'Goodness, is he still in the union?'

'Yes, he's still employed by British Railways so he's still represented. Mind you, he hardly ever goes to any meetings so the dear Lord knows why he chose this one tonight. I think they give them a good feed—it'll make a change from my cooking, I suppose.'

Alan smiled at his mother.

'There's nothing wrong with your cooking, Mother—that looks delicious.'

As he set to on his plateful, Isa looked affectionately at her handsome son.

'Something's bothering you, Alan. What is it?'

He shook his head.

'Och, it's nothin' Mother.'

'If it's bothering you, then it is not nothing. Come on, there's just the two of us here...'

~~~

Between mouthfuls of sausage and fried potato, Alan voiced his concerns once more about Niven Fairbrother. His mother remained silent until he had finished both his narrative and his meal. As he had talked, he realised once again that his feelings towards Fairbrother were neither those of envy nor dislike; they were feelings of mistrust. Finally, his mother spoke.

'Have you mentioned this to anyone else, son?'

He hesitated before answering, not wanting to incur his mother's disapproval.

'Erm, yes, I spoke to Sergeant Tait about it earlier today.'

'And what did he have to say?'

Alan shrugged.

'He said that I should let the matter drop and that if there was a problem then it was up to Inspector McGinn to deal with it.'

'And how do you feel about that?'

Alan wasn't quite sure; he trusted McGinn but, somehow, he felt that, despite the obvious enmity between the two officers, the inspector seemed to turn a blind eye to Fairbrother's apparent shortcomings.

'Well, Mother, the thing is, I've realised that I don't really trust Sergeant Fairbrother. There's just somethin' about the man, I can't put my finger on it but I get the feeling that he has his own agenda, if you know what I mean? It's obvious that the inspector doesn't really like him either—he often makes snide little comments—but he never really seems to take action.'

Isa poured herself another cup of tea. She stirred in some sugar, took a sip then placed the cup carefully down on the saucer. Alan recognised the signs; she was about to give her forthright opinion.

'Well, if I were you, Alan, I'd take Donny Tait's advice; he's a good and honest man—you know that—and if he thinks you should drop it then that's exactly what you should do.'

Somehow, her defence of Tait irritated him.

'That's all very well, Mother, but I think that there's something decidedly suspicious about Fairbrother's behaviour—despite what Sergeant Tait says.'

He frowned.

'Maybe I should talk to Inspector McGinn...'

'NO!'

Alan jumped at his mother's half-shouted response; she went on, leaning forward and with a stern expression her face.

'Alan, even I know that it's unwise to criticise a senior officer. For goodness sake, son, take Donny's advice—after all, he is your...'

The word remained unsaid, but Alan stared at his mother with an expression of near-horror.

'Mother—you said we'd never speak of that!'

She bowed her head.

'Yes, I know, I know we did, but you can't deny the fact, Alan, I'm sorry.'

'But my father lives here—he's your husband, for God's sake!'

'Alan—there's no need for profanity. Yes, of course Gilbert is your father to all intents and purposes but...well, we both know the truth and Donny only has your best interests at heart.'

Alan was dumbfounded; although the harsh reality of his mother's confession the previous year would be forever etched in his mind, he tried to suppress it on a day-to-day basis.

'Mother...'

'No, you listen to me, Alan. You know that Donny Tait won't let you do the wrong thing—you need to take heed of what he says. If you try and take this matter any further then your career in the police could be over before it's really started. You don't want that—think of your future, think of Nancy! You're going to be a married man soon and you don't want to jeopardise any of that, do you?'

'No,' he mumbled.

'Good. Now, just you put any thoughts of talking to Inspector McGinn about this out of your mind. Away through and watch the television—it'll take your mind off things. I made a wee chocolate sponge earlier, I'll bring you through a piece and another cup of tea.'

~~~

Alan had been staring unseeingly at the screen when his mother came in, handing him a plate with a large slice of chocolate cake.

'Thanks, Mother. '

She walked across and switched off the television; her son seemed to barely notice.

'Alan, son, we need to have a wee chat.'

He looked up at her and, in a gesture of maternal affection, she reached out and wiped chocolate from his chin.

'I know we said we'd not mention it again, but...'

'Please, Mother, it's hard enough, on a day-to-day basis, having to work with Sergeant Tait and knowing that he's...well...'

'Yes, and I can understand that; but it is an undeniable fact, I'm afraid, and you just have to accept it. In situations such as this, Donny Tait will act not only as your superior officer but in...in...'

She paused, searching for words that wouldn't cause further upset.

'Well, in a paternal manner, let's say.'

Alan glowered down at the remains of the cake.

'Mother...'

'No, son, I can only imagine how this must have upset you but, believe me, it has caused me a great deal of upset over the years. Your father—Gilbert—still finds it hard to come to terms with, naturally, and doesn't like to hear Donny's name mentioned in the house. Unfortunately, with you being in the police, that isn't always an easy thing to achieve. It all happened so long ago now, a chance meeting...'

Alan jumped to his feet.

'Mother, I don't want to hear any of the sordid details. Look, I can accept that Tait may be my...my natural father. I can forgive you—you're my mother, after all, and I love you. But I find it hard to forgive Donald Tait. So, please, let's drop the subject. I'll listen to your—and his—advice but, if I witness any further peculiar behaviour on the part of Fairbrother, then I'll have to re-assess the situation. Now, I'm going up to my room, thanks for the cake, it was delicious.'

He made to leave then, almost as an afterthought, leaned down and kissed his mother's cheek, seemingly unaware of the tears that were rolling down it.

~~~

It was a troubled young man who lay in his bed, staring up at the ceiling. While his earlier conversation with Sergeant Tait had merely disheartened him, the later conversation with his mother had unsettled him considerably. The discovery the previous year that Donny Tait was, in fact, his biological father, had caused him great confusion and, indeed, hurt; however, although the passing of the months had eased these feelings, they had now returned in full force. He closed his eyes but, as always when his mind was racing, sleep eluded him. He swore softly under his breath, wishing that his family life was as straightforward as that of his fiancé, Nancy; and, in almost the same instant, a wave of guilt at the ingratitude of his thoughts threatened to engulf him. He turned on his side and swore again; somewhat more violently this time!

~~~

As sleep eventually overcame Alan, a shadowy figure crept along the deserted streets of the little village, avoiding as far as possible the pools of white light from the recently installed mercury vapour streetlamps. A dog barked, the figure paused, crouching down behind a hedge. Two cats screeched at one another, a window opened, a voice hissed angrily in the darkness. When silence ensued once more, the figure moved on; up through Cruicksfield Oval, along Cruicks Crescent. With a glance to right and left, they climbed the steps and, with great care, pushed a missive of some sort through the letterbox.

Retracing their steps, blending into the shadows of the night, the figure was soon safely enshrouded in the velvety darkness of the outskirts of Barloch. Any residents still awake might have heard the starting of a motorbike, the revving and the changing through the gearbox as it sped into the night, carrying its anonymous rider to an unknown destination.

Chapter 21

'Another fine mornin', Sergeant.'

'Aye, it is that, Brodie. Mind, it's tae be cold the nicht, so they say,' replied Sergeant Tait, before swallowing a mouthful of tea. 'Aah, that's good...'

He pulled out his watch and frowned.

'No,' like McInnes tae be late. Here, d'ye think the lad's all richt? Seems tae me he's been a wee bit peaky the last few days.'

'He's no' said anythin' tae me, Sergeant. Actually, between you an' me, despite what Ah said the other day, Ah'm wonderin' if Alan actually is cut oot for CID work—this is the second time he's been involved in a case an' it never seems tae dae him any good. He takes it awful serious.'

Tait nodded his agreement, taking his pipe from his jacket pocket.

'Aye, ye're richt enough, Brodie; no, he's best off doon here, a nice quiet wee place...oh-oh, is that him noo?'

The outer door opened slightly and a head appeared round it, glancing nervously about; once it was clear that there were no other members of the public inside, the figure entered; it was Douglas McSween.

'Aye-aye, McSween, an' whit is it ye're wantin' this mornin'?'

There was a note of suspicion in Tait's voice; he still wasn't in full agreement with McGinn's strategy and didn't trust the young man one iota. McSween approached the bar, clutching a scrap of paper in a trembling hand. Tait took it.

'This wis through the letterbox last night, sir. Ah thocht Ah'd best bring it doon richt awa".

Tait fished his spectacles from his tunic pocket and read the note out loud.

"Friday morn. Two o'clock. Be ready." An' that's it? Did ye see who left it?'

McSween shook his head vigorously.

'Naw, Sergeant, we wis aw asleep. Never heard nothin' either, must've sneaked up durin' the nicht.'

The door opened, causing a look of near-panic to flash across McSween's face as he turned his head.

'Jesus...!'

Alan McInnes entered, dark circles under his eyes, tie slightly askew and an apologetic expression on his face. A plaster adhered to his cheek where he had obviously cut himself shaving.

'I'm really sorry, Sergeant, I didn't sleep well last night. I'll make it up.'

Tait gave him a long look.

'Aye, weel, ye micht have tae, sooner than ye maybe think.'

He handed the note to Alan, whose eyebrows rose in surprise.

'Tonight then?' He glanced at McSween. 'You're sure?'

McSween looked confused.

'Erm, weel, Ah...Ah only just got it last nicht, there's been nae phone call or nothin".'

'He's as sure as he's goin' tae be, McInnes,' interjected Tait. 'Richt, Ah'll awa' an call Inspector McGinn. He'll need tae get arrangements in place.'

He consulted his watch once more.

'McSween, nae use o' you hangin' aboot here. Awa' up the road an' come back down here at eleven sharp, see whit the inspector wants ye tae dae.'

As the nervous young man opened the door, Tait added, 'An' no' a bloody word o' this tae anybody—or ye'll hae me tae deal with!'

McSween nodded

'Aye, Sergeant, Ah'll no breathe a word—Ah promise.'

~~~

Inspector McGinn strode purposefully into the small Barloch police office, closely followed by Sergeant Fairbrother. The three local officers were standing behind the bar, awaiting the CID's arrival.

'Mornin, Tait—lads.' He consulted his wristwatch. 'Right, half an hour 'til McSween's due—he'd better bloody arrive.'

'Ah'm sure he will,' replied Tait. 'The laddie's scared oot o' his wits an' Ah think he believes that we're the only ones who can get him oot o' this jam. Brodie, awa' an' put the kettle on.'

As Brodie left, McGinn lit a cigarette.

'Aye, well, he's no' far wrong. Right, let's get a plan of action goin'—we don't want to let this Scanlon character slip through our fingers! McInnes, you've been up there—can you draw us a plan of the house, the garden an' the shed?'

'Yes, Inspector, it's all pretty straightforward.'

He pulled a sheet of foolscap from the typewriter and, with his pencil, quickly produced a reasonably accurate sketch of the house and its environs. McGinn studied it carefully for a few moments.

'Right—are those bushes to the side of the shed?'

'Yes, between the two gardens. There's another shed next door too, that we could maybe hide behind.'

'Right. We'll need to be well out of sight—ah, good man, Brodie, I could be doing with a cup. Anyway, I reckon that one o' us takes position behind McSween's shed—Brodie, that'll be you.'

The constable nodded as he passed around the beverages.

'McInnes, you go behind the adjacent shed—you'll need to

speak to the householders though, in case they see us an' make a fuss.'

'Right-o, sir, I will. It's a Mrs Barr that's through the wall, if I recall. I'll go up as soon as we're done.'

'Good. Fairbrother, same goes for you, only round the back of the house next door—there's a hedge of sorts, according to McInnes' plan. You stay there an' you can watch the proceedings until we make our move. McInnes, you'll need to speak to the householders there as well.'

'Yes, sir.'

He turned and looked at Tait, wondering if the older man was up to the job. Sensing his hesitation, Tait spoke.

'Inspector, Ah ken the man that lives across the road—he's a retired constable, gettin' on a bit noo but he'd be happy for me tae keep watch from inside his hoose. He'll welcome the company too—an' the excitement.'

'Well, let's just hope there's not too much excitement—but that'd be fine, Tait, I don't want you to be standing about in the cold for hours. I'll tuck myself away across the road and wait for Scanlon to arrive. We can follow him an' the McSween lad round the back.'

'How will we know when he gets there?' asked Alan.

'Aye, that's a point, McInnes. Look, he said he'd arrive at two—keep an eye on the time. It'll be dead quiet by then, listen out for footsteps; you should hear him chap the door at least. I don't want to shout or use a whistle—he'd be off like a bloody shot. No, let's just keep our ears and eyes open. Right, now we just need to wait for McSween.'

~~~

Douglas McSween was punctual if nothing else; at exactly eleven o'clock, the door opened and the young man slunk in,

220

cowering once more at the sight of the five officers gathered in the small front office. McGinn pulled a chair forwards.

'Right, son, sit down there and listen very carefully.'

McSween did as he was bid, chewing frantically at his fingernails. McGinn lit a fresh cigarette, adding to the already fuggy atmosphere.

'I've seen the note you gave to Sergeant Tait—have you any reason to doubt that it's genuine?'

McSween shook his head.

'Naw, sir, Ah havenae. It wis pit through the letterbox last nicht, jist as Ah said tae Mister Tait.'

'Has this happened before?'

Another shake of the head.

'Naw, never, it's aye jist been the phone call on the Sunday. Naebody's ever pit anythin' through the letterbox afore.'

'Right, I see.'

McGinn turned towards the others, speaking in a low voice.

'I don't like it—I'm worried that Scanlon's got wind o' something if he's acting out o' character like this. We'll have to tread carefully.'

He turned back to the nervous youth.

'Okay, McSween, here's what's going to happen; we'll be in position a couple o' hours before, just in case anyone's watching your house. You go about your everyday business, whatever that may be, don't do anything stupid and try an act normally. What usually happens when he arrives?'

'Weel, he jist comes tae the front door, Ah go ootside wi' him an' we go roon the back. Ah open up the shed an' stand ootside, Ah jist let him take whitever he's needin' then, once he's done, he gie's me...'

The youth stopped mid-sentence, mouth agape.

'Aye, I get the picture, McSween; but he doesn't go into the house?'

'Naw, never, sir, we jist gang roon' the wee path tae the back green.'

'Right. we'll be in position, well out of sight. You take him round as normal then, once he's in the shed, we'll move and catch him when he comes out. Understood?'

'Aye, sir, Ah understand.'

'And McSween?'

'Aye, sir?'

'Don't even think about running off when all this is happening. If you do, we'll find you an' then God help you. Got it?'

McSween nodded; his bravado of a few days previously had evaporated and, once again, he looked to be on the verge of tears. Alan couldn't help but feel slightly sorry for the youth.

'Right, get yourself up the road; get some sleep to make sure you're fresh come two in the morning—the last thing we need is you falling asleep and not hearing your door being chapped!'

The young man almost ran out of the office, leaving behind a silence and a haze of tobacco smoke. Finally, McGinn spoke.

'Right, I think we should be able to handle this between the five of us, but I'll maybe draft in a couple of extra men to sit in the car, in case he does slip away from us. It also means that none of you will need to accompany me back to Paisley once we've made the arrest.'

'You'll no' be keepin him here overnicht, then?' asked Tait, a note of relief in his voice. McGinn gave him a grim smile.

'It's one thing locking up a petty thief like McSween, Tait, but I'm pretty sure we've got a double murderer here. No, I'd rather get him back up to Paisley—I'd feel a lot safer and I'm sure you would too. Anyway, McInnes, you and Fairbrother away up the road just now an' speak to the neighbours, tell them that you'll be on surveillance duties in their gardens an' that they've not to act suspiciously. Tait, what about this retired policeman?'

'Ach, Auld Lawrence will be fine, he doesnae get oot much an', as Ah said, he'll welcome the excitement. Ah'm sure he'd widnae mind you comin' in as well, Inspector.'

'Thanks, but I'll stay outside—I want to be able to hear Scanlon approaching. If he's not local, he must be using some form of transport and it might just give us a bit more warning. Right, do we all know what we're doing?'

The others mumbled as they nodded their assent.

'Good. Right, let's leave it at that. Tait, I think you can shut up shop about four o'clock, on my authority. It'll let you all get something to eat an' a bit of rest, it could be a long night an' I want everyone alert. If we can rendezvous back here at ten o'clock, we can run through the plan again, get a cup of tea then head to our positions. See an' wrap up well—McInnes, Brodie, you stay in uniform. The rest of us—wear dark clothes; oh, an' Fairbrother...'

'Yes sir?'

'Wear a hat—your red hair stands out a bloody mile.'

~~~

Alan felt decidedly awkward; this was only the second time he had been alone in the company of Sergeant Fairbrother and he didn't really know what to say. However, he also had a vague feeling of self-importance and he wondered if, perhaps, he should have joined the CID after all. Fairbrother interrupted his thoughts.

'So, I take it you're born and bred here, McInnes?'

'Yes, sir, I am.'

He was about to add 'and proud to be' but thought better of it.

'I see. A quiet wee place, right enough. No ambitions to move on, then?'

Alan had assumed—wrongly, it appeared—that McGinn would have told Fairbrother that he had approached Alan about joining the CID.

'Not really, sir, I like it here—I've passed my sergeant's exams and I'm hoping to take over when Sergeant Tait retires. I'm engaged to be married as well, it seems best to stay in Barloch, if you see what I mean.'

Fairbrother gave a wry smile.

'Hm, I suppose I can see your point of view, although Tait doesn't seem to be showing any signs of stepping down, does he?'

Alan gave a grimace.

'No, he doesn't.'

They walked on in silence for a few moments, then Fairbrother asked, 'Never thought of applying to the CID?'

The question took Alan by surprise and his instinct was to conceal the truth.

'Erm, well, I'd not really thought about it.'

'I'm sure the inspector would put in a good word—you seem to be a bit of a favourite with him.'

Before Alan could reply, the door to the cottage that they were passing opened and an elderly, white-haired woman stepped out.

'Ah, Constable McInnes—the very man!'

'Hello, Mrs Munn—what can I do for you?'

'They weans were playin' chicky melly last night—gie'd me the fricht o' ma life, so it did. Ah want ye tae dae somethin' aboot it.'

Alan was aware of Fairbrother smiling—in a rather condescending manner, he thought.

'Did you see who it was, Mrs Munn?'

'Ah recognised wan o' the brats—it was that Scott laddie frae doon the street.'

'Fine, I'll have a word—now, we're on important business, Mrs Munn, you must excuse us.'

They walked on, leaving a disgruntled Mrs Munn staring after them. Fairbrother smirked as he spoke.

'A far cry from CID work, eh, McInnes? What, exactly, is chicky melly?"

Alan could feel his hackles rise.

'Och, it's just a daft game the kids play; you stick a short bit of string to a window using chewing gum or sticky tape, with a wee stone hanging on to the end. Then you tie on a longer bit, hide somewhere and pull on it to chap the window. A good strong tug on the string pulls the whole thing off, getting rid of the evidence. By the time Mrs Munn got to the window, or the door, they'd be away down the street, or round the corner.'

Irritated by the sergeant's contemptuous attitude, Alan asked, 'It's Greenock you're from, isn't it, Sergeant?'

Fairbrother momentarily paused in his stride.

'How d'you know that, McInnes?'

Alan detected a wariness, a subtle change in the tone of the conversation. It only served to heighten his suspicions about the detective sergeant; and, of course, his dislike.

'Erm, och, I think Constable Brodie mentioned it—his father used to work down in the Greenock office.'

The sergeant gave him a keen glance.

'Did he, indeed? But, yes, he's correct, I started my career down there, although I've been in Glasgow City for the last few years. Wanted to get away from the parochial constraints of the district and Glasgow certainly has more to offer in the way of future prospects. Anyway, are we just along here?'

~~~

Come four o'clock, Alan trudged back up School Street.

Despite a feeling of excitement about the forthcoming operation, he was exhausted and he just wanted to sleep. He arrived home to find Isa in the middle of preparing dinner; she gave him a concerned look.

'Oh Alan, son, you're early—is everything all right?'

He smiled—his mother was always worrying, always fretting.

'Yes, Mother, everything's fine, In fact, Inspector McGinn has an operation planned for tonight, he's hoping to catch a fairly important criminal and I'll be helping him. I can't really tell you much more at the moment, but we're meeting back at the station at ten o'clock. It's going to be a long night, though.'

'And a cold one, son but, goodness, that is exciting. You just watch yourself though, Alan McInnes, I don't want you to get hurt.'

He chuckled, putting his arm around her shoulder.

'Aye, I will, Mother, don't you worry. Inspector McGinn knows what he's doing.'

'Well, I certainly hope so; here, I'll make you up some sandwiches, if you're out all night you'll be hungry.'

'Now, there's no need, Mother...'

But Isa already had the bread bin open; he might as well have tried to stem the tide.

Chapter 22

'Mother, will you stop worrying!'

'That's all very well for you to say, Alan McInnes, but it's your poor father and I that will be sitting here, wondering if you're all right.'

'I told you, it's just a routine operation, we're just waiting for our suspect to turn up, then we'll take him into custody. There's five of us so there's nothing to worry about, nothing at all.'

To Alan's surprise, the normally taciturn Gilbert raised his own objection.

'Aye, jist like those in authority tae rope the foot-soldiers intae all this. It should jist be the CID that's carryin' oot ye'r so-called 'operation', no' the likes o' you an' Kerr Brodie.'

Alan felt his hackles rise; he considered himself to be something more than a 'foot-soldier.'

'But Sergeant Tait will be there too.'

As soon as the words were out, Alan regretted them. Isa looked aghast, whilst Gilbert allowed himself a bleak smile.

'Aye, it'll dae the auld bugger some good, get rid o' some o' the weight he's carryin...'

Isa's expression changed in an instant.

'Gilbert McInnes. We'll have none of that language in this house. Sergeant Tait is far too old to be taking part in escapades like this.'

Alan interjected, trying to avert any further recriminations.

'Mother, I told you, it's all just routine—anyway, the sergeant will be waiting in a house across the road, there's a retired policeman lives there. He'll be fine.'

Isa put a hand on her son's arm.

'Alan, son, just make sure nothing happens—do you hear?'

As Alan patted his mother's arm reassuringly, Gilbert gave a snort of disgust.

'Huh, seems ye care a bit too bloody much aboot—'

'Gilbert—I warned you—'

'Ach—Ah'm awa' tae ma bed.'

He put down his newspaper and hauled himself out of his chair.

'But ye'r mother's richt—you see an' take care o' yersel.'

Then, as he shuffled towards the door, to the utter astonishment of both Alan and his mother, he turned and gave his son an odd, fierce look.

'Ah'm richt proud o' ye, Alan McInnes, an' Ah dinnae want anythin' happenin' tae ye.'

~~~

The mood in the small police office was one of quiet excitement. With a hint of a late frost in the night air, Brodie had banked up the fire to ensure that their return would be warm. After a final drag on his Capstan, McGinn threw the butt into the flames and consulted his watch,

'Right, we know the plan—make sure we stick to it. Are we all clear on what we're doing and where we've to be?'

The four officers nodded their assent.

'Good. Keep your eyes peeled and keep alert. I've parked the Wolseley round in the entrance road to the barrel factory—I doubt they'll be needing access durin' the night. The two officers will have the window open so, if by any chance Scanlon gets away, we'll blow a whistle an' they'll be ready for him. Let's try and make sure that doesn't happen, though, don't want us to look like a bunch o' prize idiots! Right, time to make a move. Stay quiet, lads—Tait, I suggest you turn off the lights in your friend's house and just leave a crack in the curtains.'

'Aye, Ah've already discussed it wi' Auld Lawrence, he'll be a' ready for us. Oh, an' if any o' ye need tae pay a visit...'

McGinn smiled as Tait closed and locked the office door.

'Aye, that's good to know, it's a cold night!'

~~~

They made their way silently up School Street without meeting a living soul, the streets of the little village being deserted on such a chilly evening. Once the five officers reached their destinations they separated, with only Sergeant Tait benefiting from the refuge of a warm house.

Alan's mother had insisted on him taking a scarf and gloves; as the minutes ticked by and the temperature dropped, he became increasingly grateful. He could see frost glistening on the tufted grass of the back green and his breath was forming clouds of steam. A quarter-moon cast a gloomy light on the scene and he wasn't sure if this was an advantage; after all, it increased the chances of any of them being detected. There was nothing he could do about it, however, and he concentrated on trying to move his limbs as much as he could without making any noise. Despite the layers of clothing, he could feel the chill seeping into his body when suddenly the thoughts of his discomfort vanished. Somewhere in the distance he could hear the growl of a motorcycle engine. He shivered, partly from the cold but partly from excitement—was this it? The sound was coming closer now until, suddenly, silence ensued once more. Alan reckoned that the bike had stopped somewhere on the edge of Barloch and, if this was Scanlon, then it would take a brisk ten-minute walk for him to reach their position. He flexed his arms and legs for a final time, pulled up his collar then crouched behind the rotting garden shed.

~~~

The wait seemed interminable and he was becoming increasingly colder; maybe it had just been just a householder returning home late. Then he heard a faint knocking—three taps that sounded clearly in the still of the freezing night. He tensed. A few moments later, he heard footsteps coming round the side of the house and he hoped McGinn would soon be following close behind. Although he knew that his colleagues were on hand, he felt extremely lonely.

In the ghostly moonlight, he could make out the figure of Douglas McSween, wrapped in an old army greatcoat. Behind him was a second figure, leather-jacketed, a muffler around his neck and wearing a black balaclava, presumably against the chill of the night air while riding the motorcycle. They crossed the frost-rimed grass and McSween proceeded to unlock the shed door. It opened silently, the hinges presumably having been well oiled to avoid unnecessary noise. Alan rose to his feet as the second figure entered the shed. He couldn't see McSween but presumed that he had remained outside. He was aware of further movement at the side of the house, then he saw Fair-brother appear from behind the bushes at the opposite side of the garden. McGinn came into view, stalking silently across the grass. Alan came out from behind his hiding-place but, before he could make a move, he heard angry shouting emanating from inside McSween's dilapidated structure. The youth's voice responded, carrying a note of fear.

'Eh? Whit's that? Ah dinnae understand ye—whit're ye talkin' aboot...?'

'POLICE! Do not move—you are under arrest. We have the

230

shed surrounded—come out with your hands above your head.'

As McGinn's barked command sounded, the beam from his powerful torch shone on the door. In an instant the figure inside charged out, grabbing McSween and throwing him violently to the ground. Brodie, who had appeared from the other side of the shed, tried to stop him but he, too, was roughly pushed aside, letting out a yelp of pain and clutching his arm. The man was running as fast as a hare, his speed and agility catching them all by surprise. Fairbrother gave pursuit but appeared to stumble on the slippery grass as the balaclava-clad figure hurtled towards the side of the house. McGinn, already in pursuit, caught the sergeant's foot, causing him to trip and land heavily on the ground. He yelled.

'You fuckin' idiot, Fairbrother—Jesus, man, get on your feet and get after him.'

Several lights had now appeared in the nearby windows, the shouting and frantic activity having wakened most of the householders. As Alan sprinted past the now-standing—and furious—McGinn, he heard a grunt from the side of the house; fearing the worst, he turned the corner to see Sergeant Tait standing, truncheon in hand, above their escapee, who was lying on the ground clutching his stomach and groaning in pain. Filled with a sense of relief, Alan could see that Tait had a wide grin on his face.

'Aye, there's life in the auld dog yet, McInnes; best get the cuffs on him afore he gets his wind back!'

McGinn was at Alan's heels and he looked at Tait.

'What the hell happened?'

'Ach, when Ah seen him racin' towards me, Ah jist stuck oot ma truncheon and let his ain momentum dae the work. Winded the bugger.'

Alan was already kneeling and placing handcuffs on the

still-groaning figure. Somehow, Scanlon didn't look as powerful and intimidating as Alan had expected from the various
descriptions. Fairbrother arrived on the scene.

'Sorry, sir, I—'

'Shut up' snapped McGinn. 'Your bloody stupidity nearly let
him get away. Thank God Tait was on the ball. Right, let's see
what we've got here...'

He knelt down and grasped the balaclava, pulling it roughly
off the man's head.

'...John Scanlon, I'm arresting you on suspicion of...'

Their captive stared back up at McGinn; even in the faint
moonlight, Alan could see two dark eyes, set in a narrow, ol-
ive-skinned face; two eyes that bore no sign of a squint. McGinn
sat back and shouted, 'Who the hell are you?'

The figure stared back.

'I said, who the hell are you—an' where the hell is John Scanlon?'

'Non capisco.'

'What? What did you say?'

'Non capisco.'

'I think it's Italian, sir,' muttered Fairbrother. 'I think it means
he doesn't understand.'

McGinn glared up at the sergeant.

'Italian? Good God Almighty, what the hell's goin' on—where's
Scanlon? An' where's Brodie—I need him to get back down to
the car, see if we can find this bugger's motorcycle; Scanlon's
probably down there waiting for him. Brodie—BRODIE—
damn, where in God's name is the man?'

Brodie appeared from the rear of the building; he was clutching his left arm and, despite the poor light, Alan could see the
blood seeping through the fingers of his right hand.

'Sir, Ah think you'd better come an' see this.'

McGinn got to his feet, a furious expression on his face.

'Good God Almighty—Fairbrother, Tait, you two stay here an' keep an eye on this bugger, whoever the hell he is. Brodie, are you all right?'

'Ah'll be fine sir, Ah think he's just nipped the flesh.'

'Let's see.'

Brodie took his hand away to reveal a clean cut through both his coat and his tunic. The shirt below was soaked in blood as McGinn used his torch to inspect the wound.

'Hm, I think it's a bit more than a damned nip, by the looks o' it, you're losin' a fair bit o' blood. We'll need to get you seen to as soon as possible. Are you fit enough for the time being?'

'Aye, sir, Ah'll be all right, I think.'

McGinn slapped Brodie's uninjured shoulder.

'Good man—right, what's happenin' round the back?'

As they made their way round to the rear of the property, Alan was aware of several back doors sitting open, the occupants peering curiously into the darkness. A light came on inside the McSween house as they crossed the grass.

'There, sir,' said Brodie, pointing to a figure lying on the grass. The large bloodstain around the area of the heart was obvious, even against the khaki-coloured greatcoat.

McGinn muttered an oath as he knelt beside Douglas McSween; reaching for the youth's neck, he felt for a pulse as the others looked on helplessly. After a minute, McGinn turned, shaking his head.

'Poor bugger's had it, I'm afraid.'

Suddenly, a piercing wail rent the silence of the night. Mrs McSween rushed down the steps, clad only in a thin dressing down and a pair of shabby slippers.

'Ma boy! Ma boy—whit the hell have ye done tae ma boy, ya bastarts!'

McGinn stood up as the woman rushed towards them

'Now, Mrs McSween, calm down...'

'Calm down—Christ, Ah'll calm ye down, let me see!'

She looked at the inert body that had been her son and let out another despairing wail.

'Oh, sweet Jesus, is he...is he...?'

'I'm afraid so,' replied Alan. 'Please, Mrs McSween, there's nothing you can do, best to go back inside. '

As she started to sob uncontrollably, a figure hirpled towards them.

'Noo then, Jessie, whit's aw' the fuss?'

Alan recognised 'Auld' Lawrence, Sergeant Tait's acquaintance. He ushered the retired constable aside.

'I'm afraid her son's been killed, Lawrence, stabbed, by the looks of it. Could you possibly get her inside, she'll catch her death out here.'

'Aye, aye, son, leave it tae me.'

The old man crossed to the hysterical woman and put a gentle arm around her shoulders.

'Noo, Jessie, come awa' ben the hoose wi' me an' let the offi-cers dae their job. It's freezin' cauld oot here, Ah'll get ye a nice wee cup o' tea.'

'Naw, leave me, leave me here wi ma wee Duggie.'

Another wail sounded out from the doorway.

'Maw, Maw, whit's happenin'? Maw, Ah'm feart, whit's hap-pened tae Duggie?'

The voice of Ann McSween seemed to bring the woman to her senses. She allowed herself to be helped to her feet then, with Auld Lawrence's arm around her shoulder, she crossed to the steps.

'Awa' inside, pet, the polis is takin' care o' Duggie.'

The door closed behind the tragic little group and silence

ensued once more, although Alan was aware of several pairs of eyes focused curiously on them.

'Christ, what a bloody mess,' muttered McGinn, through gritted teeth. 'McSween murdered an' all we've got is some bloody Italian who can't understand a damned word we say.'

He took a deep breath, exhaling slowly as he considered the situation; he delved into his coat pocket for his cigarettes but seemed to think better of it.

'Right, Brodie, are you all right to walk back down to the station?'

'Yes sir.'

'Good—I'll send Tait with you. You'll need to call an ambulance and also Dr Miller, the police doctor; oh, an' let the uniformed boys in the car know, send them up here pronto. An' while you're at it, tell Sergeant Fairbrother to stay where he is an' not let the killer out o' his sight.'

Brodie smiled, despite being in obvious pain.

'Aye, sir, will do.'

'Right, off you go. McInnes, we need to find the weapon, it can't be far away unless he lobbed it somewhere—I didn't see him throw anythin' though, did you?'

'I couldn't be sure, sir, but I don't think so.'

The two officers began to comb the frosted ground; a few minutes later, Alan found the offending weapon under one of the bushes.

'Here, sir, got it!'

'Right, don't touch it!' He walked over to where Alan was peering, the bloodied blade glinting in the moonlight. McGinn took a handkerchief out of his pocket, reached for the handle and lifted it up,

'Hm, looks like one o' those stilettos, by all accounts the weapon of choice for our friend back there. McInnes, put something in the ground to mark where we found it, might be relevant.'

Alan searched about, eventually lifting a piece of broken fence post, shoving it, with some difficulty, into the frozen ground next to where he had found the knife. McGinn finally removed his cigarettes from his pocket and lit up, inhaling deeply before breaking into a paroxysm of coughing.

'Dear God Almighty...right, we've got the weapon an' we've got the killer, all we need is someone who can speak the bloody lingo! Any ideas, McInnes?'

'Yes, actually, sir. The folk who own the cafe down the road are Italian. Mr Janetti doesn't speak much English but Mrs Janetti is pretty fluent; she'd be able to understand him.'

McGinn consulted his watch.

'Hm, it's nearly three o'clock, she'll no' be best pleased if we waken her up in the middle o' the damned night...anyway, that sounds like the car coming, let's get this bugger down the road. I'll feel a lot better when he's safely behind bars.'

Chapter 23

Alan could barely keep his eyes open as he sat on the back doorstep of the McSween house. He was drained both emotionally and physically, and he was chilled to the very marrow of his bones. Auld Lawrence had brought a welcome cup of tea and he clutched it gratefully, aware of his teeth chattering loudly; McGinn was standing beside him and Alan could hear the inspector let out a sigh of satisfaction as he took a sip from his own cup. A few moments later, Dr Miller stood up and walked over.

'Well, it's a straightforward enough case—the blade, being narrow and very sharp, entered the body between the upper left ribs and, judging by the amount of blood, punctured the aorta. The hemorrhaging is, of course, extensive and death would have been almost instantaneous, mercifully. The time of death is, of course, already known to you. We'll need to wait for the ambulance to return, then we can get the poor lad off to the mortuary. I should be able to fit in the postmortem tomorrow. I'll give you my findings as soon as I can get them written up. I hope your constable is all right—I'd guess that he'll need a good few stitches to fix his wound.'

Half an hour earlier, Kerr Brodie had collapsed, semi-conscious due to the considerable loss of blood; the ambulance that had arrived to collect McSween's body had immediately been dispatched to Paisley's Royal Alexandra Infirmary with the unfortunate constable inside.

'Aye, Doctor, I hope so; I daresay he'll be pretty sore for a

237

few days.'

The doctor nodded.

'Yes, he certainly will; I just hope the wound doesn't get an infection of any sort—after all, the knife had already received blood from the other poor chap. Anyway, I'll get on my way; damned cold here tonight, I think I'll treat myself to a wee nip when I get home—just to keep the circulation going. Good-night, gentlemen.'

As the doctor left, McGinn put his hand on Alan's shoulder.

'You get yourself home too, son, it's been a bloody rough night. Where's Tait, by the way?'

Wearily, Alan rose to his feet.

'Erm, I think he's back across the road.'

'Right, I'll away across and have a word. There's no point in interviewing the prisoner tonight and, if you think this Janetti woman may be able to translate for us, then it makes sense to keep him here and for me to come back down tomorrow.'

'I don't think Sergeant Tait will be too happy about that, sir. You'd said you'd be taking him back to Paisley.'

'Aye, I did, but plans change with circumstances, McInnes; anyway, I'm going to leave the uniformed constables here, so Tait can get to his bed. Poor old bugger must be exhausted.'

Alan managed a feeble grin.

'He was pretty pleased with himself, mind you.'

'An' well he might be—if it hadn't been for him, there's a good chance we'd still be searching for our killer. No, that was a damned good piece o' work from your sergeant.'

His expression became more serious.

'What's bothering me, though, is the whereabouts of John Scanlon. There's still a possibility that he was on the motorcycle and we've yet to track it down. It must be parked off the road somewhere—I daresay we'll find it tomorrow but I'm not happy at the idea that this fellow's accomplice might still be roaming around, looking for trouble. Mind you, if he's any bloody sense, he'll be far away from the scene by now.'

It took a moment for the words to sink in to Alan's weary brain.

'What—you don't think he might try something?'

McGinn shrugged.

'You just never know—desperate people often take desperate measures, that's why I'm leavin' the two constables on duty. Right, get yourself away home an' try to be down at the station for ten, if you can.'

As Alan turned to leave, McGinn added, 'It's been a hell o' a night son, and you did well; aye, very well indeed.'

~~~

He was home in less than ten minutes, hearing the church clock chiming five times as he closed the door. The house was cold, silent and in darkness, but he made his way to the kitchen where, sitting on the table, was a flask and a plate of biscuits. Silently blessing his mother, he sat down and poured himself a cup of cocoa before creeping upstairs. He was asleep within minutes.

~~~

'Come on, son, it's past nine o'clock; I got your wee note but you'd best be getting ready if the inspector wants you down for ten.'

Alan felt as if he was being dragged from a deep, dark pit.

'Erm...oh, aye, Mother, thanks, I'll be down in a few minutes.'

'Well, don't be long, your breakfast is on. My, you must have been late, your father and I sat up for a while waiting for you—when did you get home?'

'The clock was striking five when I got in—oh, and thanks for the cocoa, that was grand.'

Isa smiled.

'Och, I wouldn't let you be getting to bed on such a cold night without a wee hot drink. By the way, did you get your man?'

The memories flooded back and Alan tried not to let them show in his expression.

'It's a long story, Mother; look, I'll get a wash and a shave and I'll be down in about fifteen minutes.'

~~~

The church clock was striking ten as Alan made his way to the police station; he still felt exhausted and somewhat disorientated due to his lack of sleep but he was determined not to let himself, or the Barloch office, down. As he approached, the police Wolseley drew up outside and Inspector McGinn stepped out. He appeared alert and fresh, causing Alan to briefly wonder if the man survived on nicotine and cups of tea! The senior officer nodded.

'Mornin' McInnes—did you get a bit o' a sleep?'

'Yes, sir, I did, although I'm still pretty tired. Erm, is Sergeant Fairbrother not here?'

McGinn turned and strode towards the office door.

'No, he's not. Right, before we get started, is there any chance you could get hold of Mrs Janetti and see if she'll come along and translate?'

'Yes, of course, sir. The cafe's just along the road and they usually open about nine. Will I go along now?'

'Aye, on you go, I'll tell Sergeant Tait. I'll need to let the other two constables get back up the road at some point but I'd rather they were there when we conduct the interview. We're dealing with a nasty piece o' work and I don't want any further incidents. Right, away an' see what she says.'

Alan set off, turning on to Main Street and entering the cafe; the aroma of fresh coffee made him wish that he was on a more sociable visit. Mrs Janetti was mopping the floor, humming cheerfully to herself.

'Ah, good-a morning, Alan, an' how are you today?'

'Not too bad, Mrs Janetti, although I'm a bit tired. Look, can I ask a wee favour?'

The woman placed the mop back in the bucket.

'Sure—what-a can I do for you?'

Alan explained the situation, causing Mrs Janetti's normally cheerful countenance to darken.

'Oh, that is very worrying, Alan. But I'm not-a sure, will I be safe?'

Alan tried to give the woman a reassuring smile.

'Of course you will, Mrs Janetti. The inspector and I will both be present, as well as two CID constables, so there'll be no need to worry.'

She considered his request for a moment.

'Well, if you're sure—just let me say to Aldo. We have a girl coming in at ten-thirty and it's-a quiet at this time of day. Let me get my coat—it is still very cold, not like Napoli, no, not at all!'

~~~

As he made the introductions, Alan could sense Mrs Janetti's unease. Inspector McGinn was trying his best to reassure her but it was clear that the woman was highly nervous at the thought of being involved with what she had called 'a dangerous criminal'. Barloch was a small village and it was possible that news of Douglas McSween's murder was already common knowledge.

'...really nothing to worry about, Mrs Janetti, and I'd be very grateful. It's just information such as his name, his address, that kind of thing. He doesn't seem to speak any English at all so I'd be much obliged.'

'Oh, very well, Mister McGinn, I will-a do what I can.'

McGinn gave her a broad smile.

'That's excellent! Right, if you just take a seat here, Sergeant Tait will get you a cup of tea.'

'Hav-a you no coffee?'

McGinn gave Tait a somewhat helpless look.

'Och, Ah'm sorry, Mrs Janetti, we dinnae tend tae drink such exotic stuff in here. Ah'll awa' an' get the kettle on.'

He beat a hasty retreat, leaving McGinn to continue.

'Aye, well, as I said, you wait here an' we'll get everything organised. I'll be conducting the interview, Constable McInnes here and one of my CID men will be in the room with us—you'll be perfectly safe.'

'I hope-a so.'

~~~

Mrs Janetti sipped her tea with obvious distaste. Alan stood beside her. He was curious as to how the interview would proceed—having witnessed McGinn in action on several occasions, he knew how much the inspector relied on threats and on what he considered to be bullying tactics. That would be extremely difficult when working through an interpreter. The door to the rear of the premises opened.

'That's them ready,' said Tait. 'An', like we said, Mrs Janetti, dinnae you worry, just translate whit the inspector asks. Richt, awa' through.'

Alan led the nervous woman into Tait's cramped office. As usual, McGinn was seated behind the desk. To the right of the prisoner stood a broad-shouldered, balding man with a pug

242

face and fists like hams. He nodded at Alan as he entered and McGinn introduced him.

'McInnes, this is detective constable McCloy, he'll be keeping an eye on our man. As you can see, we've put him back in handcuffs—I wouldn't trust him an inch.'

The young man appeared indifferent to McGinn's words, presumably failing to understand any of them.

'Right, Mrs Janetti, if you just have a wee seat by my side here, McInnes, bring that chair over and take notes of the interview. Right, are we all ready?'

They mumbled a collective 'yes'.

'Okay, Mrs Janetti—can you ask his name, his address and his date of birth please?'

Mrs Janetti nodded then spoke in a torrent of fluent Italian. The young man responded, more slowly.

'He'a say his name is Luigi.'

'His second name?'

More Italian.

'He-a say just Luigi.'

Alan noticed McGinn scowling but he controlled his anger.

'I'm afraid 'just Luigi' isn't good enough. Mrs Janetti, tell him that he must give his full name, his address and his date of birth. Please.'

Mrs Janetti spoke again and, even in the foreign tongue, Alan could detect a note of anger and impatience in her voice; it appeared that the woman had lapsed into the role of a mother and, after what seemed like a few heated exchanges, she replied, 'He say his-a name is Luigi Grimaldo. He was born on the fifteenth of February in-a nineteen forty-one, during the war, He say his father was killed in the war. He has-a no address, he stay here an' there with friends, he say.'

McGinn grunted as Mrs Janetti added, 'It is-a quite common

for young Italian men—and women— to come over here for a few months, usually about this time of year. They stay for the summer; they work in cafes an' restaurants as waiters. They learn to speak some English, then they go back home when it-a becomes too cold for them!'

She gave a little giggle but it elicited no response from the stony-faced inspector.

'I see; so, can you ask where he is working please?'

She spoke again and the young man answered.

'He-a say he works in a fish an' chip shop, Aldo's, somewhere in Glasgow.'

'Erm, I think I might know it, sir,' Alan interjected. 'At least, there's an Aldo's in Paisley Road West, not too far from where Nancy lives. Mrs Janetti, ask if there's a big car garage along the road.'

She spoke and the young man nodded, saying, 'Si, si!'

'That'll be the one, sir, Paisley Road West. I think it's quite well known.'

'Good, we can check up later. Right, Mrs Janetti, I'm very sorry to have to involve you in this, but Mr Grimaldo stands accused of the murder of one Douglas McSween, last night at approximately two a.m. The murder was witnessed by me, Constable McInnes and Sergeant Fairbrother. He also assaulted and stabbed constable Kerr Brodie, who is currently receiving treatment in hospital. These are very serious charges and it is important that the accused understands fully the nature of them. Can you explain this to him, please?'

The colour drained from Mrs Janetti's face, but she nodded.

'Si, si, I will-a do my best.'

She turned to the young man and spoke at length; he became increasingly agitated until he rose from his seat, shouting in Italian. Constable McCloy immediately placed a beefy hand on the young man's neck and squeezed it tightly, causing him to cry out in pain. As he pushed the prisoner back into his seat, McCloy leaned over and, in a broad Glasgow accent, muttered a few words of what sounded like Italian in the prisoner's ear. Mrs Janetti's eyebrows rose but the young man immediately became silent and still. McGinn looked astonished.

'What the hell did you say to him, McCloy—an' how the hell d'you know Italian?'

McCloy grinned, revealing a missing tooth.

'Och, Ah worked a wee while in a chip shop ma'sel' when Ah wis a lad— Ah learned a few useful phrases, like. Ah just told him to sit doon an' be quiet.'

Mrs Janetti giggled again and McGinn didn't press the matter.

'Right, Mrs Janetti, what did he say?'

She gave him a shocked look.

'No, not Constable McCloy—Grimaldi.'

'Grimaldo,' she corrected. 'Well, he say that he acted in-a self-defence, he say that this other man attacked him an' it was an accident.'

McGinn half-rose from his seat, bellowing across at the young man, who cowered slightly in the chair, although his expression remained impassive. A cool customer, Alan thought.

'Rubbish—that's a damned lie! We were there, we saw you—'

'Inspector,' interrupted Alan.

'Damn...sorry, Mrs Janetti; can you tell him that I don't believe him—and ask him why he happened to be carrying a knife?'

She asked.

'He-a say that he was to collect a parcel an' that he just had the knife to open it an' check what was inside it.'

'An' what, exactly, did he expect to find?' snapped McGinn.

She gave the inspector a rather frosty look, but asked the question.

'He say it-a was some kind of herbs. He say that is why he had the knife, he did not mean to hurt anyone, he say again that it-a was an accident.'

McGinn took a deep breath then exhaled slowly; his face was red and he was balling and un-balling his fists. The interview certainly wasn't proceeding as he would have liked. He spoke once more to Mrs Janetti.

'Could you ask Mr Grimaldo for whom he was collecting the parcel?'

The young man shrugged in response to her question, shaking his head.

'He say he does not-a know, it was just someone where he works. They gave him a few pounds an' told him where he was to go an' what he was to collect.'

'I see; can you ask if he knows someone by the name of John Scanlon?'

Again, the captive shook his head and shrugged.

'No, he has not-a heard of anyone called Scanlon.'

McGinn pulled a face.

'Mrs Janetti, I know this is a difficult question for you but, when conducting an interview such as this we very much rely on the way the accused answers our questions; the way they speak, their body language and the like. Now, obviously, we have no idea what Mr Grimaldo is saying; can I ask, then, d'you think he's telling us the truth?'

'Uno momento.'

Once more, Mrs Janetti lapsed into a stream of rapid, fluent Italian that went on for a considerable time. Grimaldo sat back in his chair, the expressions on his thin face changing from insolence to surprise, then to fear. Finally, she stopped and he replied, his voice low and the words coming out more hesitantly. Their dialogue continued for a few more minutes then she turned to McGinn.

'Inspector, I have explained the seriousness of his situation an' I have asked if he is-a telling me the truth. He understands what is happening, he accepts his actions, but he cannot—or will not—tell me anything about the person who gave him this...this task. He is-a very afraid—more of them than of you, I think! But I do not believe he has anything else to say. I am sorry, I have-a done my best.'

McGinn smiled at her.

'Yes, you have, I really appreciate it, Mrs Janetti—if you can just tell him that he will be remanded—kept—in custody until he appears before a judge, probably in a few days' time. He'll be taken to jail in Paisley; he won't be kept here.'

She translated these facts and the youth nodded, mumbling a few words. Alan noticed that the Italian was now shaking and the colour had drained from his face.

'He understands, Inspector.'

'Good.' McGinn stood up and extended his hand. 'Mrs Janetti, I can't thank you enough, you've been a great help and you're free to go now.'

She gave him a rather sad smile as she got to her feet..

'You are-a welcome, it just makes me so sad to see a young life wasted—well, two young lives, I feel-a so sorry for the other that died. Tragico, tragico.'

She walked around the desk then, to the surprise of the other occupants, she bent down and kissed Grimaldo on each cheek before cradling his thin face in her hands and speaking softly and gently. For a moment it looked as if he was going to burst into tears but he quickly regained his composure, his expression becoming impassive once more. Alan escorted her out of the office and to the front door; as she left, she looked up into his eyes.

'As I say, it is all so sad, please make-a sure he is looked after, Alan, I hear such bad things about young men and what happens when they go to jail. He is-a just a young foolish boy, a long way from his home.'

'I'll do my best, Mrs Janetti.'

Then, once again to his surprise, she kissed him on each cheek, then grasped his hand for a moment..

'You are a good-a boy, Alan McInnes. Your mother must be very proud of you.'

~~~

Under the watchful eye and the heavy hand of Detective Constable McCloy, Luigi Grimaldo was safely incarcerated once more in one of Barloch's cramped cells. The fight appeared to have gone out of him, however, and Alan wondered if it had anything to do with what Mrs Janetti had said to him. Although he was undoubtedly guilty of killing Douglas McSween, nonetheless the woman's kindly words had tugged very slightly at Alan's heartstrings. Grimaldo *was* a young man, very far from home; a home he certainly wouldn't see for a long time—if ever. Alan shuddered at the thought.

Lifting his notes, he followed Tait and McGinn out to the front office, where the latter two immediately lit up, creating the usual fug of tobacco smoke.

'Right,' said McGinn. 'I'll organise a Black Maria to take Grimaldo up to Paisley—I'm not going to risk him in the car, even under the tender care of Constable McCloy. I'll try and get hold of an official interpreter, have another go at him and get a full and formal statement but I don't think there's any chance of him giving anything away. Have you ever heard the term 'Omerta'?'

Alan and Sergeant Tait shook their heads.

'Well, it's an Italian code of loyalty and silence that folk like him adhere to. They refuse to say anything to the authorities, despite the consequences for themselves. If that's what we're up against here we haven't a hope in hell o' getting any useful information out o' the bugger, I'm afraid. I'll have another try, though. It wasn't really fair to pressurise Mrs Janetti any further.'

He lit a second cigarette from the stub of the first.

'Then, of course, there'll be the usual damned paperwork; McInnes, can you get the statement—or what statement we managed to get—typed up as soon as you can? By the way, any word on Brodie?'

'Ah called earlier,' replied Tait. 'The lad'll be fine, had six stitches an' a blood transfusion. He should get oot at the start o' the week.'

'Good. If I've got time later, I might go and visit him, just to corroborate what he's already told us and to thank him personally.'

He let out long, weary sigh, shaking his head.

'Of course, this wasn't the outcome I'd hoped for, but you acquitted yourselves well an' I'm very grateful for all your help. Which is more than can be said for some.'

Tait and Alan exchanged a knowing glance but remained silent.

'Whit's yer thoughts on this Scanlon fellow?' asked Tait.

'God knows. Grimaldo claims to know nothing about him an' he's still our prime suspect for the other two murders. Back to the bloody drawing board, I suppose, but I'd really hoped to have him in custody now, not some foreign laddie who can't even speak our language. No, the whole thing's a bit of a bloody disaster, to be honest. Still, that's the way of it. Right, McInnes, if you can get on with that report, I've a few calls to make. Of course, you'll both be called as witnesses at the preliminary hearing and subsequent trial, but I'll brief you before then. Should be pretty open and shut—after all, we witnessed the whole damned thing. It's my fault, we should have acted sooner, it might have prevented McSween's death.'

'Ye cannae go blamin' yersel, McGinn. Efter all, it wis Scanlon we thought we'd be arrestin'—we certainly never expected thon Italian bugger tae turn up, carryin' a knife intae the bargain; nane o' us could have foreseen that. Naw, it wis just an unfortunate series o' events, no' your fault at all.'

McGinn gave the sergeant a rather half-hearted smile.

'Well, I hope the superintendent sees it that way. Right, let's get on.'

Chapter 24

A slightly uneasy calm lay upon the small Barloch police office. Luigi Grimaldo had been unceremoniously bundled into the back of a black police van, still handcuffed and accompanied by the formidable DC McCloy. The motorcycle had been found parked on a farm track on the outskirts of the village and had been taken to Paisley to check for fingerprints. There had been no indication that John Scanlon had been a passenger and McGinn felt that a door-to-door enquiry would be a waste of time, given the late hour of the events and the absence of any houses nearby.

Despite any personal misgivings, Alan felt it wise not to voice Mrs Janetti's appeal for good treatment—after all, the young man was a murderer, whether accidentally or not. With Alan's hastily typed report in hand, McGinn, too, had finally taken his leave, the sharp tang of Capstan full strength replaced by the more mellow aroma of Sergeant Tait's pipe. As Tait puffed away ruminatively, he turned to Alan.

'Aye, been a hell of a day, richt enough. Interestin' that Sergeant Fairbrother didnae grace us wi' his presence, mind.'

There was a twinkle in his eye that encouraged Alan to speak up.

'Aye, wasn't it? I'd mentioned it to Inspector McGinn but he gave no explanation.'

A short silence ensued, then Tait asked, 'So what the hell happened last nicht—McGinn was in one hell o' a mood up the road.'

'You know, it all happened so fast; Grimaldo came charging out of the shed—he'd been shouting in Italian, although I didn't realise it at the time, but he was obviously angry about something. Probably because the parcel wasn't there. Anyway, Kerr came round from behind the shed just as I did, we thought he'd just pushed McSween over but it turned out...well, you know.'

'Aye, that wis a poor do, richt enough. He was a bad laddie but he didnae deserve tae be stabbed.'

'No, he didn't! So, Kerr tried to stop him and he got stabbed in the arm. We made after Grimaldo, as did Fairbrother, but he seemed to slip on the frosty grass—I didn't really see exactly what happened but, next thing, he's on the ground, the inspector tripped over his leg and he fell too. If it hadn't been for you...'

Tait gave a smoky chuckle.

'Aye, jist as weel, eh? Ye ken, it's just instinct tae stop a runaway like that, Ah suppose it never leaves ye. But McGinn wis furious at Fairbrother—damned stupid mistake, if ye ask me, but Ah suppose it could hae happened tae any o' us.'

Could it though, wondered Alan. Once again, he silently questioned Fairbrother's actions; surely, the sergeant wouldn't have wanted Grimaldo to get away? Tait was speaking again.

'Naw, Ah'd think that Sergeant Fairbrother is 'persona non grata' at the moment, be interestin' tae see if he keeps his position efter a' this.'

He winked at Alan, who grinned in return.

'No, Sergeant, I've no inclination to join the CID; even less so after last night's carry-on. I'm quite happy here.'

He was about to add 'biding my time' but thought better of it. Tait gave him a knowing look, however.

'Aye, ye're quite richt, Ah'll no' be here forever an' you're surely first in the runnin' tae take over.'

Another silence, companionable, peaceful. Tait spoke again.

'D'ye think it was the poor McSween lad that was responsible for those arson attacks?'

Alan had almost forgotten about the earlier investigation; it all seemed rather trivial now, in light of recent events.

'I suppose we'll never know. The site manager at the new estate did get back to me, seems McSween had asked for a job as a labourer. The manager got in touch with Miss Shaw and she'd given the lad a bad reference, so maybe he was just holding a grudge against them both. He certainly had enough paraffin in his shed to set fire to half the village!'

'Weel, ye're probably richt enough; an', like ye say, we'll never know.'

He consulted his watch.

'Aye-aye, nearly three o' the clock. Listen, McInnes, ye're done in. Get yersel' awa' up the road. Ah'll shut up the office; if anyone needs me Ah'm only next door an' Ah can aye call ye if Ah need help.'

'Are you sure, Sergeant? To be honest, I am pretty exhausted after last night.'

Tait was already switching the lights off.

'Aye, Ah'm sure; anyway, Ah've got few things tae see tae ma'sel'. Mind an' tell your mother Ah wis askin' for her—an thank her for the sandwiches last nicht—no' tae mention the breakfast!'

~~~

It was a weary climb up School Street; the previous evening's frost had disappeared and the sky was clouding over, heralding the possibility of a mild, but wet, weekend. Although exhausted, Alan was eager to get home and he quickened his pace as best he could; a decent meal, an early night and he would be fresh for Saturday, when he would be spending the afternoon and the evening with Nancy. He had booked dinner in a fancy restaurant in Paisley. It was stretching his resources a little but he planned on using it as an opportunity to finally settle on a date for their wedding. He was also looking forward to unburdening himself to his fiancé, as he felt the last week had caused him a great deal of anxiety and stress. He smiled as he opened the gate and walked up the path; thank God for Nancy!

He expected his mother, at least, to be at home but, when he opened the door, there was an unusual and unsettling silence in the house. He opened the kitchen door and stopped in his tracks. Isa McInnes was sitting at one end of the kitchen table, arms folded tightly across her chest. Opposite her sat Gilbert, a sullen, hangdog expression on his craggy features. Between them, on the table, lay an old grey woollen sock and a rolled-up bundle of one-pound notes. Neither of his parents gave him as much as a glance as he stood in the doorway, surveying the odd and troubling scene.

'Mother? Father? What's goin' on?'

Isa turned and looked at her son; her eyes were glistening, not with sorrow but with anger.

'Well might you ask, Alan. Indeed, you might ask your father as he refuses to tell me.'

'There's nothin' tae tell, woman.'

She turned on him, her voice laden with fury.

'Nothing? NOTHING? You call fifteen one-pound notes, nothing, Gilbert McInnes? We've been married for nigh on thirty years and, in all that time, you have never given me an unopened wage packet. NEVER! I give you whatever you need, for tobacco, your newspapers, the occasional drink down the pub. I have trusted you, absolutely, implicitly. And now...THIS.'

She banged her small fist on the table, causing the notes to jump slightly; Gilbert McInnes jumped rather more. Alan walked across, looking from one parent to the other.

'Will someone please explain what the hell is goin' on?'

Isa looked back up at her son.

'I was clearing out your father's sock drawer, seeing if any of his socks needed darning. I found this old sock at the back of the drawer and I realised that there was something inside it. And that something—' she pointed '—is lying there. Fifteen pounds, and your father refuses to tell me where he got it from.'

Alan looked at his father.

'Well, Father, will you answer Mother's question—actually, will you answer mine. Where did you get that money?'

Gilbert looked belligerently at his son.

'Nane o' your damned business, Alan McInnes.'

'GILBERT!' screamed Isa 'I will NOT have you swearing in this house; and I will ask you again—where did that money come from?'

Gilbert appeared to back down slightly.

'Ah...ah saved it up.'

Isa looked as if she was about to have apoplexy.

'You—saved—it—up? And how, may I ask, Gilbert McInnes, did you manage to 'save it up'?' You take about ten shillings a week from me which you spend on your own bits and pieces. I cleared that drawer out only a month ago and there was no sign of any money then. Are you telling me that you saved fifteen pounds from your small change in the space of one month? Because, quite honestly, I don't believe you!'

With some effort, McInnes senior hauled himself out of the chair.

'D'ye no', woman? Weel, Ah'm tellin ye an' ye can believe whit the hell ye like.'

He leaned forwards and swept both sock and notes on to

the floor.

'Ye can keep the damned money—Ah've nae bloody use for it an' Ah'm sick tae death o' bein' telled aff in ma ain hoose. Ah'm awa' oot tae get some peace an' quiet frae the baith o' ye.'

With that, he swept out of the room as fast as his prosthetic leg would allow, leaving Isa and Alan in a stunned silence. Suddenly, Isa broke into floods of tears and her son knelt beside her, patting her arm.

'Mother, it's all right, I'm sure there's an explanation.'

But, at the back of his mind, there was only one explanation, one that he daren't even consider.

~~~

Alan managed to calm his mother down slightly and, having made her a cup of tea, he decided that she was in no fit state to cook dinner. He made his way back down School Street to fetch two fish suppers, fervently hoping that Mrs Janetti would be too busy to quiz him on the previous evening's events. His mind was racing—fifteen pounds was more than many people earned in a week, it was impossible that his father could have saved that amount in a month. In which case, where *had* it come from? Had Gilbert McInnes's leg *really* been troubling him badly enough to prevent him covering the night shift on that fateful night, or had someone paid him to absent himself, not expecting Alex Combe to be on duty? He could feel himself shaking; should he take the matter to Sergeant Tait? Where would that lead—his father would be questioned, most likely by Inspector McGinn who, despite their relationship, would not spare him. There would be disgrace, it would affect his career; most of all, the shame would destroy his mother.

His turn came at the head of the long, Friday night queue.

'An-a what can I get you, Alan?'

'Oh—erm, two fish suppers please, Mrs Janetti.'

She shouted the order in Italian; her husband shovelled two large helpings of steaming chips on to the waiting papers before placing golden, battered haddock on top.

'You 'av come at the right time, they're just-a fresh out the fryer. Salt an' vinegar?'

'What—sorry?'

'Salt an' vinegar? Alan, are-a you all right? You don't look well.'

'Erm, och it's just with last night an' everything, I'm really tired—thanks, Mrs Janetti, how much is that?'

He paid and made a hasty exit; the last thing he needed were any more personal questions. He popped a chip into his mouth then swore as it burned his palate.

~~~

By the time Alan reached his house, Isa was bustling about in the kitchen; the table was set with cutlery and two plates, beside one of which stood a glass and a bottle of beer. There was no sign of the money or the sock that had contained it. Alan put the fish suppers on the plates and sat down.

'Beer, Mother?'

'Och, well, I'd bought it for your father but, seeing as he's not here...'

She sat across from him; her cheerfulness was decidedly brittle but she was making a valiant attempt at normality. Alan was starving and tucked into the tasty fish and chips, although Isa merely picked at hers, eating only about a third of the fish and no more than a dozen chips. Alan managed to make inroads on most of her leftovers, although he suspected he might regret it later. They ate in a silence that would normally have been companionable; tonight it was strained.

After helping his mother clear the kitchen, they watched television for a short while but Alan couldn't concentrate. Finally, about half past nine, he stood up.

'I'm heading up to bed, Mother, I'm absolutely exhausted. Are you coming up?'

She looked away.

'Och, no, I'll wait a wee while yet, I've some knitting I want to finish. Have you any plans for tomorrow?'

'Aye, I'm meeting Nancy in the afternoon then we're going for a meal in a fancy new place in Paisley.'

'Oh, that'll be nice. Is it a special occasion?'

He hadn't intended to discuss his plans but he felt that his mother needed a boost.

'Actually, I'm hoping to set a date for our wedding.'

She beamed up at her son.

'Oh, that's lovely! I'll finally be able to choose an outfit—it depends on the season, you see! Maybe Nancy could help me?'

He smiled; he had made the right decision and it would give her something pleasant to consider.

'I'm sure she'd love to, Mother, I'll ask her.'

He bent over and kissed her cheek.

'Right, I'm off. Goodnight—and, please, try not to worry.'

Her smile became more forced.

'I will, son, you're a good boy.'

As he left the room , he wondered if she would still think so if he reported his suspicions to Sergeant Tait.

~~~

As expected, his over-eating caused him severe indigestion and he lay awake, uncomfortable, agitated—and listening for his father's return. The day's events replayed over and over in his mind; the murder of Douglas McSween, the frustrating interview and the highly disturbing incident that had taken place in his own home, his sanctuary. Then there was the niggling issue of Sergeant Fairbrother; Alan was still convinced that, somehow, the man was up to no good but both his mother and Tait had persuaded him to let the matter drop. However, his doubts persisted, especially in view of the man's apparent clumsiness the previous night. He would speak to Nancy about it tomorrow; she would know what to do.

Eventually, he heard the front door open, followed by low voices in the kitchen. Whatever was being said, at least it wasn't being said in anger. After about fifteen minutes, his parents climbed the stairs; he waited until he could hear his father's snores, then got out of bed and tip-toed down to the kitchen. He opened the cupboard and, with a sigh of relief, took out the blue bottle labelled 'Milk of Magnesia'. At least there was medicine for one of his troubles!

Chapter 25

'I brought you up a wee cup of tea, son—my, you've had a good long sleep, you must have been exhausted.'

'Mmm...what? Oh, thanks, Mother. Yes, it has been a pretty tough few days.'

He stretched his long frame and sat up, gratefully accepting the steaming cup.

'I feel a lot better though, just needed a long lie.'

'There's enough hot water for a bath, seeing as you're going out with Nancy today.'

'Oh, that'd be the very thing, thanks!'

A bath was a luxury in the McInnes household and, half an hour later, Alan was relaxing in the small bathtub, although his torso and knees had to vie for position in the hot soapy water. He felt a sense of release, though, as if the water was washing away the tribulations of the previous week but, as he leaned his head contentedly against the wall, he was aware of the intrusive ringing of the telephone. He swore, then held his breath, awaiting his mother's voice summoning him; the phone was mostly used for police business. However, he remained undisturbed and presumed it had either been a wrong number or possibly one of his mother's violin pupils. He closed his eyes for a few moments. Then, feeling the water begin to cool, he rose and began to dry himself.

~~~

Half an hour later, clean, well-shaved and smartly dressed, he opened the kitchen door; immediately he could detect a change in his mother's demeanour, the slight drooping of the head, her shoulders slumped.

'Mother—is everything all right? Who was that on the telephone?'

She turned and gave him a wistful look.

'Och, Alan, son, it was Nancy.'

'Nancy?' His heart sank. 'Has something happened?'

'No, but I'm afraid she's called off your day together.'

This time his heart plummeted to his boots.

'What? Why...did she say?'

'Yes, everything's fine, but she's away through to Edinburgh instead—her mother is attending some fancy legal function with her father in a few weeks and she needs a new outfit. She wants Nancy to help her choose; oh, and she asked me to pass on her apologies.'

Alan detected the faint tone of sarcasm in his mother's voice.

'I'll away and call her.'

'Don't bother yourself, Alan, she was just leaving when she telephoned, they'll be on their way by now.'

He could also hear the disappointment in her voice and he felt a surge of anger. It was only yesterday that his mother had expressed the same wish of Nancy's help in choosing her outfit for their wedding and he realised that she must be almost as disappointed as he was.

'But why can she not just go to Glasgow—there's plenty of decent shops there, surely?'

'Well, apparently Mrs Wright has an account at Jenners, that fancy big shop in Princes Street. Didn't you say that her mother comes from Edinburgh?'

'Yes, she does.'

He let out a long sigh; he had been particularly looking forward to seeing Nancy, not just to discuss a wedding date. He needed someone to talk to about the recent events and about his misgivings regarding Sergeant Fairbrother. He hadn't yet decided if he would tell her about the fifteen pounds found in his father's sock.

'Never, mind, son, there'll be plenty more days out and nice dinners. Why don't you see if Kerr is free, maybe you could go for a drink?'

Alan realised that his mother was unaware of Kerr Brodie's injury and hospitalisation; he decided that he wouldn't burden her any further.

'Och, Kerr told me he's seeing his own lass tonight, he'll no' want to be going out with me. No, I'll probably just have a quiet night in.'

Isa placed his breakfast before him and he sat at the table, going through the motions of enjoying his food. But his mind was elsewehere.

~~~

Alan decided that the best thing to do was to go for a walk, alone with his thoughts. He pulled on his coat and strode down the path, turning onto School Street. However, he turned left into Glenhead Street, not wishing to pass either the police station or Janetti's cafe; today he needed the counsel of his own company.

He was angry and disappointed in Nancy; this day had been arranged a few weeks ago and reservations at the restaurant were difficult to obtain, especially on a Saturday. He was equally disappointed for his mother, who had been hoping not only for a wedding date but also for the opportunity to go outfit-shopping with her future daughter-in-law. The week's events had upset him more than he realised and, whilst the last year had provided the macabre experience of viewing a few corpses first-hand, Friday morning had been the first time he had been in the vicinity of a cold-blooded murder, not to mention Kerr Brodie's vicious assault. It had also brought home to him the hazards of being a police officer and how quickly events could turn disastrous. As to the money that his mother had found—his mind shied away from thinking about it, the implications and possible repercussions being too awful to contemplate.

Then there was the issue of Sergeant Fairbrother.

He let out a grunt of...of what? Anger? Dislike? Mistrust? He wasn't sure, but there was something definitely 'off' about the sergeant's behaviour. Had he really slipped that night and would he have allowed the killer to escape? What had he been looking for at Kilmirrin station? Did he, too, notice the missing buttons on Frank Kilbride's coat and draw the same conclusions as Alan? Why hadn't he recognised two well-known hoodlums that would undoubtedly have been recognisable to any officer based in Greenock? Why did he lie about where he drank and who was the mysterious man that Kerr had seen him in conversation with? The thoughts spun in his head and he barely noticed that the rain had started; a fine, west of Scotland drizzle that seeped through the fabric of his coat and sent a chill through his frame. He paid no attention whatsoever to another discarded and broken ice-cream cone on the pavement.

Having reached the far end of the village, he found himself back on Main Street, outside the Hole in the Wa' bar; the door was open and the vaguely enticing smell of beer, tobacco and wet clothing wafted out on to the street, along with the commentary on a horse race playing on the radio. Without thinking, he entered, causing a slight dip in the babble of conversation as they realised that there was a relative stranger in their midst—this was definitely a working man's pub, seldom frequented by the likes of Alan. Many knew, too, that he was an off-duty policeman and, while most of the customers would have nothing to hide, there was still a vague element of suspicion when he entered. He walked up to the bar and the barman nodded.

'What can Ah get ye, son?'

'A pint o' heavy, please.'

The barman went to the taps and poured Alan's pint; by the time the glass was full, the conversations had returned to a normal volume and he was now just another Saturday lunchtime customer. The barman placed the pint in front of him.

'Don't normally see you along this end o' the village, Alan.'

'Och, I fancied a wee change—here, could I have a glass of brandy as well, please?'

The barman gave him an odd look.

'Brandy, is it? Ah think Ah've a bottle through in the lounge, don't often get asked for it in the public bar. Mind, they say ye shouldnae mix the grape an' the grain—are ye sure?'

'Aye, an' could you make it a double please?'

~~~

His stomach was churning as, rather unsteadily, he made his way back up School Street. The barman appeared to have been correct with his advice and the combination of the cold beer and the strong brandy was having the predicted effect, not helped by the second order he had placed. The drizzle had eased slightly but he was cold, wet and in worse spirits than ever when he finally arrived home. He hung his coat by the door and entered the warmth of the kitchen, where Gilbert McInnes was seated with an empty soup bowl before him. Isa was busy at the stove and she turned.

'You're late, son—here, I'll get you some broth.'

Gilbert, however, stared intently at his son..

'You've been drinkin.'

Alan felt a wave of uncharacteristic belligerence wash over him.

'An' what if I have?'

Isa turned back, giving her son a look of consternation.

'Oh, Alan, what are you doing drinking at lunchtime—you never usually do that?'

'Can a man no' have a drink when he wants, Mother? Seems to me there's damn all to do apart from that.'

He regretted the words as soon as they were out. Isa looked on the verge of tears.

'Alan, please don't use such language, it's not like you. Look, sit yourself down, here's a plate of Scotch broth and some bread. That'll help.'

Gilbert sat with a smirk on his face.

'An' whit prompted ye to go oot an get stocious this lunchtime?'

Alan glared at his father.

'I'm no' stocious, as you put it, I've just had a few drinks. If you must know, I went a walk an' the rain came on, I was passin' the Hole in the Wa' an' I went in.'

'The Hole? Huh, Ah doubt ye'd no get a great welcome in there, there's a few that maybe like tae keep the law at arm's length.'

'Well, no-one seemed to care; I just had a couple o' drinks then I came up the road.'

'Just a couple? Aye, it'll no' be the first time that a policeman had taken tae the drink, Ah've seen it happen...'

'Oh, for God's sake, be quiet and leave me be.'

The ensuing silence was tense as Alan noisily slurped the hot, thick soup, aware of both parents staring at him; half way through the bowl, he felt his innards clenching ominously and stood up.

'Erm, sorry—excuse me...'

~~~

Gilbert McInnes didn't show much sympathy towards his son, stating that it was his own fault and that he should know better. Isa, however, had left Alan for an hour or so before bringing him a cup of tea and some toast.

'Here, son—are you feeling a bit better?'

He mumbled an affirmative.

'You were in a right state—I was quite worried about you. What on earth did you have to drink?'

'I had some beer and some brandy' he replied, omitting to tell her how much.

'What? Oh, Alan, you know that brandy's too rich for the likes of us—remember how ill you were that time when you were over at Nancy's parents! Anyway, you should never mix the grape and the grain.'

The mention of his fiancé's name jarred with him. Rather than lying miserably in his bed, he should have been out with Nancy, possibly watching a matinee in the cinema, or having coffee, looking forward to an expensive dinner and a pleasant, productive talk.

'Aye, the barman said that as well.'

'Well, he was correct—don't ask me why but the two always seem to cause an upset stomach. Anyway, this'll put something back in your tummy, just have a wee rest and you'll soon feel better.'

He thanked her as she closed the door behind her, leaving him alone with his thoughts. Despite his upset stomach and pounding head, there was no doubt that the effects of the alcohol had temporarily relieved his troubled mind but these troubles were now crowding back; he closed his eyes and fell into a restless sleep.

~~~

Dinner was a rather bleak affair. Although Alan had recovered, the atmosphere was oppressive, his father having returned to his usual morose self while Isa fussed unnecessarily, as always trying to make light of things. The meal over, the family retired to the living room to watch the television; 'Wyatt Earp', then 'International Detective' followed by 'Bernard Delfont presents'. Alan could barely concentrate as a vague idea formed in his mind; his father had fallen asleep and his mother was busy knitting. The idea developed until, finally, he reached a decision and stood up.

'Mother, I need to go and clear my head, there's just been so much going on the last few weeks. I can't seem to concentrate on the television.'

She made to protest but seemed to think better of it, although she asked, 'You're not going to the pub again?'

He smiled and shook his head.

'No. Mother, I'm not—I've learned my lesson!'

He lifted his coat from where it was drying before the fire.

'I won't be too late, don't worry.'

He bent down and kissed her cheek, ashamed of himself for lying.

~~~

Ten minutes later, he walked up the ramp to Barloch train station, hoping that Bert Oliphant wouldn't be on duty. As he approached the booking office, he was dismayed to see the stationmaster's bearded bulk in the small office. The man looked up at his approach.

'Aye-aye.'

Oliphant's welcome lacked its customary warmth.

'Evening, Mr Oliphant, how are you?'

'Aye, weel, it's been a hard few days, what wi' Alex Combe's funeral yesterday afternoon.'

He let the statement hang as Alan gaped at him; he had completely forgotten!

'I'm so sorry, Mr Oliphant, I'd fully intended to attend but—well, I'm sure you heard what happened. Friday was an awful day and we were kept pretty busy, what with the investigation.'

'Aye, Ah'm sure ye were. Still, that's the poor man buried noo, jist need tae get on wi' things. Ah'm surprised that yer sergeant didnae remind ye.'

Alan thought back to the previous day, Tait's haste to close the office at three o'clock. The sergeant had obviously decided that Alan had experienced enough upset for the week—little did he realise what the young man was to encounter once he arrived home.

'Once again, I can only apologise, Mr Oliphant, I'm very sorry to have missed it.'

Oliphant leaned forward towards the window.

'An' Ah'm fair surprised yer faither didnae attend—unless he wis sufferin' frae a guilty conscience?'

The words stung Alan as if he'd been slapped in the face; did Oliphant suspect something?'

'That's a bit unfair, Mr Oliphant, I can't speak for my father, you'd need to take it up with him. Anyway, can I have a return to Glensherrie, please?'

Oliphant gave him an odd look.

'Glensherrie? Whit are ye' wantin' tae go doon there for, at this time on a Saturday?'

Alan was in no mood to explain.

'I've some business to attend to.'

The stationmaster regarded him for a moment, then reached for the ticket before pushing it into the Edmondson machine with a loud clunk.

'There ye are. Next train's due in aboot five minutes, return trains on the half-hour wi' the last one leavin' Glensherrie aboot half-past ten—dependin' on how long yer 'business' takes.'

'Thanks, Mr Oliphant, and my apologies once again.'

He went outside to the platform to await the train, his other thoughts temporarily pushed aside by an overpowering feeling of guilt. Not only for his own, but for his father's absence; he could only think that it was due to the incident of the fifteen pounds. His bleak thoughts were interrupted by the melancholy sounding of a two-tone horn, heralding the approach of the diesel multiple-unit. It ground its way into the station, filling the cold air with diesel fumes, and he opened the door, slumping into a corner seat, head against the steamed-up window. Almost immediately, he hoisted himself back upright—the journey was only a few minutes and he was concerned that he might fall asleep.

With another short blast from its horn, the train accelerated out of Barloch and, as it rumbled across the Marchburn viaduct, Alan shuddered, recalling the tragic events of the previous year. It seemed that the train had only just picked up speed when it began to slow down as it approached Glensherrie. The brakes screeched, the train stopped with a jolt and, a few seconds later, he was standing on the unfamiliar platform of the small station, although it bore a distinct resemblance to Barloch. With barely a glance, the stationmaster punched his ticket and he made his way down the station ramp. At the bottom, he paused; was this a dreadful mistake? What did he hope to accomplish, heading off on yet another unofficial investigation? Both Sergeant Tait's and his mother's advice rang in his ears but he ignored them. No, there was something very suspicious going on and he hoped to find out for himself just what it was. After all, there was no harm in just observing.

None at all, surely?

Chapter 26

Pulling up the collar of his greatcoat, Alan made his way down to Stoneyfield Road, the main thoroughfare linking Glensherrie and Barloch. The street was quiet and soon he was passing the County Police offices, an austere building sitting back from the road. As he did so, the door opened and two uniformed policemen exited, striding across to a dark and powerful-looking Rover, with a police sign atop. They were strangers to him; he had crossed the border into Ayrshire, an entirely different division, and was unfamiliar with any of these fellow officers. Adjacent to the office was a long, low building and several smartly-dressed couples were approaching, laughing happily as they walked, arm-in-arm. As the door opened, the sound of an accordion band drifted out and Alan felt a sudden pang of sadness and longing. Young couples, they appeared all set for a pleasant evening of dance, drink and companionship, the kind of evening that he'd had planned with Nancy.

He put his head down and strode on, trying to push the thought out of his mind. Once past the large, looming mill building, he turned left on to Main Street where, a few hundred yards along the road, a sign proclaimed his destination: The Masonic Arms. He stood outside for a moment, wondering if he should turn back. The door to the public bar opened and an elderly man exited, turning his collar up before lighting his pipe. Not giving himself the chance to think, Alan pushed the door open and stepped inside.

A few heads turned at the appearance of a stranger, but they quickly returned to the business of drink and conversation. He tried not to appear conspicuous, remembering that McGinn had once stated that everyone recognised an off-duty policeman when they saw one. He sauntered up to the bar and, finding a space, caught the eye of the rather buxom middle-aged woman behind the counter, her black-dyed hair swept up in a beehive style. She finished her conversation with a fellow customer then walked over to him and smiled.

'Evenin' darlin', what can Ah get ye?'

He didn't think that his stomach could handle any more beer; almost without thinking, he replied, 'Brandy, please; double.'

She laughed.

'Hark at ye—brandy ye're wantin? Fancy, eh! Ah've a bottle ben the lounge, gie's a wee meenit.'

She returned with a glass of the golden liquid.

'There ye are, pet, that'll warm ye up, ken.'

She took his money.

'Hav'na' seen ye aboot here afore—are ye local, like?'

He was reluctant to make conversation and wondered if she had guessed his occupation.

'Erm, no, I'm from Barloch but my friend sometimes comes in with his lass, I was just wonderin' if he's about.'

'Och, if he brings a lassie here, ken, he'll be ben the lounge. Once ye've feenished thon, ye can gang awa' through.'

'I will, thanks.'

The brandy tasted strong and rough, nothing like the smooth, pleasant beverage that he had been given by Andrew Wright, Nancy's father. After the first sip, he threw the rest back, swallowing it and nearly choking as it burned his already raw throat. At the side of the bar was a door marked 'lounge' and he made his way towards it. Swallowing hard, partly from nerves and partly in an attempt to get rid of the after-taste, he pushed the swing-door open.

~~~

The lounge of the Masonic was small and cosy; the clientele, consisting mostly of couples, were all seated at tables, unlike in the public bar, and the counter was on a curve, preventing a view of the far end. He stepped into the room, attracting a few curious glances and, trying to appear inconspicuous, he glanced about; Sergeant Fairbrother's red hair would be easy to spot but he was nowhere to be seen. He felt both disappointed and relieved; his journey might have been wasted but he could go back home and forget about what now seemed to be his foolishness.

He was about to re-enter the bar when a figure at the far end of the room, his back towards Alan, turned around; Kerr Brodie's words immediately came back to him—'a sleekit wee man wi' dark hair an' a wee moustache.' The description certainly fitted, but the man was alone, although he seemed to be staring past Alan. Suddenly he felt a hand on his shoulder.

'What the hell are you doing here, McInnes?'

Without thinking, he replied, 'I could ask you the same thing, Sergeant Fairbrother.'

The sergeant glared at Alan.

'And what the hell is that supposed to mean? I can drink anywhere I choose, it's none of your damned business.'

'Well, maybe it is my business, Sergeant. There's been several occasion when you've clearly stated that you were intending to drink in the Bird in Hand but you've been seen here—with that person over there.'

Alan pointed towards the dark-haired man, who was hastily rising from his seat. Fairbrother lowered his voice.

'How dare you, McInnes! My movements, where I drink and

with whom I drink are of no concern to you. What the hell gives you the right to barge in here, asking ridiculous questions?'

'I have every right, sir. You've been seen exchanging something with that stranger and, quite frankly, some of your actions during the recent investigations have been questionable, to say the least.'

Alan could see the colour rise in Fairbrother's freckled cheeks—the sergeant looked as if he was about to explode.

'Wh...how dare you, you bloody idiot! You don't have the faintest idea what the hell you're talking about!'

The dark-haired man was now making for the door and Alan turned towards him, raising his voice.

'Here, you, I want a word...'

Fairbrother grabbed Alan's arm roughly.

'Leave it, McInnes, let him go.'

Alan grasped the sergeant's hand, trying to release his grip. He raised his voice, attracting a few concerned looks.

'No, I want to speak to him—I intend to find out what the hell's goin' on...'

They were interrupted by the sudden appearance of the large, sturdy barman, who made to grab both of them by the collar. Fairbrother managed to reach into his pocket, pulling out his warrant card.

'This is a police matter, sir, everything is under control.'

The man looked at the card then glared at the sergeant.

'Polis, is it? Aye, weel, ye can take yer matter ootside, if ye dinnae mind, ye're upsettin' ma customers, who's jist wantin' a peaceful' drink.'

Fairbrother apologised and pushed Alan towards the door. Once outside, the sergeant turned on him, poking him in the chest as he ranted.

'God-Almighty-McInnes, what the hell d'you think you're

playing at?'

Alan was looking around for the dark-haired stranger, but he had disappeared; he stood his ground.

'Who was that man, Sergeant?'

'None of your damned business; now, get yourself home, Constable, and sober up.'

'Sober up...I'm not drunk, sir!'

'Well, you're bloody stinking of alcohol—get out of my sight, you incompetent fool.'

With that, Fairbrother turned and strode away; after a few paces, however, he turned back.

'And, if I were you, I'd be giving serious thought to your future because, if I have anything to do with it, your career in the police is finished—d'you understand?'

~~~

Alan trudged back to Glensherrie station in a daze; he tried to convince himself that Fairbrother was bluffing but the sergeant had appeared so furious that he doubted it. The remarks regarding his future had been the final straw; the young man was deflated, despondent and defeated and, as he climbed up the ramp, he could have wept. His life seemed to have caved in around him, everything that he valued was in jeopardy; his family, his job, even his relationship. He bit his lip as he reached the platform, only to be greeted by an apologetic-looking stationmaster.

'Sorry, son, there'll be nae mair train's runnin' the nicht.'

Alan looked at the man in disbelief.

'Wh...what d'you mean?'

'Och, it's thon bloody diesel units—wan o' they's broken doon' a'tween here an' Barloch. They're sendin' fitters oot but, if they cannae get it started, they'll hae tae send for an engine tae tow

275

it back up tae the depot.'

'But what am I supposed to do? I need to get home.'

'Aye, weel, they're tryin' tae organise a bus but the drivers dinnae want tae get hauled oot on a wet Saturday nicht. it'll be weel ower an hour afore it gets here. Where're you headed, son?'

'Barloch.'

The stationmaster patted his shoulder.

'Then ma best advice is tae take Shanks's pony—it's jist aboot three miles, ken, ye'll be hame a lot sooner than waitin' here fur a bus. Fit young laddie like yersel', the walk'll dae ye good—sober ye up a bit, ken!'

Alan headed back down the ramp and began the long, dark tramp home to Barloch. He felt that life couldn't get any worse.

Chapter 27

As far as Alan was concerned, Sunday was a day best forgotten. The atmosphere in his home was cold and distant, with neither of his parents engaging either with him or with one another; his head continued to pound, no doubt affected by the cheap brandy served in the Masonic Arms. Most of all, he was sick to his stomach following Fairbrother's harsh words. He considered telephoning Nancy but decided against it—he would wait until he could speak to her face-to-face, although he dreaded what he might have to tell her.

Monday dawned clear and bright, a new week, a fresh start. As he walked down School Street, his heart was pounding and he was filled with a sense of dread, compounded when he saw the police Wolseley already parked outside the office. As he walked towards the door, he straightened his tie, swallowed hard and entered.

Sergeant Tait was behind the desk, his pipe noticeably absent. He gave Alan a look that he couldn't quite interpret.

'Inspector McGinn wants tae see ye—richt away. Just go through an' knock.'

'Yes, Sergeant.'

He did as he was bid, waiting for what seemed like an age outside Tait's office. Finally, McGinn responded.

'Come in.'

He entered the office, where Inspector McGinn was seated behind Tait's desk, several sheets of paper in front of him. He remained silent and Alan stood facing him, hands behind his back. Without looking up, McGinn barked, 'At attention, McInnes.'

Immediately, Alan put his feet together and his hands by his side, staring fixedly at a spot above the inspector's head. McGinn continued to peruse the documents in silence and Alan felt beads of sweat start to break out on his forehead; he was beginning to understand how suspects felt when kept waiting in such a manner. Eventually, McGinn placed the sheets together and looked up at the nervous young constable. When he spoke, his voice was unusually quiet, although Alan could see the glint of anger in his eyes.

'McInnes, what the hell were you playing at?'

He opened his mouth to speak, but before he could get a word out, McGinn banged his fist on the desk.

'I'M NOT BLOODY LOOKING FOR AN ANSWER!'

Alan's mouth clamped shut as McGinn continued.

'You're a bloody fool, McInnes, an absolute stupid, bloody fool! Yet again, you seem to think that you can go off on your own, ignoring protocol, acting as if you're some kind of damned detective in your own right. Well, on this occasion, you've stepped way over the line.'

Alan fought back the tears.

'Sergeant Fairbrother has made a formal complaint and requested that you be dismissed from the force; under any other circumstances, I would agree with him. However, in light of the assistance you've provided over the last week—and, indeed, the last year—I have persuaded him to take no further action, on the clear understanding that I reprimand you in the most severe manner. Have you any idea the trouble you've caused?'

'No sir,' mumbled Alan.

'Well, let me tell you. As you are aware, we are facing an increased problem with the distribution and use of illegal drugs.

Sergeant Fairbrother has been working with a special division in Glasgow in an attempt to find out who is behind the supply of these drugs. He was seconded to our division, as it was believed that there was a connection to Paisley.'

He consulted his notes briefly, the leaned his elbows on the desk, giving Alan a thunderous look.

'The person that the sergeant was seen liaising with in the Masonic Arms is a police informant—and a very useful one at that. He goes by the assumed name of Marcel, and he just happens to be the head waiter at a rather exclusive Glasgow restaurant. Marcel is also an accomplished amateur photographer, with a penchant for taking photographs of scantily clad young women. In return for us turning a blind eye to his sordid activities, he has agreed to provide us with information—an' photographs—of the less-than-salubrious guests that dine in the restaurant. You can take it from me that there are a fair number.'

He paused, taking out a Capstan and lighting it. He exhaled a cloud of blue smoke.

'Sergeant Fairbrother and Marcel meet in the Masonic Arms as it's out of the way for both o' them. The exchange that Brodie witnessed was of the sergeant passing Marcel a payment and receiving a packet of photographs in return. This arrangement has worked well for a number o' months; until now, that is.'

He paused for effect, narrowing his eyes as he took a deep draw on his cigarette.

'UNTIL NOW, McInnes. Now, and thanks to your interference, not only is Sergeant Fairbrother's identity compromised, but if word gets out about the identity of our friend Marcel, the man's bloody life could be in danger!'

'I'm sorry, sir, I had no idea—'

'SORRY! You bloody should be sorry, McInnes—in the space of an evening, you've jeopardised an entire operation an' you've

put a man's life in danger! Sorry doesn't even come close to bein'
sufficient! D'you understand?'

Alan, chastised beyond his comprehension, cast his eyes down
and nodded.

'God only knows what got into your bloody head, McInnes,
but you've overstepped the mark so far that you've all but ended
your career. D'you hear?'

'Yes sir—I'm really sorry, sir.'

'Aye, well, like I said, you bloody should be sorry. As I already
mentioned, I've managed to convince Fairbrother to hold off on
taking this matter to the superintendent, but there's no guarantee that he won't change his mind. So, keep your bloody head
down an' your nose clean, let's just hope for the best.'

'Yes sir. Thank you, sir.'

McGinn shook his head despairingly.

'Good God Almighty, McInnes, I don't know what the hell
to do with you. It's just lucky for you that you've proved your
worth to me in recent times.'

He sat back, took a deep draw on his Capstan before stubbing
it out in the overflowing ashtray.

'Right, ask Sergeant Tait to come through—I want a word
with both of you.'

~~~

The two Barloch officers stood in front of McGinn; underneath
his notes was an envelope and he took out a photograph.

'Right, Sergeant Fairbrother has given me this. It was taken
by our friend, Marcel, a few months back.'

The three looked at the grainy, black-and-white image. It
showed the back of a man's head; thin, with longish hair, his
face unseen. Facing the camera, a man and woman were seated
beside each other, in full view, the man sporting an expan-

sive smile that, even in the poor-quality photo, didn't seem to reach his eyes. He was wearing what looked to be a loud, double-breasted suit—the archetypal 'Spiv.' The woman was attractive yet hard-faced, more soberly dressed and with a sullen expression. To their side sat a burly man, middle-aged and with thick dark hair. The expression on his face indicated that he was ill at ease somehow and, indeed, his suit looked too tight across the shoulders, the sleeves very slightly short. His face was in profile, clean-shaven, heavy-jowled, with dark eyes under bushy eyebrows.

'So, it seems that the man an' the woman are Londoners, as far as we can gather from Marcel. They booked into the Central Hotel but under assumed names, needless to say. They had separate rooms, which indicated that they're likely not a couple.'

Alan peered at the photo, opening his mouth as if to speak; he thought better of it but McGinn noticed.

'Spit it out, McInnes.'

'Erm, well, I'd say they look alike, sir—same eyes and nose; d'you think they might be brother an' sister, maybe?'

McGinn looked intently at the image then gave Alan the ghost of a smile.

'Aye, you might be right at that, McInnes.'

He pointed at the more heavy-set individual.

'This is the man that we're interested in, though. Our friend Marcel says that this bloke was a local, tough as they come but he seemed out o' his depth. He says that there was a lot o' talking and discussing going on during the meal, although they were quick to stop every time anyone approached.'

'An' whit are these folks supposed tae be talkin aboot?' asked Tait.

McGinn shrugged.

'That's the thing, Tait, we don't know, but from what Sergeant

Fairbrother has gleaned and from what Marcel has told us, we think that some kind o' deal was takin' place.'

He leaned back in the chair.

'Fairbrother suspects that the English pair are the suppliers an' that this anonymous man was being set up as their contact in the Glasgow area, more than likely the man in charge o' the local supply. The thing is, we have no idea how the drugs arrive and how they're distributed, other than this recent incident at Barloch. We're pretty certain that this particular consignment of drugs was being stolen from the usual distributor, which complicates matters. Also, after what happened, I think it highly unlikely that they'll use this method again.'

He pointed at the burly individual.

'If this man is the local contact, then my guess is that he's the one that's lost the consignment, which is now safely under lock and key at Paisley headquarters. In which case, he'll be considerably out of pocket. What I'd really like to know, apart from his identity, is who stole his consignment. I don't, for one minute, believe that Grimaldo is behind this, although, as I expected, he's saying bugger all. He's just the errand boy, collecting the goods that Scanlon stole from the goods van before he set it alight. If we could only lay our hands on Scanlon, it'd answer a lot of questions.'

Tait frowned as he digested this information.

'So d'ye think it wis anither—well, Ah don't know whit ye'd call them, exactly.'

McGinn nodded.

'Another crime organisation? Aye, that's the general opinion. The consignment arrived here and was due to be collected as normal—all above board, on the face o' it, although with false names, as we already know—the mysterious and non-existent Mr R Watson. But somebody got wind o' the delivery and set out to steal it. Unfortunately, Oliphant drafted in poor old Combe to cover McInnes senior's shift and—well, you know the rest.'

Alan's heart skipped a beat; he still hadn't resolved his dilemma regarding the fifteen pounds that his mother had found. McGinn continued.

'But what I can guarantee is that there'll be a few pretty disgruntled crooks kicking about, and that's never a good thing. Can lead to all sorts o' trouble and the last thing we need is some sort o' gang war on our hands.'

'An' does nae'body know who this bugger is?' asked Tait.

'Apparently not,' replied McGinn. 'Fairbrother has done the rounds with this photo but no-one appears to have seen him before. Y'know, there's a good few Glasgow crooks who keep themselves well under the parapet and, to be honest, up until now, it's not been a huge problem. Tobacco, alcohol, petty thieving, we just get on with our job and catch whoever we can. But this—well, it's a whole new area o' criminality. I suppose that, just like every other business, the crooks have got to move with the times, but it's worrying, I have to admit.'

He pointed to the picture once more.

'So, we need to find out who the hell this man is—I take it you've never seen him?'

Both Alan and Tait shook their heads.

'No, sir, never set eyes on him.'

'Well, I'll leave you this photograph for your information. We need to try an' stem the flow o' all this—mark my words, it's going to be a hell o' a problem in years to come if we don't.'

~~~

McGinn was in the front office and about to leave when the phone rang. Sergeant Tait answered.

'Barloch Police Station...aye...aye, he's still here...just a wee minute...'

He handed the telephone to McGinn.

'It's Sergeant Fairbrother, Inspector.'

'McGinn here...yes, Fairbrother?' Damn and blast! Right, I see, I'll be there as soon as I can.'

He handed the receiver back to Tait.

'They've found a body in the river, down at the Erskine Ferry—going by what Fairbrother says, it's our friend John Scanlon an' it looks as if he's been stabbed.'

The news hung in the air for a few moments, then Tait said, in a flat tone, 'So there's tae be nae justice for poor auld Combe, then?'.

McGinn gave a grim smile.

'Depends what you mean by justice, Tait. At the end of the day, if he'd been found guilty o' murder, the outcome might just as easily have been the same.'

'Aye, Ah suppose so, but we'll never ken noo whit actually happened.'

McGinn lit a Capstan and exhaled slowly.

'Well, the way I see it is like this; Scanlon an' his sidekick, Frank Kilbride, never set out to murder anybody— they probably thought the yard would be unstaffed, but when Alex Combe accosted them, they just intended to knock him unconscious.'

He looked at Alan, who was cringing inwardly; it could just have easily been his father, but Gilbert's absence that night was ultimately responsible for Combe's death. Was that absence coincidence—or otherwise? McGinn went on.

'From what we know, Scanlon was a violent thug but I think that Kilbride was one o' those easily-led young men, who fell under Scanlon's influence. We'll never know who struck that fatal blow but, either way, I think that Kilbride probably panicked. The only way to ensure his silence was to get rid of him as well, make it look as if he was working alone.'

He nodded in Alan's direction.

'And if it hadn't been for our friend here, we might never have considered the possibility that there was two o' them and that Scanlon had done away with his accomplice.'

Alan wondered again if Fairbrother had thought the same thing—had he been looking for the same evidence at Kilmirrin Station? He daren't ask, not after his earlier reprimand, but Tait voiced his own opinion.

'Ah must say that yer sergeant seemed awfy quick tae accept the facts at face value, mind. Like ye say, if it hadnae been for McInnes, the case would likely hae been closed an' Scanlon wid have got off scot free.'

McGinn pondered on this for a moment.

'The thing is, Tait, Fairbrother is comin' at this from a very different angle. He's been involved in this new drug investigation division and they're lookin' to catch those further up the tree, if you get my meaning. At the end of the day, the likes of Scanlon and Kilbride are just the footsoldiers—Fairbrother's lot are after the generals.'

'So would he ha'e let Scanlon go free, d'ye think?'

McGinn shrugged.

'I really don't know; but if he had, it would have been in the hope that he led them to his contacts.'

He lit a second cigarette.

'But, like I said earlier, Scanlon's murder shows just what kind o' business we're dealin' with here; this isn't petty thieving, it's high value, organised crime. I'm hoping that Scanlon's death isn't the start of something and I'm concerned about the involvement of this Italian character— it casts a very different light on things.'

'Why would someone kill Scanlon, though?' asked Alan.

McGinn shrugged.

'Probably they knew we were after him—Scanlon's just a west of Scotland petty criminal, he wouldn't be bound by this bloody Omerta caper. Whoever's behind all this wanted to make sure he didn't talk and they sent our Italian friend to collect the goods instead. Dr Miller will confirm it, but I think it's pretty likely that Scanlon has been dead since before last Friday's carry-on. There's a lot o' questions unanswered, I'm afraid.'

He made to leave.

'Right, I'd best get down to Erskine Ferry and see what's happening.'

As he reached the door, he turned.

'And for God's sake, McInnes, keep out o' bother!'

~~~

Once the inspector had left, peace descended once more on the little office, for a few minutes, at any rate. Tait puffed on his pipe, then gave Alan a dark look.

'Weel, ye had a damned lucky escape there, McInnes. Good God Almighty, whit the hell were ye playin' at? Ah warned ye, Ah told ye no' tae go makin' accusations aboot a senior officer. Whit in God's name possessed ye tae go galivantin' doon tae Glensherrie, spyin' on Fairbrother?'

'I just thought...'

Tait pointed the stem of his pipe at the constable.

'Ye see, that's the problem, son. Ye shouldnae ha'e thought! Aye, Ah ken, there's many a time when yer thinkin' has brought results but, on this occasion, it damned near got ye drummed oot o' the force!'

Alan looked, and felt, contrite.

'I know, Sergeant, and I'm sorry, I should have listened to

you—and my mother. I told her and she said exactly the same as you.'

Tait sighed and shook his head.

'Aye, she's a wise woman, is Isa. But ye're an awfy laddie, ye ken that? Still, Ah hope ye've learned yer lesson, Jist dae as Mc-Ginn says, keep yer head doon an' yer nose clean an' hopefully it'll a blow over.'

'Yes, Sergeant, I will.'

~~~

Later that afternoon, they received a call from Inspector McGinn; the body found in the Clyde at Renfrew had been positively identified as that of John Scanlon. Dr Miller had, indeed, made an initial diagnosis of the cause of death as being a stab wound to the heart, much the same as that of Douglas McSween.

'Looks like it's thon Italian fellow richt enough then,' commented Tait. 'Aye, a sad affair, a sad affair all roond. Weel, that's five o' clock, awa' up the road, McInnes, let's try an' put the whole matter behind us.'

~~~

As Alan trudged up School Street, he reached a decision: despite his conscience, he decided that the best course of action regarding the fifteen pounds was to remain silent. His career was already potentially jeopardised and to report the possible involvement of his father, albeit indirectly, in Alex Combe's murder could prove disastrous, both to him and to his mother. Alan McInnes decided that this was a secret best kept.

~~~

Bruno Carlaveri lifted his napkin and dabbed his mouth, ensuring that no tomato sauce remained; a vain man, he took almost as much care with his appearance as he did with his business. Unfortunately, and much to his annoyance, the latter had not been going exactly to plan recently.

Placing the napkin back on the table, he pushed his plate away then took a cigar from his breast pocket, sniffing it appreciatively. An attentive young waiter immediately approached and, once Carlaveri had snipped the end from the cigar, held a struck match to it before removing the plate.

He leaned his head back against the wall, letting out a stream of fragrant smoke. Cafe Verona was one of his favourite places; the food was excellent, almost as good as that in his home village. Located in Glasgow's Springburn, it was off the beaten track, which suited his purposes admirably. It was a small cafe that could seat about thirty occupants; being a Monday evening, there were few customers, just a couple of teenagers seated by the window, greedily spooning the delicious home-made ice-cream into their mouths. An old man sat nearby, nursing a lonely pot of tea as he smoked his third Woodbine.

The door opened and his expected visitor entered, making his way swiftly to the table. Carlaveri noticed him looking about anxiously and beckoned him to sit, giving him an oily, insincere smile.

'Did-a you think I had something planned something for you? Do you not-a trust me?'

The visitor shook his head; he didn't trust Carlaveri an inch but he certainly wasn't going to tell him that!

'Of course I do, Mr Carlaveri, I was just checking. Can't be too careful.'

'Huh.' He snapped his fingers at the waiter. 'Espresso. Uno.'

Carlaveri blew smoke across the table, causing the other man to narrow his eyes.

'So what-a news?'

'None, I'm afraid. The consignment is well beyond our reach, unfortunately. In the hands of the police.'

Carlaveri muttered an oath in Italian.

'How did they know about it, that is-a what I want to find out. I 'ad hoped to use that supply in order to put more pressure on that fool, Wallace.'

'More to the point, why did that fool Luigi stab McSween? If he decides to talk...'

Carlaveri banged his palms on the table, causing the teenagers to turn and stare across at him. He leaned forward, speaking in a low, menacing tone.

'Luigi will not talk, you 'ear me? Never—he is-a bound by an oath. His family back in Sicily will be looked after but, if he says a word, then...'

He drew his hand across his throat.

'No, Luigi is a good boy, he will remain silent, no matter what.'

'I take it he was responsible for Scanlon's death?'

Carlaveri gave a slight nod, then took another puff on his cigar as his coffee arrived. Silence ensued as he sipped the strong, dark brew.

'Have you found out anything more about Wallace? I need-a to know who is supplying him—once I do, I can cut him out altogether.'

Again the man shook his head.

'Nothing yet, sorry.'

Carlaveri hissed.

'I do not want your damned 'sorry', I want information and that is-a what I pay you for.'

'I'll do my best, Mr Carlaveri.'

The Italian reached into the inside pocket of his grey silk suit and removed an envelope, passing it to the other man.

'Here—you 'av been of some use but I need more—more information.'

Nervously, the man stood up.

'Thank you, Mr Carlaveri, I appreciate it. I'll get in touch as soon as I find out anything.'

The Italian glared.

'You 'ad better; and remember...'

Again, he drew his finger across his throat.

'...Omerta—silence. I expect that from all those in-a my pay, Mr Fairbrother.'

Chapter 28

A leaden September sky greeted Alan as he opened the curtains of his bedroom. Although it was only autumn, it felt as if the chill of early winter had already descended upon the little village and he shivered as he wiped the condensation from his window. He intended to spend a bit of time finishing off his renovations of the police house, although Nancy's continued lack of enthusiasm had curtailed his activities somewhat of late. He knew that her heart was still set on one of the new houses that were nearing completion in the village but, even with their combined salaries, he felt that such a purchase would be beyond their means. His attempts to convince her that it would be prudent to live in the police house for a year or two and save their money continued to fall on deaf ears and he was beginning to wonder if there was any point in continuing his labours during his well-earned days off. Hopefully they would discuss it that evening over dinner, as he had made a reservation at the same new restaurant in Paisley. He let out a long sigh—yet again, he would try to pin Nancy down on a date for their wedding; they had been engaged for over six months but, when pressed, she just giggled and said that there was no rush.

His rather despondent reverie was broken by the clatter of dishes from downstairs, telling him that his mother was already up and doing. He shoved his feet into his worn, comfortable slippers, wrapped his thick dressing gown around his shoulders and made his way downstairs, the tantalising aroma of a cooked breakfast gradually strengthening. He opened the kitchen door and his mother turned towards him. Isa favoured her son with a smile, although he had noticed that her smiles had lost some of their warmth of late.

'Morning, son. Sit yourself down, breakfast's nearly ready. Pour yourself some tea.'

He did as he was bid and a plate laden with sausage, bacon, eggs and potato scones was laid before him. As he began to eat, he heard the rattling of the letterbox and Isa made her way through to the hallway, returning with a handful of mail. She looked through the envelopes, handing a light blue one to Alan.

'One for you, Alan; Basildon Bond envelope—what nice handwriting too!'

Alan stared at the envelope, recognising the neat, feminine script. He placed the letter on the table and continued to eat.

'Aren't you going to see who it's from?' asked his mother.

'No, I'll have my breakfast while it's still warm.'

They sat in a companionable silence as he ate, then heavy, uneven footsteps on the stairs indicated that they were about to be joined by Gilbert McInnes. Isa stood up and returned to the stove as Alan's father entered. He had aged considerably over the last few months, his skin grey, his face unshaven. He sat down heavily, dropping his stick to the floor, then poured the dregs of the tea through the strainer and into his cup.

'Your breakfast won't be long, Gilbert, I was just making sure Alan got his.'

McInnes senior grunted and picked up the meagre bundle of mail.

'Bloody bills, that's aw' we seem tae get these days.'

Alan could see his mother's shoulders tense at the mild profanity but she refrained from comment; it seemed that his father was all too ready to pick a fight at the least opportunity. He stood up, picked up his letter and crossed to the door.

'Thanks, Mother, that was grand, I'll away up and shave.'

As Isa smiled across at him, Gilbert caught sight of the envelope.

'Who's been writin' tae you in thon fancy envelope, eh? Some high-falutin' friend?'

Isa responded.

'Leave the boy alone, Gilbert. It's his own business who he corresponds with.'

'Ach, Ah wis only teasin', for God's sake.'

Alan made a hasty exit; such scenes were becoming increasingly common in the McInnes household.

~~~

One in the privacy of his bedroom, he sat on the bed, clutching the letter in his hands. Finally, he reached for his penknife and slit the envelope open, removing the single sheet. The handwriting, as with the envelope, was small, neat and all too familiar.

Dear Alan,

I know that this is the coward's way out but I really think it is for the best as I couldn't bear having to face you.

Earlier this year I applied for the position of deputy headmistress at a private school in Edinburgh. Mummy went to school with the headmistress and she had been in touch to ask if I might be interested. I didn't tell you as I wasn't really sure what my intentions were but I heard today that my application has been successful. It's an excellent position and one that I really don't want to turn down, as I feel that my career isn't really progressing in Barloch.

I know that you have your own career to think about too and I don't imagine that you would want to transfer to Edinburgh so, after a lot of soul-searching, I think it would be best if you and I went our separate ways. I'm so very sorry to break it to you like this but everything seems to have happened so fast and I thought that writing to you would be easier than meeting you and possibly having a scene.

We've had a really nice time, haven't we, but I just don't know if we're right for each other any more and I hope you understand. You're a fine young man, Alan, and I'm sure that there are plenty of nice local girls who would be happy to be your sweetheart.

I will send the ring back to you separately by registered post, as I wouldn't want it to go astray.

Once again, I'm so sorry, but as I said, I think it's for the best.

Affectionately yours,

Nancy.

Alan stared at the letter for a few moments, then read it once more with a growing sense of despair. Finally, he folded it carefully and placed it on the bed beside him; despite his best efforts, two tears ran down his unshaven cheeks.

~~~

He shaved, washed and dressed in a daze, his mind reeling with the shock of Nancy's letter. Although they came from very different social backgrounds, he was a respectable young man with prospects and he had truly believed that they loved one another. Without warning, it seemed that her career was more important than his; or was it all just a convenient excuse to end their engagement?

Was he simply just not good enough for her?

He pulled on a heavy woollen pullover, stuffed Nancy's letter into his trouser pocket, then stormed out of his room before clattering down the stairs, calling out as he approached the front door.

'Mother, I'm going out for a walk.'

He didn't await Isa's response, not wanting to have to engage in conversation. He reached for his fawn duffel-coat, which was hanging on the peg, then changed his mind; it had been a gift from Nancy the previous Christmas, an attempt to modernise his appearance. Was he really that outmoded, he wondered? Instead, he wrapped a scarf around his neck and grabbed his worn, gaberdine raincoat; less warm, perhaps, but free of any attached sentiment.

A few minutes later, he was striding down the hill towards The Cross, with no idea where he was headed. Briefly, he regretted not wearing the hooded duffel-coat; the morning held a chill that permeated the gaberdine of his raincoat and his head was already covered with moisture from the cool, damp atmosphere. He strode on, averting his gaze from the police houses on his right; across Main Street, down Kirk Street, finally he turned right along the road leading out of the village, stopping at the bridge over the Millbank Burn, the dark, peated stream that fed the Bar Loch.

He leaned on the parapet, gazing unseeingly at the swirling waters below; for a moment, he felt he could understand the actions of Inspector Nisbet, a man so troubled that, over a year ago, had jumped to his death from the Marchburn railway viaduct.

Had it really only been a year since he had been looking forward to the ceilidh that would herald in nineteen-sixty? His great plans—promotion, proposing to Nancy...all just smoke in the wind. He had been looking forward to a new decade but now it had just been another dull and disappointing year. He still had feelings of guilt regarding the money found in his father's drawer, although he had heard from Sergeant Tait that Alex Combe's widow had received a gift of fifteen pounds, posted anonymously through her letterbox and presumed to be a collection from those who knew her husband. He allowed himself a bleak smile—trust his mother to do the right thing!

He cringed slightly as he recalled the humiliation following his ridiculous and unfounded suspicions about Sergeant Fairbrother, that ghastly dressing-down from Inspector McGinn. Then there was this latest, final blow, Nancy's letter. No, nineteen-sixty had been a truly dreadful year.

But, as he gazed at river below, he gave a wry laugh and straightened himself; this wouldn't do, he wasn't going to allow himself to wallow in sentiment. He was young, he had a future before him.

He became aware of a figure approaching and he turned to see a young woman, wrapped snugly in a warm coat and a headscarf, an aged black labrador panting wearily at her side. She smiled at him.

'Good mornin' Alan McInnes, it's a gey dreich day the day—how're you keepin'?'

Alan had been in the same class at school as Alice Quinn, who now worked as secretary to the manager of the local cooperage. He managed a half-hearted smile.

'Mornin', Alice. I'm not too bad, thanks, how are you?'

'Och, doin' away, just like the rest of us. You're lookin' a bit down in the dumps—everythin' okay?'

He had no intention of sharing his troubles with Alice; he shrugged.

'Och, just a few concerns, that's all. What about you—are you still workin' in the cooperage?'

'Aye, still workin' for the high an' mighty Neil Lawson, dirty old bugger that he is!' She grinned as she spoke.

Alan frowned, both at Alice's choice of language and her assertion.

'What do you mean, Alice?'

She shrugged.

'Och, I dinn'a really like to say, but he's got what ye'd call wanderin' hands, if you ken whit I mean.'

Alan knew only too well—he had witnessed it first-hand in the Greenock Police office and he felt a slight surge of anger.

'Here, that's terrible, Alice; look, if there's anythin' I can do...'

She grinned and held up her hands, showing off her long, scarlet-lacquered nails.

'Thanks, Alan, but these have already done the trick; next time, he'll have tae explain tae his wife how his cheeks got scratched!'

He smiled again— this time it seemed to take less effort; Alice's cheery, cheeky demeanour was, perhaps, just what he needed. They chatted for a few minutes more, about school friends, exchanging village gossip, until Alan became aware that the chill of the day was seeping further through his clothes, causing him to shudder visibly.

'Aye, it's getting right raw, so it is,' Alice said. 'Listen, you could buy me a coffee in the cafe if you like. I'm thinkin' we could both be doin' with a hot drink.'

He hesitated momentarily, then grinned.

'Aye, that'd be fine, Alice. You're right, I could do with something to warm me up.'

They walked back up Kirk Street in a companionable silence, the aged labrador trotting along at Alan's heels. Janetti's cafe was busy but they managed to find a table, sandwiched between the flashy new juke-box that had recently been installed and an advertising board for Players cigarettes. The waitress came over and, almost without thinking, Alan spoke.

'Two cappuccinos, please.'

Alice grinned.

'Listen tae you, Alan McInnes, all fancy wi' ye'r cappuccinos! Never had one of those before, it's aye just been a cup o' coffee!'

He smiled back.

'Well, just watch you don't burn your mouth, the coffee's a lot hotter than the froth.'

As the waitress left, she gave Alice a rather odd look and, once she was safely behind the counter, Alan asked, 'She gave you a bit of a once-over there, Alice. D'you know her?'

Alice grinned again—Alan had the impression that she had been grinning quite a lot since they had met. He had also noticed that, when she did so, her cheeks dimpled in a particularly becoming way.

'Och, I may as well tell you, I was seein' Johnny Patterson for a wee while—mind, he was a year above us—but we went our separate ways a few weeks back. Sometimes we used to come in here on a Saturday and the lassie's probably just puttin' two an' two together.'

Alan could feel the colour rise in his cheeks; as far as anyone who knew him was concerned, he was firmly engaged to Nancy Wright, a respected local schoolteacher; would his innocent coffee with Alice Quinn set local tongues wagging? For a brief moment, he was tempted to get up and leave but, as the coffees arrived, he decided to stay. After all, it was just an innocent coffee, although Alice Quinn, whom he had known for nigh on twenty years, had turned into a rather attractive young woman; then there was that cheeky grin...

~~~

They stayed for over an hour, chatting easily in the warm, steamy and smoky atmosphere of the cafe. Alan had kept his news to himself, however; it was far too soon to confide in

Alice and he knew that he would need to tell his parents before anyone else. They parted company outside the cafe, with a vague mention of meeting again the following Saturday. As he left Alice and walked along Barloch's Main Street, Alan realised that, perhaps, it wasn't the end of the world after all. However, as he turned the corner into School Street, he froze. His mother was walking down the other side of the street, carrying a wicker hen basket. His suspicion as to where she was headed was confirmed when she turned on to the path leading to Donny Tait's house; Isa was obviously expected, as the door opened at her approach. Alan hurried up the road, but he was unable to resist the temptation to stare across at his sergeant's house. The afternoon was still overcast and gloomy and the light was on in Tait's living room. Alan slunk into the entranceway that led to the local undertaker's premises and gazed across; even from that distance he could see the animated smile on his mother's face as she crossed to the window and closed the curtains.

~~~

The house was empty when he arrived home, his father presumably out on some business of his own; Alan didn't really care. He entered the living room, where a glowing fire was banked up behind the brass fireguard. He removed the guard, lifted the poker and thrust it angrily into the embers, feeling that the warmth and security of his home had been sullied somehow. As the fire brightened, he reached into his trouser pocket and removed the missive from Nancy. Briefly he stared at it, tempted to read it once more in case he had misconstrued her meaning, but he knew perfectly well that he hadn't. Finally, he dropped it on to the glowing coals, watching expressionlessly as it flared briefly before catching alight. The

299

neat handwriting showed momentarily before it turned to ash, just another small morsel to feed the fire.

~~~

Connie Lumsdale adjusted the top of her pink, frilly nightdress just as the bedroom door opened. Jock Wallace came in, a lascivious leer on his heavy features. Although the attractive young woman smiled at her paramour, her stomach lurched at the thought of what was to follow. However, hopefully Wallace would reward her adequately—after all, that was why she was here. He sat on the bed and opened his bedside drawer.

'Here, hen, a wee present for ye.'

He handed her a wooden cigarette box, at which she frowned.

'Aw, Jock, these aren't the usual ones!'

She had been hoping for her customary gift of the fragrant Sobranie cocktail cigarettes.

'Aye, Ah know—open it.'

She did as she was bid, her frown deepening. She was tempted to get out of the bed and storm off but her innate common sense, not to mention her insatiable desire for the money, prevented her; after all, that way she would receive no reward whatsoever.

The box contained about thirty fat, hand-rolled cigarettes, each with a little twist of paper at one end. She looked up at the big man, her red-painted lips twisted in a grimace of disgust.

'An' just what the hell are these, Jock? You know whit Ah like—Ah dinnae smoke roll-ups, for God's sake!'

He grinned and reached back over to his bedside cabinet picking up a heavy onyx-cased cigarette lighter.

'Aye, Ah ken richt enough, but these arenae any old roll-ups, pet. Here, try one, Ah bet you'll like it.'

He clicked the lighter into flame and, with some considerable reluctance, she selected what looked to be the smallest of the cigarettes and placed it between her lips. Jock lit the end and, rather tentatively, she inhaled, then coughed violently.

'In the name o' God, are ye tryin' tae poison me?'

He grinned.

'Take it easy at first, hen, just a few gentle puffs until ye get the taste fur it...aye, that's it!'

Ten minutes later, Connie lay on her back, her blonde hair spread across the white pillow, a beatific smile on her pretty features. The atmosphere in the room was thick with the unfamiliar, sickly-sweet smell of the cigarette. Jock Wallace raised himself on an elbow and stroked her pale skin with the back of his rough hand.

'See, whit did Ah tell ye?'

'Oh Jock, Ah don't know whit the hell's in them but Ah feel just great—all kind o' floaty, if ye ken whit Ah mean.'

He gazed down into her dilated pupils.

'Ah knew ye'd like it; now whit Ah want ye tae dae is give them tae all your pals. Ah'm sure they'd like them every bit as much as you did; there's plenty mair where they came from...'

ACKNOWLEDGEMENTS

This is a very hard thing to do. At the end of the long editing and production process, I always ask the authors to mention the people who have helped them bring their act of creation into the physical world. Sadly, I can't ask Diarmid MacArthur to do that as he died unexpectedly this summer.

The loss of Diarmid leaves a devastating hole in the lives of his family and also the Sparsile pantheon of authors. His cheerful confidence and practical help often spurred us onwards when it seemed we would never overcome the obstacles in the way of the finishing line.

I know he would have wanted me to thank Jim Campbell, who edited Diarmid's last manuscript and also Stephen Cashmore who went above and beyond in proofing the text and layout. Their selfless help and dedication has allowed us to bring Diarmid's last book into the life.

He chose to name it *To Feed The Fire*, and I hope it will last as beacon of his work forever more.

Lesley Affrossman
Sparile Books